THE COAT IN THE WOODS

Kat MacVeagh

ORLEBAR POINT PUBLISHING
GABRIOLA ISLAND, BC

Copyright © 2009 Kat MacVeagh

All rights reserved. No part of this publication may be reproduced, distributed, or transmitted in any form or by any means, or stored in a database or retrieval system, without the prior written permission of the publisher.

Library and Archives Canada Cataloguing in Publication

MacVeagh, Kat, 1945 –
The coat in the woods / Kat MacVeagh.

ISBN 978-0-615-29132-1

I. Title.

PS8625.V42C58 2009   C813'.6   C2009-901235-9

Design and typesetting by
Toby Macklin (www.tobymacklin.com)

Cover photograph by Ellie Speare

Orlebar Point Publishing
182 Decourcy Drive, V0R 1X1
Gabriola Island, BC
Canada

*To Ed, the love of my life
and the most resilient man I know*

PROLOGUE

April, 1956

The recess bell clattered into my head. I rushed to catch up with Sammy and Ellie, my best friends. Together we burst out of the double doors, loving the ga-clunk of the metal bars that opened them. Ignoring the jungle gym, merry-go-round, and swings, we dashed out to the wide expanse of the playground, towards the lush, damp smell of the grass at the back.

We were still kindergarteners, but that spring we considered ourselves almost first graders. We loved watching the fifth and sixth graders, who were allowed to climb the ancient oak tree that had been hauled in by a group of fathers to create a more interesting playground out of the flat prairie land. The old trunk was stripped bare of bark, but rubber-soled shoes made it easy to climb. A chinning bar had been installed a few feet from one of the highest limbs. The most adventurous kids jumped from the limb to the bar. A teacher was already down by the tree. There were some other younger kids watching, but none of them was planning what we were today. It was against the rules. We eyed the line of kids waiting to climb the enormous trunk. The tree was so big, I could just barely see over it. My stomach felt queasy. I looked at Sammy and Ellie on either side of me. They looked a bit nervous too, but we had shaken on it yesterday when we made our decision.

Sammy had dared us, and since Ellie and I figured we could do anything a boy could do, we dared him back. So here we were.

Finally we had our chance. The line of sixth graders had dwindled and the teacher had turned away, talking to some of them. Sammy was already on the tree, heading towards the higher end, Ellie right behind. We had made it this far without the teacher seeing us. I scrambled up behind Ellie and scooted out to sit on a limb right beside her, holding tightly as I noticed how far up we were. A gentle breeze ruffled my dark curly locks. I pushed my glasses up on my nose while I watched Sammy. We knew what he was going to do. It wasn't enough just to climb the tree, we had to do "it".

Ellie and I both held our breath in suspense as Sammy climbed up to the top part of the tree and picked his way out to the end of the highest large limb. He didn't even bother to steady himself with the branch overhead that extended from a nearby birch tree, but catapulted himself towards the chinning bar, caught it with his hands, held on, and then dropped about four feet. When he landed, the teacher turned, but Sammy was too fast and danced around so the teacher couldn't tell where he had come from.

My stomach clenched. Ellie and I crouched down.

"What are you up to, Sammy?" The teacher knew he was a mischievous boy.

"Just playing around. I'm hiding from Pru and Ellie."

"Well, head back towards the younger kids. You could get hurt here."

"Yes, Mr. Brown." He chanced a quick look over his shoulder at us and mouthed, "Sorry", as he did what he was told.

Ellie whispered, "You still want to do it, Pru?"

"We swore. We got to," I replied.

"Come on. I'll go first. If you come right after me the teacher won't notice."

I wasn't at all sure about that but I didn't want to end up crawling back down the tree. We were explorers, all three of us. I couldn't break that. At almost six we had the daring without the smarts. "Okay."

I inched my way off the branch back to the trunk. I sat and let Ellie scrunch past me to go ahead. I watched her. All of a sudden, I realized I was still straddling the trunk and Ellie had already crawled up to the jumping-off place. If I didn't get up right behind her, I was going to be left perched like one of those ducks in the shooting gallery at the fair.

I scurried up behind Ellie, ready to launch myself at the bar the minute she landed, so if the teacher saw her it would be too late to stop me.

Ellie stood up, held onto the limb above her, leaned forward a bit *towards her target which was only about three feet away, and leapt. She made it! She swung with both hands and jumped down, landing almost on all fours.*

I felt glued to the tree, but it was now or never. I could do this.

My stomach was fluttering again, as if the butterflies in it were doing somersaults. But I was determined. I inched out towards the abyss. I stood up, holding on to the reassuring thickness of the overhead branch. The chinning bar seemed far away. I counted to three and took off.

I was flying through the air!

I reached out for the bar. It seemed like forever. It wasn't there.

My stomach fell into a bottomless pit. Whump! My body slammed into the ground like a plane that had lost its landing gear. Then blackness.

The next thing I knew I was lying flat on my back. I couldn't breathe. The teacher was leaning over me saying something but I couldn't hear his words. My ears were thundering with my own heartbeat and all I could focus on was trying to catch my breath. Nothing happened. I was going to die. And on top of it all, I had failed my friends.

Finally, my lungs were able to take in some air. I tried again. I took a deep breath and exhaled. I struggled not to cry in relief. The teacher held my shoulders and told me to lie still a bit more. I could hear what he was saying. He was telling me that the wind had been knocked out of me.

My head hurt. My back hurt, too, but I sat up. The teacher handed me my glasses, which had fallen nearby. Nothing broken at least, on the glasses or me.

Ellie was sitting next to me, as was Sammy who had run back to us when he heard what had happened. The teacher helped me up. He told me I should go to the nurse's office. He said he had to report this to the principal, but added that we probably had been punished enough already. Beyond him, it seemed like the whole school was staring at me.

I braced myself, expecting to get grief from everyone, but something else happened instead. As Ellie and Sammy walked beside me to the building, all I noticed were smiles and comments like, "Wow! Did you guys really jump?" "How did you do it?" "Are you all right?" Sammy and Ellie straightened up and grinned a little. I just felt like my head was full of pillow stuffing and my body was a jigsaw puzzle that hadn't been put together properly. But I breathed a sigh of relief as I gingerly walked back to the school. I hadn't made it but I had tried to keep our pact. Maybe some day I would try again when I was bigger.

I had to lie down in the nurse's office while she called home. She couldn't reach Mum. I had forgotten that she was leaving for New York that day for her annual visit. The nurse tried Dad's office but he was in class. Should they interrupt him? I guess they decided not to because the nurse made one more call and then told me my Grandmother was coming. I must have dozed a bit, as the next thing I knew Grandma was leaning over me, telling me it was time to go home.

As we reached the school door, it started to pour – one of those storms that stops as fast as it starts. A flash of lightning that lit up the whole parking lot followed a clap of thunder. I hurried into the car as fast as I could. Once inside I crouched down under the dashboard. Grandma reached out for me as she got in her side of the car. I snuggled up to her.

"I'm scared, Grandma."

"It's only a storm, Pip. It will be over soon."

"Are you mad at me, Grandma?"

"More worried, Pip. It was a pretty foolish thing to do."

"I thought it would be easy. We climb trees all the time."

"From what I understand it wasn't the climbing that was the problem." She looked at me with her sharp green eyes, patted me on the shoulder, and then moved me over so she could start the car. "The nurse said I should take you to the doctor. Let's get you some dry clothes beforehand and see what your Mum's up to. I don't know why the nurse couldn't reach her. I'm supposed to take her to the train in an hour or so."

Grandma sounded more worried about Mum than me, so I just kept quiet. I hoped I'd be sent to my room after the doctor. My head still hurt.

As we turned into our driveway, the worst of the storm had moved on but I still heard noises. Then I realized they were car noises and people talking. Ours was the only house down this way so I wondered what was going on. I sat up a bit and peeked out the window. I could see an ambulance and a police car, lights flashing, and two big guys carrying a stretcher out to the ambulance. There was somebody on the stretcher covered up. Where was Mum? Had something bad happened? Was it because I got in trouble at school?

I choked. My head spun. I cried, "Grandma!"

She turned and hid my head in her bosom. The tissue she tucked there tickled my nose.

Arthur Dillen, Journal
October 6, 1944
Day One

I purchased this notebook before we set sail in order to record the experiences that are in store for me.

During training, it was frustrating not being able to tell Adrienne what I was doing. I called a few times but I could just listen to her news and tell her and the children that I love them. Even if I was allowed, how could I explain to my dear wife that I know more about explosives than I ever thought possible, that I've learned the ins and outs of the Sten gun and the Thompson machine gun, and that I now know how to snap a man's neck with my bare hands – hands that until now I have used only to till the soil, write lectures and love my family? Perhaps writing about it all will help Adrienne and the children understand some day.

CHAPTER ONE

June 15, 2000
Pru's Story

I slowed down as I approached the driveway. My small SUV had done a yeoman's task of pulling the U-Haul trailer all the way from the West Coast to my birthplace of Avon, Minnesota. All I needed was an axle to break if I bounced too hard over the potholes I suspected would be in the driveway ahead of me. I turned on my left blinker. Not that it made any difference. I hadn't seen any other cars on the country road this early, just the occasional tractor.

A weathered wooden sign with faded red letters indicated that the opening to my left was *Dillen's Hideaway*. In my mind, the letters were still as bright as the day Dad painted them. Thick pine branches brushed the sides of my car, but there was more than enough headroom for me to pass. Velvet, my Malamute-Husky cross, who was riding shotgun in the passenger seat, had to pull her head in quickly to avoid getting snapped on the nose. She looked at me, offended.

"Hey, I never told you to stick your big furry self halfway out of the car. Don't look at me!" She "woooed" and turned her head back to the window, just poking her nose out.

The tunnel, as we used to call it, formed by a canopy of oak and pine branches, led to the clearing by the lake where my parents had built our house. I slowly rolled over the dips in the driveway like a boat in a heavy sea. I was rarely seasick when sailing our boat, but today my stomach felt unsettled. I hadn't slept much the night before at the rest stop I'd found – too tired to make it all the way home and not tired enough to still the anxious thoughts running riot through my head.

I carefully pulled the car and trailer into the open area by the garage. As I sat staring at the house, thinking about how long it had been since I was last here, I thought I saw a flash of light out of the corner of my eye, but when I turned, it was only a reflection off the garage windows. Velvet's "woof" chastised me for my immobility, so I opened the car door. The cool morning air brushed my cheeks and the distinct yodel of a loon drifted up to me. I walked down to the shore and there, in the middle of the lake was a pair of loons. Velvet was dying to get at them, and each time they called, she woofed back.

The cry of a loon. Now that was a Minnesota sound. The loon's call was as familiar here as the eagle's twitter was out west where I'd lived since my marriage twenty-three years ago. I felt a measure of calmness flow over me and thought that maybe this would work out. I whistled for Velvet and we climbed the wide wooden porch steps to the gray clapboard house, my feet naturally seeking the worn places where they had always stepped.

The porch curved around from the side to the front where it opened out onto a broad deck that stretched across the width of the house, offering a postcard view of what we always called "our lake". With a longing backward glance at the loons and the two

Adirondack chairs on the deck, I retraced my steps to the kitchen door. I opened the storm door into the kitchen, grateful that Celeste had left it unlocked for me, and noticed she had left a cobweb between it and the inside door. I glanced up at the lone spider hanging there, paying my respects as I passed carefully beneath it into the house.

As soon as Velvet and I entered, she trotted off exploring the unfamiliar odors. Only the clicking of her nails on the hardwood floors interrupted the deep quiet of the house. The smells that greeted me were of polished wood and an old house that had been shut up for a while, maybe a hint of mildew, the acrid smell of mothballs thrown under the sink to discourage any enterprising mice or squirrels, and a faint whiff of something that reached me from my childhood and told me I was home.

I wondered if others were struck only by fond memories when they revisited places of their youth. As I looked around, what bombarded me was an overwhelming feeling of sadness and loss.

My mother Adrienne, an architect, had designed this house in an open style that was ahead of its time. Unfortunately, I didn't have a whole lot of memories of her, but standing in the kitchen, it seemed as if she was everywhere. Suddenly I had an image of coming home after my first day of Kindergarten.

* * *

"Hey, Pip," she called from the living room as she heard me close the door. "How did it go?"

"Okay," I mumbled as I unbuttoned my coat and untied the matching woolen cap. I carefully hung the coat on the rack by the door, but kicked the cap underneath it. Mum arrived at the doorway in time to see me.

"Why are you doing that to your cap, Pip?" I stood there with my back to her. "Turn around please." I obeyed, and as soon as I saw her, I started crying. She scooped me up, and I clung to her as we passed back into the living room. She sat on the couch, settled me on her lap, and held me until my sobs abated. "Can you tell me what happened?"

I breathed in her comforting lavender smell and nodded. "The kids in the car pool teased me about my cap 'cause it is pointy on both sides. They said with my green eyes I looked like a kitty cat. 'Kitty cat, kitty cat, Pru is a kitty cat!'" Mum hugged me harder. "And that's not all. I couldn't find my desk and I didn't know all the letters that were up on the wall. I hate kindergarten. Do I have to go back?"

"Oh, Pip. What a hard way to start your first day of school. As for the letters, no one expects you to know all of them your first day. That's why you're going to school, to learn. If you don't want to wear the cap, you can wear your old hat. You can be sure the other kids won't be teasing you when I drive. And I'll talk to the other mothers." Her dark brown eyes flashed. She shifted me in her lap, easing me off, and stood up. "I have an idea." She led me to her drafting table in the corner of the living room. Sitting on the high stool, she hoisted me again onto her lap, and leaned forward to pick up a pencil and a small piece of paper. With me folded into her, her salt and pepper hair tickling my cheeks, she quickly drew the face of a beautiful green-eyed tabby cat, who managed to look like me. She held it at arm's length, added a few whiskers, and then said, "Here, Pip. Tuck this into your lunch box. If anyone teases you again, whether it's about the cap or something else, you can take this out and look at it. It's to remind you of how much I love you."

I turned my face into her and hugged her hard. She handed me the picture and after carefully folding it, I hopped off the stool and walked back into the hall to get my lunch box. I reached under the hat rack and retrieved the pointy cap which I hung up, then I took my lunch box into the kitchen ready for tomorrow's lunch. Mum met me in there. "So, you think you might go back tomorrow?" She nodded at the box.

I stood up straighter and said, "Now I do." I opened the box, put the drawing in it and snapped it shut.

"Good, let's have some applesauce to celebrate." She pulled out a jar of the applesauce I'd helped make on the old iron cook stove, using the apples from my grandparents' farm. My favorite afternoon treat.

* * *

I looked around the kitchen, trying to remember when Dad had removed the old stove. As I glanced towards my father's study, my stomach lurched and I decided to save it for later. Instead, I climbed the stairs. Velvet bounded up ahead of me and stood at the top, waiting. I quickly skipped over the second to last step where I would crouch, eavesdropping on my parents' arguments. Arriving upstairs, I looked around at the four bedrooms opening off the hallway. Two were at the front, two at the back. My parents always put the youngest child in the bedroom next to theirs as it was easier for them to hear a baby's cry. As the last child, the small front room had remained mine. A door from my room opened onto a balcony shared by the master bedroom. I unlocked the balcony door and took a moment to enjoy this view of the lake. Velvet wandered out and lay by the railing. I left the door open to air out the upstairs while I explored the rest of the bedrooms, first crossing the dated hall carpet to Paul's room. A stale odor of old socks met me, left behind from Paul's teenage years when he played baseball. I pushed up the window and then approached Celeste's room. Here I noticed a familiar flowery smell. I opened that window and left her door ajar as well. Next, I pulled at the door that led up to the attic. It was locked. I'd have to ask Celeste about the key. I returned to my room and sat in the old rocker where Mum used to rock me. Gazing out at the lake, I could feel the cool cross-breeze freshen the house.

As I rocked, other pictures lurked at the edge of my memory. They seemed a bit closer than ever before, but whether I didn't remember or couldn't wasn't clear to me. I decided I had better things to do than try to figure that out now.

"Come on, Velvet, Let's get some stuff unpacked." I clambered down the stairs, Velvet rumbling down after me. She whipped around me and made for the door. I pulled her water bowl out of the back of the car and filled it for her. She slurped it down in a very un-lady-like manner and lay down on the porch, looking as if she had lived here forever. Easy for her. I hauled my suitcase out of the car, added my purse and backpack and climbed up the stairs to at least start making my nest in this new old place.

"Yoo Hoo!" My activities were interrupted by a First Soprano call. Celeste! I thundered down the stairs again. Part of me wanted to fling myself into her arms, but something in the way she stood stopped me.

"Is this creature yours? I found him poking around the bushes." Celeste pointed to Velvet.

"Yup, and he's a she. Her name is Velvet." At the sound of her name, Velvet wagged her curly white tail and snuffled her nose into Celeste's hand looking for a treat. Celeste bent down to pat her.

"Oh, I must smell good. My two dogs, not to mention oats and carrots and all sorts of horsy odors. She's beautiful."

"Yeah, I know, but she's part Malamute and the saying about them is that they are great watchdogs – as in watching while the thieves come and take everything you have." Celeste chuckled then fell silent. She stood up from patting Velvet and looked at me.

I folded my arms across my chest, hands stuck in opposite armpits, and said, "So, how are you?"

"Fine," Celeste said, continuing to stare. "You look good," she added, with a peculiar lack of enthusiasm that told me I probably looked terrible. I hadn't washed my hair in two days and the brown strands stuck to my head, while the white streaks sprung out around them in a bed-head arrangement.

"Likewise, Sister." However, I meant it. Celeste was almost sixty-seven but looked a decade younger. As a child, I had envied her thick curly hair. It had turned white since the last time I saw her, but it was still curly, resulting in a wild mane that framed her face, emphasizing her dark brown eyes and still black eyebrows. Even dressed in old riding pants and big rubber Wellingtons she looked elegant, mostly due to her long graceful legs which she inherited from Mum.

"Been mucking out stalls?" I glanced at her boots. Straw was stuck to some indeterminate dried stuff on the toes.

"Yep. How long have you been here?" She gestured to the U-Haul sitting out front, still unpacked.

"Not long. I just brought my suitcase up and put it in my old room. Before that, I was wandering through the house getting flashes of pictures in my mind of Mum and Dad."

"Oh?" Celeste raised an eyebrow, then looked at me with narrowed eyes. "Like pictures or real flashing lights?"

"Both. Why? Am I missing something?"

"Hard not to, after all these years." Celeste's eyes drilled into me, then slid sideways.

I tensed. Good old Celeste. Some things never change.

"Still not holding back any, are you, Celeste?"

"Guess not." Her shoulders hunched, then relaxed. "Let's leave it for now, Pru, and get you unpacked. Any big stuff you need help with?"

I decided not to push it, so I matched her lighter tone. "Not really, since you said a lot of the old furniture was in pretty good shape. By the way, how is old Hank? I'm surprised he decided to go into a nursing home. Paul said he was always such a free spirit even if he was a little odd." Paul was my older brother with whom I actually had communicated over the years.

"Well," replied Celeste, "Hank didn't exactly decide to go in on his own. The odd part started usurping the free spirit. He stopped taking care of the house to the extent that I had to have one of my men come over and paint it last year. He had stacks of magazines and newspapers all over. You could barely make a path through.

At times he'd barricade himself in and wouldn't open the door when I brought him food. I had to lock the attic as he started rummaging around up there. He kept mumbling about something he had to find. Finally, I contacted the Veterans Administration hospital and they found a spot for him on their elderly unit."

"Does he have Alzheimer's?" I asked.

"I'm not sure," answered Celeste. "Since I'm not real family, the staff doesn't tell me much when I visit. Sometimes I feel badly that he's there, but," she paused, "I can only do so much." Before I could respond, Celeste brushed her hands together. "So, let's get to work. Does Velvet carry anything useful?"

I walked briskly after her, trying to keep up. "Nope. Hopefully, she'll stick around while we carry stuff. She seems to sense that I need her."

"Oh?" Celeste raised her eyebrow again. I ignored the look and reached down to grab the canvas strap to pull up the back of the U-Haul. The door spring was so well oiled, I had to let go before it pulled me up as well.

For the next hour we carried in boxes, lamps, small tables, suitcases, and pictures. Occasionally we'd bump into each other while carrying boxes too big to see over. At times it seemed like a competition to see who could finish first. Either that or a bad Laurel and Hardy movie. We finally collapsed on two old wooden chairs we had plunked down in the hall. Celeste leaned forward, hands on her knees, elbows out.

"Jeeze, Pru. I thought telling you the house was furnished would make your trip light. What is all this junk?"

"I thought maybe I could turn my love of flea markets and auctions into some sort of income for myself while I'm here. David won't need much, living on the boat."

"Oh?" Celeste leaned back and crossed her legs, bouncing one big rubber-booted foot.

God, was she going to keep saying that every time I told her something? And didn't she ever sit still? I couldn't believe how much she was already getting on my nerves. I took a breath. "Look, Celeste, obviously we both need to start somewhere with each other, and I promise I will explain why I have suddenly appeared after all these years, but I'd rather get settled first. I know you have to get back to the horses. I can take the rest from here."

Thankfully, Celeste got the hint. "Oh, sure. But come over for supper later. About six? You can walk over on the old road. Velvet can come and meet my dogs. *They'll* get along." She stood up and swept out the door, tossing the last comment over her shoulder.

"Thanks," I called with mixed feelings. From my summers home during college, I remembered my sister was a fabulous cook but her housekeeping skills were far inferior to her barn cleaning ones. One never knew whose hair would end up in your meal. "By the way," I added as she opened the door to her truck, "speaking of old memories, is there anything left of the old fur coat that used to hang in the woods?"

But she was already starting the engine so she didn't hear me. I would just have to check for myself.

October 8, 1944
Day Two

I've been away from my darling Adrienne and the children for a month already, and I miss them more than I can say – their laughter, their touch, their smell. Adrienne gave me one of her handkerchiefs sprinkled with her lavender toilet water that I inhale when I feel particularly lonely. The scent is already getting faint.

CHAPTER TWO

I spent the rest of the afternoon moving boxes and furniture, most of which I stored in my father's study. I recalled him napping on the old green leather sofa, his glasses perched on the edge of his nose, *The Minneapolis Tribune* and *The New Republic* scattered on the floor. Then I remembered being woken up by the sounds of his nightmares. When I would check on him, I could still smell the whiskey left in the glass by his bedside. I have racked my brain for years wondering why a man like him ended up needing to anaesthetize himself in order to sleep.

Was I really ready for all the images this coming-home business was bringing up? I wasn't at all sure. My breathing sped up and I started feeling a bit nauseous, so I beat a hasty retreat from the study and sat down in the comfy chair in the living room. I breathed deeply and counted to one hundred. Focus on the present moment, Pru. Put the food away, feed Velvet, and unpack. I took another long slow breath and went to work.

Once upstairs, I opened my suitcase and the first thing I unpacked was a small three by five photo of my mother's portrait. She had been twenty when it was painted, just before she married my father. For a moment I wondered where the original was, with Paul or Celeste? When I set the photo up in whatever bedroom I inhabited, I felt like she was watching over me.

I never knew the woman who looked that young. By the time I came along, Mum had been through the Depression and World

War Two and thought she was at the end of her childbearing years. I must have been quite a surprise.

I sat down on my bed. Exhausted from the trip and feeling a bit surreal from all the events of the past two weeks, I found myself staring at the picture. I wondered if the young debutante in the photograph ever dreamed of the life she was to live.

The loons calling to each other brought my thoughts back into the room. Time to get ready to go to Celeste's.

An hour later, feeling better after a shower and change of clothes, with Velvet trotting along beside me, I started for the farm.

Celeste lived on what used to be Grandpa and Grandma Dillen's dairy farm. Replacing the cows were fifteen horses of various breeds and lineage, not to mention temperament.

Dad and Mum had bought Celeste her first horse, Sunrise, when she was a horse-crazy teen. The year after I was born, Celeste had graduated from high school, skipped college and went straight into the jump circuit, winning ribbons and trophies urging Sunrise over massive stadium jumps. Then, all of a sudden, she stopped, and was working at the stables with Glen, the man who had trained her. She was still living at home the year Mum died, but I rarely saw her and since I was just five, she never talked to me about anything going on in her life. It wasn't until I was sent to live with Uncle Hugh and Aunt Alice in Boston when I was nine that I learned that Celeste had battled a serious drug and alcohol problem while on the circuit. Mum and Dad finally convinced her to go into treatment, and Glen gave her a job. Celeste found out she had a love and talent for working with all kinds of horses and riders. By the time I was in high school out East, Celeste had taken over the farm and was running a training and boarding stable. Her skills were so well known in the horse world that she rarely had empty stalls. It would never occur to Celeste to give a name to what she did, but to those who knew her, she was not only a horse trainer, she was a horse whisperer. Too bad it didn't transfer over to her family.

The trail I was following was created when my parents built the house. Once graveled and well-kept, in the time I had been away, the road had deteriorated into nothing more than a footpath. Ferns and moss lined the path's edge, while evergreens, oaks, and basswood soared overhead. Every so often I would catch the murmur of the brook that ran from the bottom of the farm's fields into the lake. Velvet was absorbed by the new smells and sniffed at a plant so long that I figured she was tracing the ancestors of the animal who last peed there. Then she got a whiff of something else and nose up, she started pulling me.

"I don't think so. That's why you're on a leash." Of course she ignored me and pulled some more. I yanked her back. She sat down with an injured look.

The late afternoon sun still shone brightly through the trees, casting dappled patterns on the ground.

* * *

One of my few positive memories of Dad was working in the woods with him the spring I was eight. He gave me a small pair of clippers and I helped him as best I could, cutting back the underbrush while he cleared the area around a beautiful stand of maples. On one of these occasions I got bored with my task and wandered off to find the thickest, softest moss to line the granite clearing I had found for a make-believe house. Dad gave me the job of keeping track of Chloe, our Pomeranian-Chow mix, so she came with me, snuffling here and there after intriguing smells. I found a lush patch of moss that I carried back to the clearing, not aware that Chloe was no longer behind me.

As I was laying my moss carpet carefully in a neat square, I heard Chloe's high-pitched yipping. Dad turned to me, using my family nickname.

"Pip, where's Chloe?" he asked.

"Oops! Sorry, Dad. I'll get her!"

I left my tidy carpet and worked my way out to the road, remembering the boulder that marked my exit from the part of the woods Dad was clearing. Following Chloe's yips, I ran down the path towards Grandpa's farm, my sneakers crunching on the gravel.

"Chloe, come!" I called as I ran.

I heard her off to my left and pushed through the undergrowth, feeling a bit like a fish swimming upstream. Chloe's barks grew louder. Finally, exhausted, I found her. And that wasn't all.

There, in front of me, was our little dog, orange fur fluffed up, a ridge of it standing straight up on her neck, pointed ears forward, nose quivering. She was yapping her head off at what looked like an old, ratty fur coat hanging on a wire hanger from a basswood tree branch. The fur was dark and mushed down. The hanger showed through one shoulder and the coat was torn at the bottom, as if an animal had tried to pull it off the hanger. I was so flabbergasted that I plopped down on a rock hard enough to make my bottom sting. I tried to quiet my frantic dog.

"Hush, Chloe. It's all right." But then I thought maybe it wasn't.

Having done her job of calling one of her humans, Chloe calmed down. I stood up and inched my way towards the tattered coat, not at all sure it was real. Chloe crept up with me and sniffed the hem. She sniffed it so intensely that it looked like her nose was glued to it. I patted the rough fur and took a whiff. Just the odor of mildewed fur and maybe something else very faint but familiar. It reminded me of riding up in a department store elevator, standing behind a lady whose mink stole wafted a fancy perfume. (Grandma Dillen used to raise her eyebrows at me as I would sidle closer to get the full scent, reaching out to barely touch the fur with my fingers.)

But this was the woods. Maybe it was just the smell of the sweet basswood flowers dipping towards me. I stared at the coat some more and noticed a breeze was moving the leaves of the tree. I looked around. None of the other trees was moving. A flashing spot on the coat caught my eye and I turned around to see where it was *coming from.* As I did so, I almost stumbled down the steep ravine that fell to the babbling brook below.

The sun glittered on something halfway down. I looked harder. It was a mirror attached to a rusty blue car that looked like it, too, had been there for ages.

More excited than scared, I carefully moved away from the edge of the gorge and called Chloe. Together we crashed through the underbrush to the road. After breaking a branch to find my way in again, I ran pell-mell back down the road to Dad. I saw the boulder and heard the whack of his axe. I turned in, yelling as I ran.

"Dad! Dad! Come see what Chloe found!" I rushed to his side. He stood with his hand on the axe handle, looking at me in a peculiar way.

"What, Pip? If it's a skunk we're not going anywhere near it."

"Well, it has fur but it isn't a skunk. I'm not that dumb! Come on!" I grabbed his other hand. He was forced to drop the axe and follow however awkwardly, as I wouldn't let go of him. We reached the road, and still pulling him along with me, I headed back to Chloe's mysterious find.

"See?" I waited for his reaction.

"What the Hell?" Dad saved swearing for special occasions. His face turned white.

"How do you suppose it got here? How long do you think it's been here? Whose coat do you think it was? Oh, and there's more." I turned him around towards the edge of the ravine. "Look! An old car!"

My Dad glanced down and looked strange, like he was somewhere else. I squeezed his hand and he seemed to come to his senses. He looked at me and then looked around.

"This is quite an interesting find, Pru." All of a sudden he sounded like the professor he was, even forgoing my nickname.

"Do you know where they came from?"

"The automobile is probably an old moonshine car, used to transport the liquor folks around here made during a time when they weren't allowed to buy it in stores. As for the coat, Pru, that is a complete mystery."

"Oh." Then I had another idea. "Can we go look at the car? Maybe it will give us a clue to the coat."

"Not on your life Pru. And don't ever think about going down there on your own. That car is perched so precariously that just a bump could tumble it all the way down and you with it. I couldn't stand losing you, too."

That was enough to quiet me down. My Mum had died suddenly of a heart attack three years earlier. Dad had been so sad ever since, I would never want to make him sadder. "Don't worry, Dad. But if I promise not to go near the car, do you mind if I visit the coat every so often? I kind of like it." He was quiet. We turned back to the garment.

"I guess not, but let's keep it in the family. I don't want all sorts of strangers coming in to gape."

I had already thought of bringing my friends but instead I gave in to Dad's request, settling for telling Celeste and Paul. "Oh, all right."

"Now, let's get back. I have a few more dead branches to clear before we're done for the day. Do you need more moss for your house?"

Thus distracted, I bent down to gather some more, said a mental goodbye to the coat, and followed Dad back to his clearing.

* * *

After what seemed like several hours but was just a few minutes, judging by the fact that the light around me hadn't changed, Velvet's whine brought my daydreaming to a halt. Her nose was in the air again. It was the same time of year as that long ago June and the basswood flowers were out. Maybe that was what she was sniffing. Then, without warning, she jerked me to my feet, forcing me to follow, nose still high. Abruptly, she veered off the path to the left, the bushes scratching my arms as we pushed through them. The burble of the brook was louder. Finally, I could see flashes of it below me. My memory of where I was returned to me.

"Wait!" I said. I pulled Velvet back up off the edge of the ravine just in time, then stared down. There it was. The old car. Still in the same position. I turned around knowing what I would see when I did.

The beautiful basswood tree stood tall, its trunk splitting into two sturdy branches that soared up to the sky, heart-shaped leaves glowing in the sun and dancing in the light breeze, delicate white flowers hidden beneath them. Around the middle section of the trunk clung little tufts of fur as if some woodland nymph had embarked on a forest beautification project and then given up.

It was all that was left of the fur coat. The old basswood on which it had originally hung had died and rotted. If a new tree hadn't grown up inside the coat, most likely it would have just disintegrated and become part of the earth. I approached, marveling at how many tufts were still left, and carefully stroked one of the matted patches like the long-ago girl in the elevator patting the mink stole. Velvet sniffed at a few lower bits, then rubbed her ruff against them. She usually did that only with strong odors, where other animals had slept, or with dead seals on the beach. I leaned down and inhaled, but all I detected was the old flowery smell from the basswood flowers hanging in clusters right under my nose. I felt I was missing something again, like in so many parts of my life. I gave the furry tree a final pat.

"See you later." I whispered as I turned to leave, remembering to bend a branch out by the path to find my way back, like I had done years ago.

Time to face Celeste and admit that she had been right from the very beginning about David. I had gone through several boyfriends by the time I met him, but in the end, each had decided in the words of Jack, the last one, that I was "too high maintenance." I was twenty-seven when I met David, and the relationship might have gone down the same road as the others if I hadn't gotten pregnant with Jess. That was when Celeste and I began to argue. She told me I was making the biggest mistake of my life, that I didn't have to get married; I could raise a baby on my own. I had a good job and a career. I yelled back that not everyone was as unconventional as she was, and that I was lucky David wanted to do "the right thing". I was terrified of being alone with a baby "out of wedlock", as they called it back then. Neither Celeste nor I could see the other person's point of view, but kept insisting that each of us was right. Celeste refused to come to my wedding. I waited as long as I could before cutting the cake, but she never showed up. Today was the first time I had seen her since, although my brother Paul had kept me up on her general activities over the years.

It took my youngest son, Adrian, moving out and leaving me with an empty nest for me to realize my marriage was in tatters. Twenty-three years seems like a long time, but not when it is filled with a career, children, friends and activities. At times over the years, David and I seemed to click, especially after he got sober, and I started going to Al-Anon to learn how to take care of myself, but then when everything seemed smooth again, I stopped going and turned a blind eye to David's next addiction – women. Over this past Easter Adrian told me that even he and Jess had figured out long ago what their Dad's pretty graduate "assistants" were all about. At Adrian's urging, I promised to think about what I wanted to do with my life now that he and Jess were out of the house. Celeste's call gave me more to ponder, then what finally sealed it was finding David and one of the assistants on our boat when I thought he had gone to a convention. I had to do something different. I didn't work summers, so I decided to come to Minnesota to see if I could repair the rift with Celeste. As Velvet and I came to the opening at the bottom of the fields, however, my pace slowed as I wondered what the evening with my sister would bring.

October 9, 1944
Day Three

I know that Adrienne doesn't really understand why I am doing this. At times, I'm not sure myself. When I saw Hank off to Europe last spring, I realized that the chances of him coming back alive were very slim. I could no longer sit by the radio while he and others continued to sacrifice their lives to battle Hitler and his fellow Axis powers. How could I encourage Hank to sign up, if I didn't? We've been like brothers. How could I look him in the face if he does return, if I did nothing in this war? How could I live with myself doing nothing if he fails to return? And my Adrienne. She fell in love with someone she thought would go places. She says she is happy but how do I really know? I guess I still feel I need to prove myself to her.

CHAPTER THREE

Emerging from the woods, I could see the roof and upper windows of the farmhouse. In front of me was a long hill covered with the bright grass of early summer. Five horses grazed contentedly. I followed the path until it ended at the turn of the farm's driveway. Since Velvet was almost pulling me up the hill, I decided to jog the rest of the way to the farmhouse.

I stopped and stared at the house. It still looked the same. A big white square, now with green trim, formed the original homestead that Grandpa Dillen had inherited from his parents. The square houses were easier to build in the days when neighbors got together to "raise the walls". This design was also the best one to keep the families warm in the dead of winter when the glowing potbellied wood stove and the kitchen range were the only sources of heat. Placing the bedrooms right above the living room and kitchen ensured that they stayed somewhat snug most of the night. It wasn't until early morning, after peeking a cold nose out of the covers, that someone had to tiptoe downstairs to stoke the fires.

Since taking over the farm, with the help of electric heating, Celeste had built two wings that grew from the back of the house to make a big U. One was kept intact for family and guests, while the other served as a bunkhouse for the farm hands and visiting riders. My gaze shifted to the barn beyond the far side of the house. White and green as well, the stables stood at right angles to the house, imitating its U shape. As I was staring at it, two black and white streaks erupted from the house.

Celeste called, "You might as well let Velvet go. She's about to be greeted!" Velvet was already dancing at the end of the leash. I unclipped her quickly as Celeste's two dogs circled her. Velvet whipped around and circled back. Before I knew it, all three dogs were tearing across the lawn towards the barn.

As I approached Celeste I asked, "What about the horses? Velvet has never met one."

"Not to worry. She'll hang with my guys. She'll learn."

The guys in question were two different versions of black and white. One was a Border Collie with only three legs who still outran and out-cornered the other two. The other was a black and white Newfoundland almost the size of a small pony. With Velvet as the third, they made an amazing montage.

"What happened to the Collie?" I asked.

"Leg got caught in an illegal trap," was the terse reply. "Come on, Pip, Velvet'll be fine."

I looked once more, then turned to Celeste. "So, what gourmet meal did you whip up tonight?" I followed her into the kitchen, the heart of the house. The flooring had been updated, keeping the old black and white square design I remembered from my youth. The large white enameled woodstove still dominated the kitchen, with a more modern cousin beside it. An old oak drop-leaf table sat in the middle of the room surrounded by four press-backed oak chairs. I flopped onto one.

"What will you have, Pip?" Celeste asked.

"Sparkling water with lemon or lime, if you have it."

"Ah, you've come to the right place. Cold Spring water from just down the road. Hey, we in the Midwest are even yuppified enough to offer you the lime." I made a face at her as she bustled about, her white hair escaping from an old tortoiseshell barrette. She poured two waters over ice, topping each with a slice of lime and joined me at the table. For the next hour we skimmed the surface, talking like two neighbors having tea about what my kids were up to, Celeste's newest training project, and how Paul and his wife Annie were doing. When we ran out of those topics, we moved on to politics and, inevitably, the weather. Anything but the huge white elephant standing smack in the middle of the kitchen. The warm smell of melting cheddar cheese wafted under my nose.

Thinking that exchanging recipes would provide the next filler, I asked, "Are you going to give up what's for dinner?" but Celeste took the elephant by the trunk and led it right to the table.

"Aah, a secret, my dear sister. It won't be ready for a while, so you finally have time to tell me what the hell is happening that you are sitting at my table with all your worldly goods at the lake house. When I called you about Hank, I hoped it might start us talking at least, but this scenario never occurred to me in my wildest dreams."

I stood up, crossed to the window, and looked out. "Are the dogs okay?" Unfortunately for me, Velvet looked like she was in doggy heaven.

"Yep," Celeste said. She leaned forward in that way she had with her hands on her knees. I wandered around the room, stopped at the cupboard, and took down some dinner plates. Celeste watched me. "I already have some warming on the back of the stove." I returned the plates to their nest and looked at the old wood stove, my back to Celeste.

"Is that the one Grandma Dillen taught Mum to cook on?"

"Yep."

"What happened to the one we used to have?"

Celeste cleared her throat. "Um, I think Dad sold it after Mum died."

"Earlier today I was remembering Mum teaching me how to

THE COAT IN THE WOODS 31

make applesauce on that old stove." My voice caught a bit. I stood there, lost in thought. A single tear rolled down my cheek.

"Pip, what's going on?" Celeste's voice softened just a tad.

Silence.

Then before I knew it, still standing with my back to Celeste, I started sobbing. The tears were flowing down my cheeks like a brook in spring flood. Soon I was hiccuping, my nose running. Celeste stood up, took me by the shoulders, gently turned me around, and led me to a chair. I sat down. She pulled a wad of tissue from her ample cleavage and thrust it into my hand. I wiped my nose and continued crying. Celeste pulled up another chair and sat down with her hand on my arm as if I was one of her broken-down horses. Maybe I was. Finally I stopped with a big sigh and only intermittent sniffles.

"I didn't know what to do. This was the only thing I could think of, to come home. You know, like Dad after the mess in England."

Celeste tucked a straggling curl behind her ear. "Will you please talk to me, Pip?"

I blew my nose. A real honker. That was an icebreaker. We both laughed. "Things haven't been really going well between David and me for a long time." I looked down, then up at my sister.

She gave me a thin smile. "Is this where I finally get to say 'I told you so'?"

"Looks like it. Ever since I decided to drive out, I knew we'd get to this point."

"Go on. The ball is in your court."

I straightened up in the chair. "You saw something in David from the beginning that took me years to see. For a long time I couldn't bear to admit that you were right. Then, after a while, it was just easier not to call you, not to write, not to visit, and just let the geographical distance take over. After all, it's not like I was ever a big part of yours and Paul's life anyway, being so much younger."

Celeste's brown eyes turned dark. "And I couldn't stand that you went ahead and married David in spite of what I thought was obvious. Then, I decided, fine, you never did like it when I gave you advice, so I wasn't going to bother ever again."

I nodded, thinking how alike we were in spite of the years between us. It was quiet except for the ticking of the kitty cat clock on the wall over the stove. I stared at the tail, sweeping back and forth. Celeste tapped me on the shoulder.

"If you've been living that way for such a long time, what spurred you to finally come home?"

I focused back on Celeste and told her the shortened version of the last few months. "Even the kids knew, Celeste. Adrian, who has always been the kid who tells me stuff about myself I don't want to hear, couldn't believe I'd been hoodwinked all these years."

"Were you?"

"Down deep, not really. But I always hoped that I was wrong. Denial and delusion have been my friends for so long, it's been hard to give them up."

"Coming from our family, that makes sense," Celeste said.

"It does?" I asked.

"Later, Pip. When you told David what you were going to do, did he at least apologize for the boat sweetie?"

"Not a word, but that's how it was with us. If we didn't talk about it, we didn't have to deal with it. Instead, David became oh so reasonable and told me I could take anything I wanted from the house since he might go and live on the boat."

"Thus your earlier comment about him not needing much stuff."

"Right. Sometimes I think we should just have ranted and raved at each other more often over the years."

"Pip, we grew up not knowing any other way. It didn't work to show we were upset." Celeste pushed the errant curl behind her ear again.

"Celeste, I can't remember much about growing up, at least around here."

"Maybe I can help with that. But to finish up here, any thoughts beyond the summer?"

"Hey, until now, I was just trying to get up the courage get this far. If I take it one step at a time, hopefully I'll know what I want to do before the summer is over. There are plenty of younger school psychologists being churned out daily. My director won't mind paying less for someone with less experience. If I stay here I'll find some way to keep paying into my retirement until I figure out what else to do." I started sniffling again and drank some water. "I guess it's back to taking care of myself again. Are there any good Al-Anon meetings nearby?"

"You bet, even one on the same night as my AA meeting. You know Minnesota. Rehab Heaven." We both laughed.

"Good. Now, Celeste, dinner must be ready. Feed me."

October 10, 1944
Day Four

I realize I am one of the few on this ship who actually knows we are heading to the Far East. With the number of men on this freighter there must be some kind of push going on. Ed couldn't tell me where I was going, but why else would they need someone with expertise in Far Eastern languages? I'm sure that's the only reason they decided to take on an old man like me. Good thing I've kept myself in shape with farming and working in the woods. And if something happens to me out there, I will no doubt be grateful for having learned those commando techniques.

CHAPTER FOUR

Later, Celeste and I sat on the front porch and looked out at the late evening sky. Our stomachs were full of Celeste's wild rice and cheese casserole, washed down with thick Guernsey milk from Celeste's cow Sophie, who made you wish you had never heard of bad cholesterol. The dogs, exhausted and fed, stretched out around us, occasionally whimpering and moving their hind legs as if still playing and chasing. I felt calmer than I had in a long time. I glanced at my sister.

"Celeste, how did you know David wasn't good for me?"

"First, there was your track record, and David wasn't much different from the other guys you had brought home, plus the fact that observing behavior is one of the things I do. I can't just turn it off when I'm not working with horses. Then there is just gut instinct. Even Paul, who I don't think is the most intuitive person on the planet, noticed."

"Except he didn't manage to alienate me."

"You did that to yourself, Pip. All I did was tell it like I saw it. There's nothing wrong with you that a little dose of independence and reality won't fix."

I bristled. Here we went again. "I don't know about that. I'm not exactly enjoying the dose I've been taking in the last few weeks."

Celeste sat back and put her foot on her knee in that annoyingly confident pose of hers. She seemed undeterred. "Hey, life changes aren't always fun at the time but that doesn't mean they're bad. Look at you. Just by being here, you've taken a big step. Maybe you'll look back on this whole situation as one of the best things that ever happened to you."

"And what makes you the authority on that, Big Sister?"

Celeste uncrossed her leg and softly replied, "Lots of pain, Pip, lots."

"I'm sorry Cel. Why do I seem to get my back up when you zero in on me?"

Celeste perked up a bit. "Because you know I'm right?"

I had to laugh. "Probably. But you didn't hear that from me."

It was her turn to chuckle. "For my part, after Mum died, maybe I confused the roles of sister and mother a bit."

"Maybe? A bit?"

"All right, all right. But I've got to tell you, during that period when Dad wanted me to be your nanny, drinking was starting to look good again. Thank God for Grandma Dillen."

"About the drinking. Dad told me the basics, but the trouble about being the caboose in the family by so many years is that no one thinks you're old enough to handle the details. Think you can do that yet?"

Celeste rolled her eyes. "Guess it's time," she sighed and began. "I started drinking as far back as my early teens, after Mum and Dad gave me Sunrise. I loved riding him from the first day and sitting still in school had always been tough for me. So I would cut school and get a ride out to the stables and hang out with the grooms, who thought it entertaining to give me a shot of whatever they had, as well as teach me all the swear words they knew."

"That must have gone over well," I said, thinking of the reserved professor father that I had known.

"You bet. Dad backed Mum up, but she was the disciplinarian. Instead of grounding me, she would have a talk with me about how disappointed she was. That sure back-fired. Instead of buckling down, I began hanging out at the stable even more, lying to my trainer, Glen, that my folks said it was okay. I barely squeaked by to get my high school diploma. When the circuit lured me with illusions of success for those two short years, I hardly ever came home."

"Where did the other drugs come in?"

"There weren't many women on the jump circuit back then, so in order to maintain an edge, I'd use amphetamines – bennies, they used to call them. Then I'd drink hard afterwards, in addition to taking downers to relax. When I started using and drinking more than I was winning, Glen was the one who took me to my first AA meeting. I just pretended to work the program at first, so eventually I had to go for treatment. When I came out of that, I had a clearer idea of what I needed to do with my life and it didn't include going back on the circuit. Glen offered me a job, training, and with that I finally found my niche."

"It's sad you had to give up something you loved so much."

"It took me a while to differentiate between my love of riding and competing. My drug and alcohol use told me that I couldn't really deal with the competition. I finally figured out that I was only competing as a way to live up to Mum and it wasn't working."

"What do you mean? You were so lucky you knew her, Celeste."

"Yes, I guess I was, but she was a hard act to follow. She was so smart and well educated. In this day and age, you forget what a big deal it was for her to have graduated when she was twenty and land a job in a fancy New York architectural firm. And there I was. More like Grandpa Dillen than her. Happiest when I was mucking around the stables.

I smiled at her.

She looked back, scowling. "So I bare my soul and you think it is funny?"

"Relax, Cel. I wasn't laughing at you. As you were talking, it occurred to me that you're more like Mum than you think. Bolting from the East Coast nest and marrying the son of a German immigrant from the Midwest and a Catholic to boot wasn't exactly the life Grandmother had in mind for her either."

The slow smile that drifted across Celeste's face told me she was taking this in. "Not a bad observation for a little squirt."

"I did manage to learn some family history from my years with Aunt Alice and Uncle Hugh. Did you and Mum ever find some middle ground?"

"When I got sober enough to want to develop a relationship with her. We actually were starting to click once I began working for Glen. Then, of course, she died." Celeste's eyes filled with tears. She blinked them back.

"Well, she did so knowing you were going to be okay." It was my turn to be reassuring.

"I guess, but when she died, I almost wasn't again. Dad seemed to expect me to drop everything I'd worked so hard for to take care of you."

"And we all know how successful that was."

"Yes, you were a little creep, but hey, you'd just lost your mum too and Dad had disappeared into the college library, or the radio, so no wonder you were a brat."

"What about Paul? Why didn't he stick around?"

"Going into the army after college was his own way of escaping. I'm sorry Pip. We all deserted you. At that point we were thinking about our own survival."

"I understand," I said, although a part of me didn't – because feelings of abandonment and guilt were at the root of my life-long habit of creating an invisible shield of shatterproof glass around me. A habit, that come to think of it, was partially responsible for where I was today. The only time the shield didn't protect me was when I was caught by surprise. That's when the anxiety attacks hit, like something sneaking under the glass.

"Pru? Anybody home?" Celeste's question penetrated my wandering thoughts.

"Sorry, I was off somewhere else."

"No kidding."

"Tell me something, Celeste. Before I came along, what was family life like for you and Paul?"

"Life was pretty good. We seemed to have a lot of fun."

"What changed it? My birth?" Ping! A small sharp pebble flew at my invisible glass protector. A tiny spider web crack appeared in one corner. My throat started closing up again. I drank some water. The activity seemed to help as the crack stopped moving.

"Oh, Pip, is that what you have believed all these years?" Celeste leaned over and gave me a pat on the arm. "I think the war was more responsible than you. You were just a surprise baby who came along late in Mum and Dad's life – definitely more of a gift than a burden. We were all pretty excited about you joining the family. Then five years later, Mum died and so did family life as we knew it. When Paul and I were kids it seemed that things were fairly normal, and from what Grandma Dillen used to tell me, Mum and Dad lived an interesting life before we were born, apparently happy in spite of all the challenges they faced coming back to live here."

"Good. So tell me more. For a language teacher, Dad was a lousy story teller."

October 11, 1944
Day Five

It seems that the name given me during training has followed me onto the ship. We all went by nicknames during our time in camp. None of us knew if our partners were civilian or military, officers or enlisted men. My name of course is 'Pop', since most of these boys are only a few years older than my Celeste. Yesterday we crossed through the Panama Canal. Since everyone now knows where we're heading, I've been told to hold classes for the men, mainly in Chinese and Japanese, so sometimes I get called 'The Prof'.

CHAPTER FIVE

"Before I get going," said Celeste, "what do you remember about Grandma Dillen?" She dug past her tanned chest into the unknown depths and retrieved another scrunched-up tissue. She dabbed at something in her nose and returned the tissue to its hiding place. I tried not to stare. Since my boobs are the economy size from our mother's side, I always marvelled at Celeste's shelf. I often wondered whether her breasts would get caught in her belt if she didn't wear a bra. I decided not to go there. Instead I asked, "How in the world did you jump huge fences without extreme pain before sports bras were invented?"

Celeste's eyes twinkled. "Those were the days of what we called the iron maidens. Believe me, nothing moved inside those babies. I remember a sign in the department store in St Cloud where I bought them. It read: 'Nice girls don't point'."

I snickered, she guffawed, and within minutes we were both doubled over in a full-blown giggle event, reminiscent of times when we were both a lot younger. When we finally wound down, we dug out tissues again, she from the cavern, me from my pocket.

"Your question was?" I prompted, dabbing at the tears in my eyes.

"Grandma Dillen."

"I remember tissues stuffed in her bosom and the edges of them peeking out from her cleavage, tickling my nose when she would hug me. And her digging them out like you just did. I remember coming home after school when she took care of me after you turned tail, her teaching me how to make cookies, the smell of applesauce, and her green eyes, which always seemed a mismatch with her white bun and solid build. I remember she loved to tell stories about the old days, but I don't remember the stories."

"You know, you have Grandma's eyes, although they haven't been snapping recently. When you were annoyed with me earlier, it was actually nice to see that gleam back!"

Before I had a chance to digest that one, she continued, "What do you remember about Grandpa Dillen?"

"Hard to say. Didn't he die when I was about one?"

"Two"

"Oh, then that makes sense."

"What?"

"All I have is a picture of a big gnarled hand with veins standing out underneath grey fuzz, holding onto my small paw in such a way that I knew I was safe."

"Oh, yes, he was dotty over you. He was the one who gave you your nickname, you were such a pipsqueak. He was quite a guy. A study in contrasts."

"What do you mean?" With that, Celeste settled into a full two hours of stories about Grandma and Grandpa, the Depression and our family's active participation in making Avon the moonshine capital during Prohibition, including how Hank's dad, Angus, had been responsible for the formula they used. Finally, my rear told me I had to get off the porch chair. Stretching, I said, "Thanks for the stories, Cel. I'm beginning to feel like I'm almost a part of all this as opposed to a virtual stranger."

Celeste sat back and looked up at me. "Thanks too, Pip, for finally talking to me." Celeste rose also.

"Ditto. Maybe we can keep this going."

"We can always try."

I looked at her. No, she wasn't kidding. That was a good start.

"Want some milk and eggs for breakfast so you don't have to shop in the morning?" Celeste pulled the milk and a partially filled egg carton from the fridge.

"Sure. Oh, before I forget, do you have the key to the attic at the house?"

"Yep. I'll get it." She handed me the eggs and milk and headed out into the hall. I could hear the sound of a drawer opening and closing. I looked at my dog.

"Com'on, Velvet."

Velvet didn't move, just looked up at me and thumped her tail.

"Hey, I know I'm not as much fun as your doggy friends, but I'm all you've got right now. Let's go. We'll be back."

Recognizing the last two phrases, Velvet slowly rose, stretched front and back, and trotted to Celeste's truck with me. Celeste followed us out and handed me the attic key which I put in my pocket. The ride home was pretty quiet, but I swear Celeste hit every pothole in the road. When we pulled up, I opened the door. Velvet hopped out across me, and disappeared into the bushes. I stepped down from the truck.

Just as I was about to close the truck door, Celeste bounced in her seat and cried, "Oh! Menopause memory strikes again. I almost forgot. Guess who's also back in town for a while?"

I looked at her. "Celeste, I'm too tired for guessing games."

"Okay, okay. Sam Barrett."

"Little Sammy?"

"Yep, your childhood playmate. But he sure isn't very little anymore, and he's pretty sexy."

"Celeste!"

"He's been living in Canada all these years and came down to settle his dad in one of those retirement complexes. He opened a second-hand shop over by the Hair Connection and the laundromat. He and his dad dropped by the farm last week. Actually, he may want to see some of your treasures. Go check him – I mean it – out."

I made a face at her, then I grumped, "Yeah, maybe. Thanks for everything. I'll give you a ring tomorrow. 'Night."

"Night, Babe. Sleep tight." Celeste spun out and sped off down the driveway a whole lot faster than I'd go on the paved roads.

As she disappeared, I realized I had forgotten to tell her I'd found the coat tree. Maybe tomorrow. I called Velvet and we climbed the steps to the house and headed upstairs for our first night in the old homestead.

October 12, 1944
Day Six

Now that everyone knows we're headed to the Far Eastern Theater of the war, there are bets abounding about our assignment. The equipment issued to us gives us some clues, although the uniforms are pretty haphazard except for a good pair of canvas boots, khaki pants and shirts, an Aussie style jungle hat and a jungle knife. Sounds like it will be a far cry from the Minnesota woods!

CHAPTER SIX

The loons woke me up the next morning. I looked out over the foot of my bed and noticed Velvet on the balcony sitting up and sniffing the air. I stretched and felt every muscle in my back. If I was going to stay here very long, I would have to do something about this bed. It felt as if it still had the original mattress and box spring from my childhood. I spent most of the night trying to avoid the popped springs and ended up clinging to one side. I missed our big pillow-topped king. I pulled on a t- shirt, shorts and sneakers, and headed down the stairs, Velvet thumping after me. I wondered about letting her out without a leash, but decided everything was still new enough that she'd stick around. I hoped. Something else I'd have to do if I stayed here. Fence in part of the property.

Velvet returned looking hungry. I fed her, then scrambled some eggs, added toast, and took my plate and a large mug full of smoky Lapsang Souchong tea out to the deck. I ate while watching the loon couple. It looked as if they had a floating nest out in the middle of the lake, but I knew there was a little piece of land that jutted out just under the water. I wasn't a good enough bird watcher to know if the same pair returned every year, but two of them always did. Too bad my life wasn't that predictable.

I felt more grounded than I had in a long time. I soaked in the morning sun, listened to the loons, the gentle lap of the water, and the silence beyond. The ocean back home was never this quiet.

I wondered about all the family stories Celeste still had in store. Amazing what you can learn about the place you grew up in when you bother to look or listen. The problem was it wasn't really the place where I grew up. I had never felt I really belonged anywhere. I was sort of a Midwesterner, sort of an Easterner and then a transplanted Northwesterner. Maybe I should head to Arizona or Louisiana next to be sure I covered all the directions. I started chewing the insides of my cheeks as I pondered this, so I decided I wasn't going to dwell on it now. This was the exploration phase, not decision time.

I needed to go shopping for some food. Eggs and milk weren't going to take me very far and I couldn't ask Celeste to feed me every night. I decided to take some boxes of my treasures with me in case Sammy was at his store. If he truly was running the kind of business I had imagined, maybe he would take some of the things on consignment.

I only vaguely remembered his dad. A big man, Elias. He was a logger who did some clearing for Grandma. When he came, he used to bring Sammy for me to play with. I think Elias was friends with Mum and Dad although I don't remember anything about his wife. Did they do church stuff together? Democratic Party meetings? I'd have to ask Sammy. If he didn't know, then there was always the omniscient Celeste.

I carried my dishes back into the house, turned into the study, and picked out three boxes to take out to the car. After accomplishing that, I looked back towards the path I had walked yesterday to the farm. I'd have to ask Celeste if any of the old hiding places were still intact from the Prohibition days. Little Avon, who would have thought it. If anyone had asked me, I would have assumed that the Moonshine Capital was somewhere in Appalachia. Ah, what did Jess plague me with when I questioned any of her teenage actions? "When you assume things, Mom, you make an ass out of you and me." Who says you don't learn things from your children?

I remembered I had to return the U-Haul, or pay another full day on it. I rummaged around in the kitchen drawers until I found a phone book. I checked the yellow pages and found that one of the gas stations accepted U-Hauls. I ran upstairs to shower and change for my big trip to town and chose a calf-length light cotton dress with sandals. Besides my eyes, my legs were inherited directly from Grandma Dillen. Strong and stocky, they weren't likely to show themselves in shorts beyond my own house. I was still a size eight and my ankles were shapely, so long dresses kept up the illusion that what was hidden was as willowy as what was shown. Yes, I was pretty sensitive about my legs. One more woman affected by the media images put before us. I was glad I was getting past the age where it mattered so intensely, but old patterns hang on like Spanish moss on trees.

Once dressed, I collected my purse and keys and a bottle of water. I dug under the kitchen counter to find a water pan for Velvet. Not having had much experience backing up trailers, it took several attempts to get turned around. But finally we bumped down the driveway.

Our lake was south of Avon, on the road to Cold Spring, near Watab Lake. It wasn't as big, and, thank God, not as popular for summer activities since it didn't have a beach, only access from the houses. I turned out of the driveway onto 50, and then drove in the direction of Highway 9, since it went right over Interstate 94 and into town. It only took about ten minutes. I stopped at the Shell station first and handed the U-Haul and paperwork over to them. I asked and was reassured that Dahlin's Grocery was still about half way down Main Street with the Hair Connection at the other end. The Hair Connection was close to the old railroad track which had been turned into a biking and walking path, named the Wobegon Trail after Garrison Keillor's famous mythical town, which was supposed to have been around this area.

I drove down the street past the pizza place, Dahlin's, and the Buckhorn Bar – now that's a name. Finally, almost to Hussey's corner, I saw the Hair Connection. I turned in and parked in the shade. I poured some water for Velvet and left the windows open enough for her to stick her head out.

I checked out the front, saw only the beauty shop with the laundromat beside it, and decided to walk around back. In the middle of the building, looking as if a room had been carved from a bit of both businesses, was a small storefront. A bleached-out blue sign hung crookedly over the door announcing that it used to lead to Lars' Meats. An old white Escort with Ontario plates stood outside. Rust was peeling off around the wheel wells, and there was a jagged tear on the right edge of the rear plastic bumper, making it look like a large animal had chased the car, thinking it was lunch. As I passed it, I noticed that the passenger side was full of candy wrappers, pop cans, and old McDonald's bags. Nice. There was a big old-fashioned sleeping bag rolled up in the back, the kind you could buy at Sears years ago that weighed a ton and kept you warm even in below zero weather. Seemed like a bit of overkill for the summer.

I approached the door and peeked in. The light was on and I saw some movement behind piled-up boxes and furniture. I pushed the door open. It jingled with brass bells from India. The place smelled like vanilla incense, and something like patchouli. The latter wasn't my favorite smell, but somehow it mingled pleasantly with the incense.

"Hello?" I called.

"Back here!" a muffled voice answered. "I'll be right with you!"

"Don't hurry, I'll browse." I heard a chuckle, as stuff was packed so tightly it would take a very determined shopper to browse in here. I checked out some of the furniture and a few of the boxes in my immediate four foot area. The quality seemed pretty good. No cat pee smells on the upholstered chairs, which was a positive sign. Some nice lamp bases and cookie jars. I knelt down to see if any of the jars were McCoy's.

"Can I help you with anything? Obviously I'm not open yet, but I'll always take an offer."

I smelled him first. Obviously the source of the patchouli. Then I looked up, and up. Standing on the other side of the fat green upholstered chair was a very tall man with salt and pepper hair pulled back into a pony tail, and a bushy mustache drooping over his upper lip. As he gazed down at me with solemn brown eyes through over-sized aviator glasses, I thought, was this Celeste's idea of sexy? Someone needed to tell this guy that the 80s were long over.

"Actually, I'm looking for Sammy Barre…"

He stopped me in mid-sentence. A charming smile lit up his face, lending a softness to his eyes. All right, so maybe he was a little sexy.

"Ohmygod! You're Pip, aren't you?"

"Sammy?"

"Please, I've grown up." He bowed. "It's Sam."

"How did you know it was me? It's only been about forever!"

"You are the spitting image of your Mom." He squinted at me through his glasses. "Except I forgot about the eyes. Grandma Dillen rides again."

"You're right about growing up. You are big!"

"Yeah, I get that all the time. I usually forget about my size until I run into someone new. Both Lewis and I ended up taller than Dad and he's a pretty big guy."

"How's he doing? Celeste said you brought him here to a retirement home. Why didn't he want to stay up in Canada?"

"When Mom died a few years ago, Dad started talking about Avon, saying he wanted to come home. He's almost eighty and he gets a bit drifty and talks more about the years here than the thirty some in Canada. My brother Lewis lives out in Calgary and I needed to come back here anyway, so I figured what the hell, why don't I bring Dad with me? I found a nice assisted-care apartment for him."

Thinking of the car outside, I asked, "What about you? Do you stay there with him?"

Sam's brown eyes dulled and darted around. "I'm not much for small spaces. Besides, I'd just get in his way. He's getting to know people there and the staff is great. He can be as independent as he wants but he still gets one square meal a day, and there are folks coming and going, which he likes. He is pretty gregarious, unlike me."

"So where do you live?"

"Here for now. I've got my old sleeping bag in the car, and that couch over there is pretty comfortable." He pointed to a faded maroon sofa.

I raised my eyebrows and gestured around the cramped store. "Uh, this doesn't seem exactly spacious."

Sam shifted his feet. "I mean other people's small spaces. This is all my stuff, so it's different."

"You carted every bit of this junk all the way from Ontario?"

He looked mildly affronted. Then ducked his head and smiled that smile.

"Long story. And don't call it junk. Remember the saying about one man's junk…"

I started laughing. There I went again, the old assuming routine. "… being another man's treasure," I finished. "Who do I think I am? I lugged at least a dozen boxes from Washington to try to start a store just like this. Sorry. Maybe I'm just a bit miffed you got here first."

"So, why did you…?"

I made a face.

"Right. Long story. So when we were kids, remember we both liked trains? Now it's collectibles. Not so odd."

"Depends on your definition of odd."

"I guess so. Anyway, let's at least look at some of your stuff. Notice *I* avoid the word junk." He started towards the door.

"I'm out front, and I have a big dog in the car. Sometimes she gets possessive when I leave her in it by herself."

THE COAT IN THE WOODS

"I love dogs. What kind?" My comment didn't seem to stop him. He swung the door open and strode around the corner as I hop-skipped to keep up with his long legs.

"Mixed breed. Malamute-Husky. Her name is Velvet."

"Perfect. I used to have a Husky, but my girlfriend at the time took it with her when we broke up. I think I missed the dog more than the girl."

We came in sight of the car. Velvet sat up and put her head out the window. Before I could warn him again he put his hand out, palm up, like giving sugar to a horse. Velvet smelled it and then licked it. Traitor.

"Hey, Velvet, nice to meet you." He turned to me. "Bring her into the store. I get a bit of the air conditioning through the vents from the other two stores, so it'll be cooler for her. Where are your boxes? I'll take some while you get Velvet."

I indicated the back. I clipped Velvet's leash on and opened the door. She leapt out of the car as if she were starting a race. Sam knelt down so they were eye to eye. He stroked her soft ears. She slurped his face. Love at first sight. Better her than me. "The boxes?" I pointed to the back of the car.

"Oh right. Come on Velvet, we'll get you some more water." He lifted the back gate, leaned in and took out two boxes. I fished the third smaller one out, tucked it under my arm, resting it on my hip and slammed the gate. With Velvet straining on the leash in the other hand, I carried my treasure, crab-stepping after Sam. By the time I reached the door he was already holding it open for us. We slipped into the cooler air. Velvet had her nose up. I put my box down and let her off the leash. She started snuffling around the store happy as a toddler in a room full of balloons. Sam disappeared into the back and returned with a stainless steel cooking pot filled with water. He placed it by the door and started looking through my boxes.

"Here, let me show you what I have," I offered, trying to take control of the situation.

"No, that's okay. Go ahead and look around if you want."

Sam was already focused on my boxes and didn't seem to notice my reluctance, so I wandered off. I wound my way around the sofa, about five rocking chairs in various states of disrepair, a couple of dressers that looked as if they were partially refinished, boxes of baseball cards and Hot Wheels, McDonald's toys still in their plastic boxes, Native carvings that looked like they came from the Northwest, and boxes of old books. And that was just the front half of the store. I found Velvet sniffing near a door that must have led into the beauty salon. Even I could smell the chemicals. She turned to another door leading to the laundromat and cocked her ears at the sound of the washers and dryers.

"Quite a smorgasbord for the senses huh, Girl?" She stopped and sniffed at an oddly shaped metal jug. It was a dull brownish color, with a spout from which tubing coiled down and around to a wooden barrel behind it. An odor of vinegar hung in the air. A pickle barrel? "Sam, what is this weird metal thingy back here?"

"Hang on!" I heard a thump as he put a box down, and then swishes and bumps as he made his way through the maze to the back of the store. "Oh, that. Some old guy brought it in the other day. That's a copper cow, for distilling moonshine."

"Celeste was just regaling me with stories of our parents' milking this baby during Prohibition."

"Yours and everyone else's around here. The Buckhorn Bar even used to have a big hole behind the bar to throw the liquor jugs down when the agents came by. Everyone had hiding places like that for the moonshine, not to mention the stills where it was brewed. Back then, there were more federal agents assigned to this area than anywhere else in the country. My parent's place has turned into the Quik Mart but if the old buildings were standing, I'd go look for their still."

"I was thinking about looking around the farm for ours."

Sam's eyes sparkled. "We can explore it together if you want. Just like the old days."

"Maybe." I started closing down. I wasn't ready to interact much with anyone except Celeste for the time being. "I just got here and have a lot to do to get myself settled. Do you mind if I let you know?"

"Oh, sorry. Sure, anytime. I'm not going anywhere."

"So. Is there anything in the boxes that might sell?"

"Yes. You have some great things. Come on. I'll show you my favorites and we can haggle about prices."

I followed him to the front of the store. Sam leaned over and pulled out an old model of an Edsel.

"Now this is wild."

"Too bad it never caught on. I kind of liked it."

"I like old cars, period."

"Obviously." I looked out the window at his.

"Oh, when we were talking about the copper cow, I meant to ask you if that old automobile is still down the ravine at your parent's place."

"Yeah." I decided not to mention the fur coat.

"Do you mind if I check it out if I come to look for your still? I always wondered if there was a bootlegger's cashbox hidden under it somewhere. My Dad wouldn't let me go near the car after they found your silverware in the trunk. He was afraid it was too unsteady from the searching."

Sam's enthusiasm for this topic was almost catching. I was feeling badly I had put him off, but then something else he said hit me. "What silverware?" I was getting confused.

"You know, your parents' silverware that the guy stashed there – the guy they think killed your mother."

"Some guy did *what* to my mother?" My stomach lurched. I plunked down onto a wooden chair.

He looked at my face. "Ohmygod. You didn't know?"

I started shaking, then sweating. I was having trouble breathing and I felt like I was going to puke all over his nice old furniture.

"I'm *so* sorry. What can I do?"

I could hear the concern in his voice, but I didn't care. I just knew I needed to leave. Velvet put her nose in my lap and I held onto her collar to stand up.

"I have to go," I croaked.

"Are you sure? Can you drive? Should I call Celeste?"

I hit Sam with a green laser stare. "No. Come on, Velvet." I clipped the leash on her and somehow got out the door.

Thankfully, Sam didn't take on the guardian angel role and follow me out. I let Velvet in the car and then collapsed onto my seat, in spite of the hot upholstery. With a sigh, I dug some tissues out of the glove compartment and wiped my face. I then took a deeper breath and drank some water. With each breath the shakiness faded, but a large lump just under my ribs replaced it. I finally started the car and pulled out of the parking lot, but instead of heading home I turned almost automatically in the opposite direction, towards the elementary school where I was a Kindergarten student that awful spring.

October 26, 1944
Day 20

I stopped writing for a while as the lethargy of the endless days took over. It was all I could do to prepare for my language classes and join in the daily exercises held to keep up our level of fitness. We have been out of sight of land for two weeks now. To keep ourselves amused, the current bets are on where we will land first. Obviously it will be somewhere in Australia, our ally. Out here it's hard to believe we're heading into a war zone, although we've gone a bit more out of our way, I've heard, due to fear of German submarines.

CHAPTER SEVEN

I pulled into the school parking lot. I hated things I couldn't control, and images were bombarding my brain without my say: trees swaying, branches against the sky, a feeling of looking down from something high, feelings of pain and discomfort in my back and head, flashing lights, thunder, Grandma Dillen's soft hair, riding in the car with her, having her press my face into her comforting bosom, Dad crying. And Mum – Mum wasn't anywhere.

What did all this mean? What was I doing here? I couldn't figure it out in my head but my gut told me to follow its lead. I sat for a few minutes until the worst of the images faded. There were only a few kids playing on the merry-go-round. I clipped Velvet's leash on her and she hopped out of the car. She trotted ahead thinking we were going for a walk. We were, sort of.

We walked to the edge of the playground where a housing development began. I followed the fence, not sure what I was looking for, only that I'd know when I saw it. Then, behind the school building I found it. Beyond the chain-link fence, in the back yard of a sizeable house, was the trunk of an old tree, bare of bark, shiny from the imprints of many sneakers. It bowed over a man-made fish pond – all that was left of the climbing tree that had dominated the playground of my youth. I moved over to a bench that had been placed by the fence and sat with my back to the playground, staring at the tree trunk. All of a sudden I was back to the last days of Kindergarten. Finally, the images that had swirled through my head a few moments ago made sense. I remembered everything about that day.

* * *

With the last sensory memory of Grandma's tissues tickling my nose, I found myself sobbing, leaning over with my head in my hands, Velvet's nose occasionally poking my arm in concern. Luckily no one else was around, although at this point, I didn't really have a choice about what was happening to me. I felt like I was never going to stop crying. Where was my shield?

After what seemed like a long time, I stood up on wobbly legs and slowly walked back to the car. Part of me felt lighter, but with that came a million questions.

I unlocked the car and rolled down both windows, as the car was hot and stuffy from the late afternoon sun. Besides that, I needed air, big time. I poured some water for Velvet and myself and, with a breeze cooling my face and the back of my neck, I drove home.

When I reached the house I noticed Celeste's truck. She heard my car and came around the side of the house from the deck.

"Where in the hell have you been?"

"That pretty much describes it," I fired back, still sitting in my car.

"I thought you knew." Celeste approached me.

"Someone would have had to tell me, which hasn't seemed to be a priority in this family." I gathered my stuff up and got out of the car, Velvet pushing behind me with her nose to hurry up.

Celeste peered at me. "I brought you some supper, but when you didn't show up I called Sam. He's really worried about you. He said it was all his fault. I wasn't sure what he meant."

"I do. But I'll explain after we eat, then *you* need to talk."

THE COAT IN THE WOODS 55

October 30, 1944
Day 26

It feels like I've lived on this ship most of my life. The acrid smells below deck of engine oil mixed with the sweat of the men bother me, so I spend as much time on deck as I can. One thing I'll say – the food isn't bad. Who knows what I'll be eating once we land. I've been pretty lucky at Poker and Red Dog. If Pa could only see me now, all those years he beat me at Poker. Well, I better go squeeze into my smelly bunk. I told Adrienne and the children to look at the evening star when it appears, because it would be as if we were seeing each other. It has been out tonight and I haven't wanted to leave it.

CHAPTER EIGHT

Finally, after consuming Celeste's black bean chili with warm cornbread and a salad full of local goodies, Celeste and I sat in the Adirondack chairs on the deck. Dusk had arrived and the loons were calling. I wished that my peaceful surroundings were mirrored inside me. I sighed and drank my decaf coffee, loaded with hazelnut creamer.

"Celeste, why wasn't I ever told how Mum really died?"

"We didn't have any choice at first. Dad decided you were too young to be told it was anything but a heart attack."

"And what about later, when I got older? Why didn't anyone tell me the truth then?"

"I don't know about Paul, but I guess I just assumed that Dad or Uncle Hugh had told you later on."

"So do I grace you with Jess's favorite phrase about assuming here?"

"Just listen. After the funeral, no one talked about Mum's death. It got locked away in a closet of family secrets. It was clear even years afterwards that Mum's death was so painful for Dad that neither Paul nor I could talk to him about it. Grandpa and

Grandma followed Dad's lead either out of sympathy for him, or because it was hard for them, too. I know they loved Mum like she was the daughter they never had, and losing her in a violent manner like that was just too much for all of them. But I swear, Pru that I would never have kept that information from you if I knew you might get blindsided like you were today. You do believe that, don't you?"

It took me a while to respond. "I guess. However, now is when you get to tell me in *what* violent manner she was killed." It was even hard to use that word instead of 'died', but I decided to make myself do so as part of my effort to face the facts.

Celeste heaved a sigh. "All right. This is all I know. There was an escaped convict from the St Cloud Reformatory who had committed a number of burglaries. He seemed to have worked his way west, through St Joe, then to the Avon area. At least the cops assumed so. Yes, I know. There's that word again. Whatever their assumptions, they were unable to catch him. Do you remember that Mum was leaving for her yearly trip out East that day?"

"Just this afternoon."

"Really?"

I nodded.

"Oh." Celeste looked at me intently for a moment, then continued. "The police think the guy might have approached the house, figuring no one was home since Dad had the car. Grandma Dillen was planning to take Mum to the train later that day. None of the previous break-ins reported anyone assaulted or killed. Maybe Mum was in the kitchen and heard the thief as he was pulling the silverware box out of the sideboard. She might have come to the dining room doorway, seen him, and asked him what the hell he was doing. She was found in the kitchen, so the police thought the robber might have pushed her back into the kitchen and in doing so, shoved her so she fell, hitting her head on the corner of the cast-iron wood stove. The doctor told Grandma that Mum died instantly, so she didn't suffer."

At these words, I found my familiar glass shield somewhere and pulled it up around me again. The spider web crack was still there, but the rest was strong. Good. I wasn't going to fall apart. I could do this. With my shield in place, I could talk almost normally. "Where were you and Paul that day?"

"I was working at Glen's, but I was saving money by still living at home. Paul was at Tech." She referred to one of the two major high schools in St Cloud. "We didn't know anything until we came home. I guess they decided to let us have one more full day of so-called normalcy before our world collapsed. By the time I got home, Grandma Dillen was here, you were napping, and Dad had been sedated and was also in bed."

Celeste's eyes glistened. She paused and looked out at the lake. "I think that was the worst day of my life. We didn't learn until later that Dad had decided to come home for lunch to see Mum before she left. He was the one who found her. He was the one who finally told us the next day about the convict."

Pwaak! The spider web crack was shifting as another small rock hit my invisible protector. A second crack appeared in the middle, stretching towards the spider web. I could feel Celeste's sadness. Oh damn! I pushed myself out of the chair, kneeling down next to her, my arms around her waist.

"Oh, Cel, sitting in my pity bag, it didn't occur to me how hard this might be for you." She leaned forward, resting her head on mine. We sat like that for a bit. She snuffled. I sniffled. Then she sat up, I let go, and we both pulled out the inevitable tissues from their hiding places, suddenly laughing as we did so.

"How can we be laughing at a time like this?"

"How can we not," responded Celeste. I stood up and sat back down in my chair.

"So they never found the guy?"

"Nope. Never did. When the police were hunting for him and the silver, they checked out the old moonshine automobile in the ravine. The silverware box was stuck in the trunk, but the guy seemed to have vanished into thin air."

"Now I know why Dad looked so strange when I found the car that summer I was nine."

"Probably. You now also know the real reason he got rid of the old cook stove."

"I wonder where the old fur coat fits in. I forgot to tell you. Velvet and I found what's left of it last night."

"I've also thought about that periodically over the years. Especially since the police never mentioned seeing it when they found the silver."

"Which means it showed up some time later?"

Celeste looked thoughtful. "Hmm", was all she said. Then she changed the subject. "By the way, what did Sam mean when he said it was all his fault?"

"Well, obviously letting the cat out of its long-ago bag. Then I think he was also talking about the day I fell out of the tree, which I didn't remember until just today after I left his store."

"Do you feel like it was his fault?"

"Maybe I did for a bit today, since the fall wiped out my memory for so long. But now that you've told me I never knew the whole story anyway – I guess not. I never could figure out why Mum dying of a heart attack was such an awful thing that Dad didn't want to take care of me any more. I didn't understand why I was foisted on Grandma Dillen who wasn't getting any younger, or why Dad started having thrashing dreams, why everything changed so much, even Hank stopped coming over. I didn't understand why I had to be sent out East to Aunt Alice and Uncle Hugh after Grandma Dillen died. All these years I was afraid it was something I had done that made Mum die." The cracks on my shield spread a bit wider. Tears started slipping down my cheeks again. Oh God. And here I naively thought that the crying jag at the playground had been my catharsis.

It was Celeste's turn to come over and hug me. I leaned in to her. It felt like being lovingly smothered in Grandma Dillen's bosom again. Then, suddenly restless, I shrugged Celeste off and sat up.

"And all this time, the only thing I did wrong was to try to jump out of a damn tree!" I leapt out of the chair and paced the deck. "You know, you would think someone would have realized I might have thought something like this, and told me the truth so I could have had a different kind of life, rather than live with guilt like that." The web of cracks was moving towards the edges, my anger pushing it.

"I'm so sorry I didn't figure it out and tell you years ago. If it makes any difference, I don't think Dad had a clue what his behavior was doing to you. He was so soaked in guilt himself."

Curiosity stopped the cracking shield for a bit. "For what? He was at school."

"For not planning to go out East with her, for getting to the house too late, for it not being him, then finally I think just for living. He and Mum were just beginning to regain the life they had before the war. Mum had finally persuaded Dad to refocus on home life, especially after you were born."

"What do you mean?"

"Because of Dad's previous work with the embassy and his service during the war, his reputation spread and he was asked to be part of the rebuilding of Japan, headed by MacArthur. This required him to travel a great deal and Mum was not happy about that. I think she was also getting tired of being left with the task of taking care of Hank when Dad traveled. She didn't have the same connection to Hank that Dad did."

"Why did they have to take care of Hank?"

"He didn't come back from the war in very good shape."

"Boy, a whole other segment I'm missing. Although I do remember Mum and Dad arguing about Dad being gone so much."

"Yeah, you'd come into my room when it got too loud. I hoped because they had always been energetic in everything they did, that the fighting was just an extension of that, but it made me so nervous that I had to go work it off at the stables. So sometimes I just left you and Paul alone."

"I was too little to figure anything out. I was just scared. If Mum didn't like him going, why did he keep doing it?"

"Who knows? Making up for past mistakes? Maybe he was flattered that the government wanted him. Who wouldn't be?"

"I know there is a profound response to that but my brain is so tired, I can't think of one, Cel. However, there is something else that I need to ask you."

"Which is?" My sister was starting to sound as tired as I was.

"Did Dad actually fight in the war? I remember him talking about being in the Far East during it, but usually it was when he had woken up from a nightmare, and he didn't make much sense."

"I think so."

"But wasn't he a bit old to be fighting? If he was forty-eight when I was born, he must have been almost forty-three by the end of the war."

"You're right. They didn't take too many men in their forties. Usually guys in their early thirties were considered 'old men.'"

"Then how…?"

"You remember that tall red-haired guy who was a friend of Dad's? He used to visit in the summers with his wife before the war, then afterwards just by himself."

"Vaguely." I just said this. I didn't really remember him at all.

"Well, anyway, I think he had something to do with Dad going into the service. It was 1944, and there was a big influx of soldiers going to Asia. They had run out of translators and language instructors for the new batch, so Dad was contacted. I was eleven and not really interested, so I don't remember much more than that. I think later Dad talked to Paul about it, especially after Paul finished his military stint. Perhaps he can enlighten us."

I couldn't think of any other questions. I was at the point where I wasn't sure I could digest any more revelations anyway. Celeste looked at me.

"You know, Pru, Mum used to keep a very well-organized photo album. Dad put it away after she died."

"You're right. The first summer I returned from Aunt Alice and Uncle Hugh's, I was eleven. I poked around in the attic once and found it in a trunk, but it was one of those summers when the bats nested up there and they kept swooping down on me, so I left it and never ventured back up there." I shuddered at the old fear of the batwings ruffling through my hair.

"It's still up there in Mum's trunk. Now that you have the key, go and look for it. It might tell you more. Also, get some food in here. You owe me a meal."

I had completely forgotten I hadn't shopped. "Will do. Thanks, Big Sister. You really are the best."

"Glad you're finally seeing the light." Celeste got up. "Now I have to go. Barn chores start early."

I followed her out to her truck. When she got in, I patted the arm that was propped on the window. With that, she revved the motor and performed an Indy 500 spin out of the driveway. I looked around for Velvet, then called her.

I heard rustling. She came up behind me, her wet nose touching the back of my leg. I jumped.

"Whoo! You startled me!" She put her head down, ears back and wagged her tail. Her version of "Sorry". I bent down and hugged her around her ruff. We rubbed noses. "That's okay, girl. Let's go to bed. It's been a pretty tough day."

I locked the doors and turned off the lights. We climbed upstairs to my room. Velvet headed out to the balcony and curled up on an old quilt I had found for her. I thought about going to the attic to look for the album Celeste mentioned, but just the idea of it started my spider web moving again. Better wait until I felt stronger. I undressed and slipped on my old soft oversized T shirt that had *101 Dalmatians* printed on the front. The June evening had cooled, and there was a breeze off the lake. I checked the top of the closet and found another old quilt. As I pulled it down, an old black and white stuffed panda bear fell at my feet. Pandy. He and I had spent many a night snuggled up together. I picked him up. Hell, why not. I didn't have anyone else to sleep with. I draped the quilt over the covers, tossed the bear onto the bed, and climbed in.

I curled onto my side and pressed Pandy against my stomach, but instead of feeling comforted, more memories assaulted me: curling up to my panda when Celeste and Paul weren't home, listening to Mum and Dad arguing, years later waking up to the sounds of Dad's nightmares, waiting until he returned upstairs with his whiskey before I could go back to sleep, waking up later to make sure he was still asleep.

The spider web crack spread. Lying motionless didn't stop it. The whole shield I had lived with all these years was almost in pieces. I couldn't control all the sadness, regret, resentment, and anger any more. It began to feel as if a ball of maggots was squirming around inside my stomach. I clutched Pandy harder, trying to still them. As I pressed, it seemed as if the worms were drenched in battery acid, eating through my intestines. My chest started heaving, although no tears appeared. I gasped and gulped. Finally as I thought about what kind of life I might have had if Mum had lived, if she hadn't died *that* way, if someone had told me the truth, my self-pity finally pushed the tears to overflowing and the pieces of my shield crumbled all around me. Years of misery, of forgotten memories, of missed opportunities finally erupted.

Sometime after I started crying and wailing, I felt Velvet's nose on my cheek, trying to reassure me. After a while, she jumped onto the space at the foot of the bed, curling up at my feet where she kept me company through the long night until finally spent, I slept, my body wrapped around my old stuffed bear.

November 13, 1944

I lost the bet on our port. It was Perth. I guessed Freemantle. We take another boat from here to Calcutta tomorrow. In the meantime it was marvelous to be on land, and I went off wandering around the city with some of the other men. Many of the young guys ogled the women, while I enjoyed the beautiful park with birds the likes of which I have never seen. The beer here is excellent, warm like the beer in England. That brought back memories, so I made sure I drank just a little.

CHAPTER NINE

When I awoke, the sun was higher in the sky than usual, and the loons were quiet. I stretched my legs. No Velvet on the end of the bed. I tilted my head to see if she was on the deck. Nope. I sat up. I felt a curious combination of exhaustion and lightness.

Then I heard the sound of a cupboard opening downstairs.

I froze. What if history was about to repeat itself? I pulled on a pair of light running pants and quietly dug back in the closet. There they were, my old baseball bat and glove. I left the glove.

As I was creeping down the stairs holding the bat as if I was the home-run champion of Minnesota, I wondered why Velvet wasn't making any noise.

At that point, Her Fuzziness trotted in from the kitchen and climbed up to me, tail a-wagging, ears back, mouth smiling. So maybe it was Celeste down there.

"Celeste?" I croaked.

"Close," called back a deep bass voice. A head poked around the corner.

"Bear! What the hell are you doing here?" I dropped the bat with a clunk, and it banged its way down the rest of the stairs, coming to a rolling halt by the door. Velvet followed it down and stood over it to make sure it had stopped making that noise.

I ran down into the arms of my brother Paul who gave the best bear hugs ever, the source of his nickname. He smelled of coffee and English Leather. No updated fancy colognes for him. He felt immeasurably safe. I finally let go of him and put him at arm's length.

"I sure hope you brought some of that coffee you smell like."

"Yep, and hazelnut creamer. Good thing too, as I found a carton with just a drop left in your fridge."

He preceded me into the kitchen, pulled two tall coffees out of a bag, then reached in and plucked out a smaller bag that revealed big, fat, juicy blueberry muffins from Perkins.

"Yes," I said. "I am very bribable. What is it you want? And again, why are you here?"

"Just wanted to see you. I have an appointment with a client in St Cloud this afternoon. Celeste called and said you were having a tough time, so Annie shooed me out of the house before I even had my coffee."

"Poor you, lucky me. Working on a Saturday, Paul?"

"Yeah. One of our father's not-so-great habits I seem to have picked up."

"What, working?"

"Overworking. You should hear Annie on the subject."

This was the first crack I had ever heard mentioned in my older brother's armor. Maybe we all had been affected in some way by our father's war experience and where it led. I reached for my cup, flipped the plastic lid off and poured in my usual good measure of creamer. Aah. I don't usually drink coffee in the morning, but good coffee from Perkins is hard to pass up.

I looked at Paul over my cup. At sixty he was still tall and trim, no osteosporatic stoop. I was struck at how much he looked like Dad, except he was taller and balder, with Mum's long legs. The hair that used to be brushed back from his forehead, etched by some encroaching baldness, was almost gone except for short grayish blond fuzz on the back and sides. Behind stylish wire rims, the slightly buggy eyes of our Germanic ancestors twinkled, but instead of Dad's and Grandpa's blue eyes, he had Mum's dark brown ones. I was the odd kid, the only one without the brown eyes. It was good to see him.

"I'm glad you came," I said, "even if you did scare the hell out of me."

"Velvet seemed to think I was acceptable."

"Velvet would welcome Jack the Ripper if he had food. I wake up, still trying to take in the 'real story' of Mum's death, and I hear what I think is an intruder downstairs. I think I've aged five years in the last two days."

"Funny, I was going to say you look young and gorgeous!"

"Maybe catharsis is good for my skin." I posed like a model for lotion that promises to keep your skin looking younger.

Paul looked over his glasses at me, grinning. Then his expression changed. "It is so strange that neither Celeste nor I caught on to the fact that you had no memory of that day, and that Dad never told you what really happened."

"Well, neither of you were around much, and even if you had been, the whole topic was definitely a non-starter as far as Dad was concerned. Celeste said Mum's photo album is still in her trunk. I was going to check the attic today. Since you're here, want to engage in a little family snooping with me?"

"You betcha. I can even do a fairly good narrative when we find the pictures. I probably remember more than Celeste."

"She told me a lot."

"But I probably know different things. Like did she tell you about the ham radio in the barn?"

"Nope."

"How about the mountain climbing and wilderness camping Mum and Dad did?"

"Another no."

"The Fourth of July picnics and the baseball games?"

"Okay, okay," I laughed. "Let me finish my muffin first."

Paul nodded in agreement, his mouth already full. We

munched in companionable silence, broken only by an occasional smacking lip. Unlike Celeste, Paul seemed to carry a calm presence with him, something I'd always treasured. He wadded up the bag, aimed it towards the basket and missed. I raised an eyebrow at him.

"Hey, I was a baseball player, not basketball." He picked up the bag and stuffed it in the basket. "Let's get going. I want to leave enough time to look through that album."

I followed Paul, who was already at the top of the stairs. He tried the attic door. "It's locked," he said.

"I know. Hang on." I turned into my room to retrieve the key and handed it to him. He took it and turned it in the lock. He paused once more before opening the door.

"Sure you're ready for this?"

"I really don't think anything else we find will surprise me, just fill in more of the blanks. Lead the way, Big Bear."

Paul chuckled as he opened the door, and we looked up the steep stairs, enclosed on both sides with wood paneling. There was a window at the top of the stairs that illuminated our climb, but we turned on the light anyway. As I followed Paul, I ducked my head automatically, even though there was no low ceiling. He sensed my body jerking.

"Ah, remembering the bats, are you?"

"Yes. I was just telling Celeste they were the reason I fled before ever looking at the album when I was a kid."

"And you were too chicken to return and try again?" Paul asked from the top of the stairs.

"Yep, that's me! Even as a college girl, the thought gave me the creeps." I caught up with him. We had to turn a hundred and eighty degrees to see the whole attic stretched out before us. First the main room, then a smaller one beyond it. I scanned the area. Over to my left was an old stuffed dressmaker's dummy from the days when Grandma Dillen taught Mum how to make her own clothes. It stood guard over the other treasures with bits of stuffing sticking out here and there. I passed a Queen Anne chair with faded upholstery. The pile of mouse droppings on it explained the tufts on the dummy. I looked up into the rafters. No bats. The whole place had a musty smell of old wood, stuffing, leather, and a sour odor that indicated an animal might have died in the walls in the not too distant past.

An antique Damascus sewing machine sat next to the chair. I leaned down, noting that the black, iron wheel still glistened underneath the wood top. I moved on. Paul was on the other side of the room. "Find anything interesting?" I asked.

"Just the old oak dining table. Also the sideboard that used to hold the silver and that old portrait of Mum."

I crossed the room and pulled the portrait out from behind the sideboard. There it was, the original of my photograph.

"I thought you had this."

"I thought Celeste did. Do you remember it hanging in the dining room?"

"It was there when I was still living at home, when Grandma Dillen was alive. When she was getting frailer she encouraged me to take a picture of it, which I did with my Brownie camera. She must have sensed I would need its company some day."

"Yeah. I think Dad took the portrait down and put it and the sideboard up here the year Grandma died and you were sent to live with Uncle Hugh. I don't remember seeing it after that in my visits home."

"Me neither. Did you ever ask him where it was?"

Paul arched both eyebrows. "As you mentioned, we weren't exactly encouraged to have any curiosity whatsoever on the topic of Mum. Grandma was the only one who would talk about her at all, and she was gone. Dad was pretty much a ghost – either in the college library or at the ham radio in the barn, except in the summer when we could lure him out to the lake."

"Yes, well. Tell me about the ham radio."

"I think there may be a photo of it. Grandpa and Dad were very proud when it was built. Let's see if we can find the album first. It looks as if the trunks are in the little room."

We turned towards the light of the other window in the attic. In the small anteroom, old hard-boxed suitcases with leather handles huddled in a group as if planning their next trip. Next to them, warped cardboard boxes overflowed with papers and folders. I heard the sound of Paul unlatching something behind me and turned around.

Paul was opening an old round-top trunk with wooden slats across the top and sides. The leather straps connecting the lid from the base weren't sturdy enough to hold the lid up by itself, so I held the top while Paul rifled through the contents. I peered over his shoulder. Mum's lavender smell wafted up out of the trunk. I inhaled sharply. Paul looked up.

"You smell it, too?"

I nodded. We both sat and just breathed it in for a while.

Paul observed, "Isn't it weird the way smells bring back such strong memories?"

I seemed to be reduced to nods. Paul turned to the contents of the trunk.

At the very bottom, covered with layers of tissue paper, were Mum's yellowed wedding dress and the Alencon lace veil she had worn with it. On top of these were baby pictures of all of us and several pairs of baby shoes. A small container enameled with blue flowers revealed baby teeth. Everything looked almost too tidy, as if someone had recently replaced it all. Then I remembered Celeste's comment about Hank searching for something up here. She probably had tidied up. I focused my attention back to the trunk.

All of the keepsakes lay almost a foot down into the body of the trunk, as if something large and thick had lain over them at one time. Right on top of the rest was an old red leather photo album, pictures sticking out from the edges of the black paper on which they were glued. Paul handed it to me. I set it on the top of a suitcase. He was about to close the trunk when I caught something reflecting the light.

"There," I pointed.

He reached down into the side of the trunk and pulled out an old mahogany picture frame. There was our father looking about the age he was when I was little – forties or so. He was standing with a solemn, far-off look on his face, his blue eyes looking somewhere else. His blond hair was swept straight back. His strong nose hooked a bit towards a long, thin-lipped mouth. A square chin balanced the nose. Surrounding Dad were twenty or so other men, wearing the same vaguely uniform-like khakis that he was. All of the men wore a blue badge over their right shirt pocket. Paul turned the picture over. The back was old cardboard, cut to fit inside the frame to hold in the photo. Written in faded pencil in Dad's handwriting was a notation: "Citation. Burma 1945".

"What citation?" I asked Paul.

"Burma was where Dad served in the war. When I enlisted in the Army, he told me a little about earning some sort of citation, but I forgot the details."

"Was Dad in the midst of much fighting?"

"I'm not sure. I just remember that a friend of his from graduate school, Ed Barstow, somehow recruited Dad for some special assignment in Burma. When he first came back, he didn't talk much at all about the war. Then later, when he did, I was still young enough that I didn't listen as well as I should have. Now I wish I had paid more attention."

"We could find out now, though, couldn't we?" I asked.

"We could."

"Then let's. There are definitely some gaps I need to fill in about Dad."

"There are quite a few holes for me too when it comes to our old man. Paul nodded towards the album. "There is this colorful record of Mum and Dad's adventures and our early family history. Then all of a sudden, after the war there are just some baby pictures of you, some of my wedding, and Celeste receiving ribbons on Sunrise, but little else. Like family life just stopped after Mum died."

"Celeste mentioned something like that."

Paul looked at me. "What do you mean?"

"She thinks the change was connected not just to Mum's death, but somehow to Dad's war service and his work afterwards." I pointed to the photo of Dad and the other men. "Maybe this citation had something to do with it."

"The Dillen family investigates their sordid past. Pretty exciting for an old mechanical engineer." With that, he pulled the trunk top down and handed me the photo. I picked up the album.

"Let's boogie," I said. I led down the stairs. Paul turned the light off and followed me, closing the attic door firmly behind us.

"Just in case," he twinkled.

December 12, 1944, Nazira

Well, here I am at Headquarters. On the boat to Calcutta we were alarmed at all the vultures and kites that welcomed us. Our distress increased when we found out they were circling the city waiting their turn at the large number of dead bodies scattered around. Apparently, these particular bodies were the victims of the Muslim government's mishandling of the rice famine brought on by the Japanese occupation which has disrupted the flow of rice to India.

As we prepare to fight in this war, it is a reminder that war touches many people at all levels of society.

CHAPTER TEN

Back downstairs, I placed the album on the dining room table and the photo of Dad and his cohorts on the table in between the love seats in the living room. I put the kettle on for tea and dug in the cupboard for two decent-sized mugs. I remembered that Paul too thought most teacups way too small. Paul opened the fridge.

"Pru, any chance you're planning to shop for food while you're here?"

"I had every intention of doing so yesterday and then events took over." I told him about my visit with Sam and the resulting trip back in time at the school playground.

"I take back the crack about shopping. What's Sam like?"

"He was really very nice. Nicer than I was. I need to apologize to him when I go back into town for food. Any chance you can stay for dinner? I'll call Celeste and see if she can join us."

"I'll check with Annie after my appointment, see if she has anything planned, then if not, sure. I haven't seen Celeste for a while. I could use a little dose of her to crank me up." He grinned. "Do you at least have some sugar for my tea?"

"Of course – another family trait." I reached up for the whole sugar bag, and stuck a spoon in it for him. I handed it and the mug filled with tea to him.

"Funny," he drawled as he scooped out four rounded teaspoons. I took my turn, although I kept to three spoonfuls so I could lord it over him some other time. We both added cream and brought our mugs to the dining room table and sat side by side, with the album opened out in front of us.

"What have we here?" I asked. I turned to the first page. "Ah, the famous society wedding!" An old newspaper clipping like the one I had seen at Uncle Hugh's was folded in half to fit the book. I opened it, and there were Mum and Dad flanked by bridesmaids and groomsmen. The caption read, "Marshall daughter wed to Language Ace." Grandmother and Grandfather Marshall were on one side, and Grandma and Grandpa Dillen on the other, one side regal and imposing, the other warm and inviting.

"Grandmother Marshall sure was formidable looking."

"She had all the warmth of a marble egg," Paul replied. "I wonder what Grandfather saw in her?"

"From the tales Uncle Hugh told, she was pretty amazing in the things she did for her time – women's rights, birth control and all."

"Maybe that's where Mum got her determination from. Good thing Mum had Grandfather though, because he definitely was the one who was responsible for her sense of humor and coziness."

"But you never really knew them, did you?"

"No, I think we visited them once when I was about six. We drove out to Washington D.C. and then went on to stay with them in New York. I think there are some pictures of that trip further on. Most of my opinions of Grandmother come from Dad. I think because Mum and Grandmother were always butting heads with each other, he was a bit prejudiced against her. Plus, it was Grandfather who supported their marriage after the events in England. If it had been up to Grandmother, she would have taken Dad up on his offer to fade off into the Midwest without Mum." He turned the page.

On one side were pictures of Mum and Dad working at various chores on the farm with Dad's two brothers and Grandpa Dillen clowning around. In one, Mum was sitting a bit unsteadily on a three-legged milking stool. One whole side of her was filthy. She had straw in her hair but a grin on her face. A youngish man was pointing to the cow as if to indicate where Mum was supposed to milk. He had a brush of dark hair and freckles so thick on his cheeks that they blended into patches. A funny-looking pig stood behind him.

"Oh," laughed Paul. "Mum told me this was her first attempt at milking. Not only did she have trouble balancing on that stool, but the cow didn't take kindly to her untrained hands and kicked her off it. Of course she got right back on and tried again."

"Who is that?" I pointed to the man I'd noticed.

"That was Hank. He was a jokester in his younger years."

"Oh," I answered. "What's with the pig?"

Paul chuckled. "That was Dirk. He was Hank's pet pig. He was born cross-eyed, and usually missed the trough when he was trying to eat. He was pushed away by the others, so Hank adopted him. He pretty much went wherever Hank did. He was Hank's best friend all through his teens. Except for Dad, Hank didn't have many friends, since his father Angus owned a pig farm. Hank was teased as a child. They called him Hank Oink, because he always smelled a little odd.

"I can't believe having a pig as his sidekick helped his reputation much," I commented.

"He was old enough by that time, according to Dad, that he didn't really care, plus Dirk was the smartest animal in the county."

"Hank is better looking than I remembered."

"He was a really unique, gentle man who just never could outlive a label put on him by a bunch of jerky kids."

I switched my attention to the opposite page. The picture showed a couple who looked remarkably like me and Paul, posed at the top of what was obviously a pretty big mountain.

"Mum and Dad again, I presume?"

"Yep. They climbed Pikes Peak in Colorado. Not just the easy path either. Real rock climbing."

"Here's another trip they liked to take." He pointed to a picture of Dad next to a canoe in the wilderness. "They'd take trips into the Boundary Waters, often crossing into Canada. Dad had great compass and camping skills. As kids, he and Hank spent days on end exploring the woods."

"Listening to Celeste the other night made me think of all the things you can learn about your parents if you bother." I paused. "How come parents stop being so interesting when they have kids?"

"*Because* they have kids?" Paul laughed.

"It's definitely a trade off. Still I don't think I would have done it differently – at least not the kid part." I made a face.

"You know, I never did think David was good enough for you." Paul scrunched up his nose and looked at me through the bottom of his glasses.

"Do I dare ask why?" I looked at him sideways.

"Sure. He just seemed more interested in how *he* related to everyone else and not nearly focused enough on you and the kids."

A brief picture of the early days with David came to mind when Jess and Adrian were young. We went everywhere together. The Four Musketeers David called us. Then a memory of being at home with just Velvet for company replaced it. I collected myself, aware of Paul's eyes on me. "It wasn't always like that, but I guess I need to avoid that topic for now. Let's stick with the subject at hand. Do you mind?"

"Not at all." His brown eyes softened. He turned the page.

More pictures of life on the farm. The dates indicated this was in 1928 – just before the Depression hit. One photo showed Mum and Dad driving cream to the market while they still could get something for it. Dad was holding the reins of two solid-looking horses. The wagon was full of cans in the back. There was Hank again, holding onto the cans to keep them from bouncing out, with Dirk poking his snout and ears from behind one of the cans.

Paul pointed to another page. Dad, Hank, and Grandpa Dillen were standing in the barn. Behind them was an elaborate contraption. "The ham radio," he announced.

"Who made it?"

"All three of them. Grandpa didn't always know what to do with his brainy son, but Dad said they could connect doing mechanical or electrical projects. Since Hank practically lived at the farm, Grandpa usually included him as well. They communicated with other operators all over the world, especially with contacts in the Far East. Did you remember that Dad started the Far Eastern Language program at St John's?"

"I thought he just taught in it."

"Nope. When Dad lost his teaching spot at Yale because of his rebelliousness, the old monks who taught him welcomed him back. A number of them had studied in the Far East – Burma, China, Japan. So Dad worked with them to develop the curriculum. An exchange program grew out of that, with students from those countries. When the exchange students returned home, Dad loved being able to keep in touch with some of the friends he had made during their year here. When I was little, I remember toddling in and hearing Dad jabber away, making all sorts of weird sounds, which I later learned were bits of Japanese, Chinese, Burmese, you name it."

Next was a picture of Mum, Dad, and another man who looked like Sam with short hair and no mustache sitting at a long table. A sign behind the table read 'DFL Regis…' The rest was lost at the edge of the photo.

"Was this some sort of political event?"

"The 1934 election. Mum and Dad supported Floyd Olson for governor. You've probably already figured out the third guy is Sam's Dad, Elias. That's how they all got to be friends. After Dad's involvement in supporting the General Strike in England, coming back to Minnesota was perfect for him, with its long history of protest politics. No one called him a Bolshevik here."

The next pages revealed baby pictures of first Celeste, then Paul. One picture showed Celeste with her ear to the old fashioned radio. "Mum took that the year the horse Seabiscuit took over the airways with his amazing race against War Admiral,"

Paul continued. "She said that was Celeste's first love affair with a horse. The only people who listened as much as Celeste were Dad and Hank, whenever the news was on. They couldn't get enough of Edward R. Murrow reporting from London on the onward march of the Germans to France. Apparently, you could even hear the screech of the guns and sirens from London. Both men would then disappear into the barn and come out telling Mum about people whom they had contacted and the horrors that were happening in Europe. I'm sure those programs had a lot to do with both Dad and Hank doing whatever they could to go overseas."

"Where did Hank end up? Burma as well?"

"No. With that scrappy nature of his, he wanted to blow Hitler's armies to hell. He even lied about his age to get in."

"But wasn't he a lot younger than Dad?"

"I think about eight years, but that still made him in his early thirties, which was old for that war."

"Yeah, Celeste mentioned that."

Paul continued, "I do remember Dad telling me after the war that he had encouraged Hank to enlist. Hank didn't have much of a life beyond our family, since his mom died when Hank was born and Angus died when Hank was in his twenties. Dad thought enlisting might give him a new view on the world and some self respect that had escaped him growing up in Avon."

"Wasn't that a good thing?" I was trying to reconcile all this information with the sad, vague man I remembered.

"Good and bad. The good thing was that Hank ended up being a great sergeant with real leadership skills."

"What was the bad? That he had to leave his cross-eyed pig?" I joked.

Paul looked at me. "Even though you're being a smartass, that was hard, too. But probably just as much for Mum as for Hank, since we inherited Dirk while he was gone. There wasn't anything that pig couldn't get into. No, the really bad part was that Hank was part of the invasion on Omaha Beach on D-Day."

I thought of what Celeste had said about Mum taking care of Hank and of the movies I had seen about that day. "Oh," I said.

"Exactly. Hank was never quite the same afterwards."

"Celeste said something about that, but didn't say how."

"I remember nights when Dad would have to drag him home from the bars. Eventually that got better and Hank kept working at the farm, but then something happened that is another one of those things no one ever talked about. All Celeste and I knew was that someone else was hired to manage the farm, and Hank ended up living in an apartment in the barn."

"Yet another mystery surrounding our family. Could we find out if that guy who recruited Dad is still alive?

"Ed Barstow? Good idea. He might be able to clear up some of these things. I may have his address in Dad's old box of radio stuff that I cleared out from the barn after he died."

"Go for it." I turned the page. "Oh, is this Barstow?" I was looking at a photo of Dad, Hank, and a tall gangly man trying to pull a stump out of one of the fields. Paul peered at it.

"Yep. He really liked working on the farm when he visited, especially after his divorce. He'd ride in the old truck with us down here to the lake for picnics. Then he'd join us for the wild family card games. You should remember those. We still played them occasionally until Mum died."

"I think I remember a lot of whooping and hollering and huge decks of cards. Also Grandpa and Grandma Dillen acting really funny."

"They were playing charades. Hank was the best at that game. All of us wanted to be on his team."

I looked at another picture. "Is this Ed Barstow again?" The same tall man, now wearing a pencil thin mustache, stood next to Dad.

"Yep. That was in Washington, the same trip we took Dad out there. Here's a photo of us starting out." He pointed out another picture of Mum, Dad, Celeste and Paul, posed in front of a car loaded down with suitcases tied to the back. Celeste looked about eleven, Paul about six.

I was still fixated on Mr. Barstow. "I thought I remembered him as being tall because I was so little, but he and Dad look like Mutt and Jeff. Did he go to Burma with Dad?"

"Can't say. Something else to put on our list of questions."

On the next page was a picture of just Mum, Celeste, and Paul all dressed up. Paul had a suit on. Celeste wore a plaid dress with patent-leather shoes. Mum looked very glamorous in a fawn colored, full length fur coat. I stared at the picture, wondering. But before I said anything, I wanted to find some things out.

"Where was that?" I asked.

"In New York City, after we left Washington. That was the visit to Grandmother and Grandfather I mentioned."

I pointed to Mum. "Where did she get the coat? From Grandmother?"

"No. Dad bought it for her with savings from his embassy work just before he went off to Burma. Even after the war, she always planned her trips to New York for cooler weather so she could wear it because she told us she felt like he was wrapped around her. I thought it was a bit gross, but what did I know? She'd pull it out of the trunk each time and then would fold it up carefully and put it back when she returned." He stopped, looked back at the picture and then at me. I grinned and nodded.

"You think?" he asked.

"Yep," I said. "Must be."

"Oh man, how dumb am I? The fur coat is what used to be in that big space in her trunk!"

"Celeste told me the day Mum was killed, she was about to leave for the East," I said. "Could she have already brought it down before she surprised the burglar?"

"And because she did, somehow it never got back to the trunk? Pru, I've lived with this so long, it never even registered on me that the coat might be missing. But where did it go?"

I voiced my other thought. "Do you think it's possible, Paul, that the coat in the woods is Mum's?"

December 16, 1944, Chabua

A few more notes on Calcutta before I forget. It is a city brimming with all kinds of sounds and smells. The noises of the taxi horns overcome the tinkling of the rickshaw bells. Women carry patty cakes of cow dung piled on trays balanced on their heads. On many walls you can see stains where the cakes had been removed after being stuck there to dry. The putrid stench from the dung fires competes with the spicy aroma of curry. Now here I am in Chabua, about 100 miles from Nazira. It is as bleak as Calcutta was colorful. I am beginning to wonder what the hell I have volunteered for.

CHAPTER ELEVEN

We looked at each other.

"Something else I missed," Paul said. "Why didn't I ever think of that?"

"Because in your mind if it wasn't on Mum, it was in the trunk."

"But if it is hers, how did it get there?"

"And the bigger question, why didn't Dad take it down once we all found it?"

Paul raised his eyebrows. "Is there any way we could confirm the coat was Mum's? Last time I walked down there, all that was left were bits and pieces sticking out of that basswood."

"That's pretty much the way it still is. I found it Thursday. Oh my God. Was that just two days ago?"

"See what a catalyst you are, Pip? Home two days and we might be on the verge of solving a forty-four year old mystery!"

"I'm thinking there is a reason for the 'ignorance is bliss' saying."

"Nah, you love this." He flipped through the rest of the album. "Not much left here, Pru. Your baby pictures, Celeste and Sunrise, my wedding, Dad and Ed with a bunch of other guys." He stopped and pulled back his cuff to look at his watch. "Holy Moly, I've got to run. I'll give Annie a call from St Cloud, but I'm pretty sure I'll be back here for dinner. Don't forget to call Celeste. We need all three brains on this conundrum." He picked up his briefcase and pulled the door open.

"Is Velvet lying down out there?" I asked.

Paul stepped out and looked around. "Not so as you'd notice."

"Damn!" I followed him out.

"What?"

"She's a roamer. Now I'll have to tramp the land to look for her."

"Why don't you check out the coat while you are at it, see if any of the pieces have a label or something still attached to them?"

"Maybe. It might have to wait a bit. Building a fence around part of this place has just risen to the top of my list of things to do." I grabbed some dog treats and Velvet's leash out of my car.

"After getting food," called Paul. "I do not want toast and eggs for dinner!" He climbed into his car, turned, and set off at a much more stately pace than our older sister.

I power-walked down the path I had traveled Thursday on my way over to Celeste's, calling Velvet. I hoped she hadn't run off after a scent because who knows where she would end up. I was working myself into a mini anxiety attack when I heard a rattle in the bushes.

"Velvet? Come here, girl!" More rattles. A snuffle. I tried to remember how often black bears came around here. "Velvet, treat!" I tried. Rattle, rustle, then whoosh! She leaped out of the brush, panting and wagging her tail. I leaned down and hugged her, gave her a treat, and clipped on her leash. I paused a minute, trying to decide if I wanted to deal with the coat remnants right now. I decided no, and we headed back to the house, Velvet prancing happily ahead of me. It was time to shower, get dressed, and plan dinner. Then I needed to call Celeste, buy food, price wire fencing and posts, and go visit Sam again.

Sam might be mad about my earlier behavior, but maybe if I apologized gracefully, he'd forgive me. Perhaps with the lure of getting to look at that old car and search for ancient moonshine hideaways, he might be willing to help me build the fence.

When I ushered Velvet into the house, I decided to close up all the windows and doors, trying to keep the cool morning air in, as it was promising to heat up. Because it gets so cold in the winter people expect Minnesota to be cold in the summer too. But it's a land of extremes – which means hot in the summer, sometimes as early as this, then it can just as easily snow the next week.

I bustled around, looked at the last few photos in Mum's album, closed it, and put it on the table with the picture of Dad and his crew. I found a small notebook in my purse and started a grocery list. After having my brain overloaded in the past two days with memories and emotions, it was a relief to focus on milk, cereal and what to feed Celeste and Paul. I checked my watch. It was getting close to lunch which meant Celeste would probably be back in the house. As I dug my cell phone out of my purse I noticed two calls: one from David, and one from Jess. David could wait, but I'd try Jess when I returned from town. I dialed Celeste's number. Someone strange answered, said "Just a minute" when I asked for Celeste, and dropped the phone with a clank. I could hear running and a voice calling for Celeste. I was just thinking of hanging up and trying later when the phone was picked up again and a breathless Celeste said, "Yeah?"

"Nice phone manners, Cel."

"Sorry, Pip. We have a new horse and he's a handful. I was introducing him to the concept of a halter when Josie said someone was on the phone. He took advantage of the distraction and nosed me into the wall of his stall. I couldn't come until I taught him that was not acceptable."

"What did you do to him?" imagining Celeste going toe to toe with a huge thoroughbred.

"Bribed him with a carrot."

"Why didn't she just say you were busy?"

"She's new – Josie, Glen's granddaughter. Doing part-time housework and part-time training. I'm breaking her in, which means I haven't let her see the sweet side of me yet, so she wasn't sure what to do. Anyway, what's up? Are you okay.?"

"Not bad. I won't keep you, just wanted to tell you that Paul came up this morning."

"I was hoping he would."

"I think he's coming back for dinner after his appointment barring any other instructions from Annie. Can you come over, too?"

"Love to sample *your* cooking for a change. When?"

"Can you come at six? Then Paul doesn't have to drive home in the dark."

"Sure. I'll let Josie and the guys close up."

"What would you think if I asked Sam? I was going to go over and apologize to him about yesterday."

"Sounds good. He's kind of like one of the family anyway."

"Speaking of which, Paul and I brought Mum's album down."

"Thought you might."

"We also discovered something else."

"What?"

"Nope. You'll have to wait until tonight!"

"Ah, Pip…"

"Bye!" I laughed and hung up. I gathered up my purse and water and called Velvet to follow me out to the car.

My first stop this time was at Lumber One to check out fencing. I looked over various kinds, shocked at the prices, having no clue how much wire I needed, or what kind of posts. I finally found a salesperson, luckily a woman. She was quite gentle with me, as she told me I might want to measure the area I wanted to fence before spending money on fencing. She directed me to the measuring tape and finally, package in hand, I paid and walked out, feeling satisfied that I had accomplished something.

I decided to drop by Sam's store next. I parked in the back this time. Sam's decrepit car was still there and the lights were on inside. I knocked on the door. Sam opened it, his hundred-watt smile dominating his face. The place was starting to look organized.

"Hey, it's coming along."

"Hi. Am I glad to see you!"

"Yeah, well," I answered. "I'm sorry for yesterday. I was pretty rude."

"Oh, God, no. I'm sorry! I shouldn't have babbled on like that."

"It's okay, Sam. I just get anxiety attacks sometimes and I hate to be around people when they happen."

"Been there."

"You, too?"

"Yup. Part of the long story."

"Oh. We really don't know much about each other, do we?"

"Guess you're right. Let's have lunch and see what we can do about that."

"Maybe later. Actually, I came to see if you could come to dinner. Paul arrived from the Cities this morning and is staying for dinner and Celeste is coming over."

"Won't I be in the way of the family reunion?"

"Hey, Celeste says you're like family anyway. Paul and I discovered some things in the attic and we could use another brain. One that isn't so close to the picture. There are some pieces that don't fit."

"Pieces of what?"

"We'll tell you tonight. What do you drink?"

"Just pop or water."

"That's easy. See you about six? Do you remember how to get to my folks' house?"

"I think so. Dad had me drive him around when we first arrived. He sure remembered it."

"Good. See you then. One other thing. I have to put some fencing up around part of the property to keep Velvet in. Would you have any time to help me measure?"

"Sure. I can help tomorrow. Monday I have to take Dad for some tests and keep working on getting this place ready to open."

"Thanks."

"À bientôt." He bowed. I laughed, returned to the car, hopped in, and drove off to finally buy some groceries for my pantry and fridge.

December 17, 1944
Waiting in Chabua

Well, I've had my first taste of the rice whiskey preferred by the mountain men our people are training. These fellows seem to be the key players in the whole operation. I was right about some sort of push. We were ordered out here for a final disruptive campaign against the Japanese. That's all I know so far.

CHAPTER TWELVE

An hour later, loaded down with necessities like toilet paper, dog food, cheese and fruit, and goodies like creamer – Amaretto as well as Hazelnut – and a blueberry pie for dinner that almost looked homemade, I rolled down the driveway back to the house. My house? That remained to be seen. Velvet jumped out and immediately went to her bowl, sucked up water, and collapsed in the shade of the porch for a nap. I hauled the grocery bags into the house. I usually try to get everything in one trip and invariably drop things, but this time I managed to open the door, juggling everything until I reached the kitchen counter. I just missed upending the whole blueberry pie.

After putting the groceries away, I made some iced tea with lemonade and cooled some beer for Paul who seemed to be the only drinker of the group. I picked up my cell phone and took it along with my iced tea out onto the deck. I tried to call Jess, but I didn't have any luck. I left a message conveying that I was all right and had lots of adventures to tell her about if she wanted to call tomorrow. I thought a moment about calling David, but changed my mind when I caught myself chewing on the insides of my cheeks again. I realized I had done so only once since arriving in Minnesota, and that was when I was wondering about my future. I had an hour before starting to make dinner and I needed some down time. I lay back in the chair and put my feet up on the deck railing, sunning myself and listening to the quiet slap of the water and the slight rustle of the breeze in the trees.

Tomorrow it would be a week since I left Washington. It felt like a year. I was surprised at how quickly the old family responses returned as soon as I was around Celeste. In spite of our long estrangement, I loved Celeste, but it didn't take long for my hackles to rise at her comments. Aunt Alice probably served more of the function of a mother as I was growing up, but I sure reacted to Celeste more than I ever did to Aunt Alice. Poor Celeste. How I was raised wasn't her fault, yet I had dumped all my anger about those years on her head.

And Paul. Celeste didn't think he was very intuitive, but he was just quieter than she was. Celeste talked everything out, whereas Paul thought about it and then said something. Maybe that was one of the things that attracted me to David – his quiet manner. Except he ended up being more like Dad than Paul, his silence more of a protective screen than a manifestation of serenity. I wondered if most people marry one of their parents in some way or other. Sometimes it works, sometimes not.

Paul's wife Annie was probably a bit like Mum – a free spirit. She was a reference librarian at the University of Minnesota and a poet as well. Very smart. However, unlike Mum, she wasn't an outdoors person. She would rather curl up with a book or write in her poetry notebook than be outside. Paul had to drag her out to fish or canoe. The fact that mosquitoes seemed to prefer her blood to any of those around her probably didn't help either. Annie was funny, compassionate, and a bit fey. She was mostly Irish and was as outgoing as Paul was quiet. It was a match that worked. I hoped I would get to see her on this trip.

I thought a bit about Jess and Adrian. How in the world had they turned out as well as they did? My brief memory of Mum when I was in the house earlier reminded me that I had experienced her love and nurturing in my early years. The imprint of that perhaps helped me know what to do with Jess and Adrian as babies. As for the rest, maybe Dad wasn't so crazy after all when he sent me to live with Uncle Hugh and Aunt Alice during the school year. They did give me some stability and an idea of how parents could be – fun and firm at the same time. And whatever feelings I had about David, I had to admit that he loved the kids and was involved at least peripherally in their lives.

I took a deep breath. My mouth twisted again in an effort to keep from biting bits of flesh off the insides of my cheeks. Stop it, I told myself. Get back to the present. Which was actually the past.

In spite of all the information inundating me about my family, I was coping better with that than thinking about my marriage. My meltdown last night seemed to have freed some things inside me. I wasn't exactly sure what they were yet, but I was beginning to believe that I would understand eventually if I kept following the family clues. Perhaps unraveling those would lead me to the answer about what to do with my marriage and allow me to explore the other parts of myself that I had buried over the years. The coincidence of all this family revelation happening at a time when I sorely needed some direction in my life was not lost on me.

Velvet whimpered in her dream, her legs running after some ephemeral rabbit. I checked my watch. Whoa! Time to get going. I finished the last of my iced tea and went back inside. Sensing food, Velvet raised herself and followed.

I minced the garlic for a clam sauce and put the water on for spaghetti. I made a salad, tossing Velvet the carrot ends. She caught them in mid air. I was slicing the French bread when I heard a car. Probably not Celeste, and too noisy for Paul. As I was congratulating myself on my detecting skills, I looked out the window and saw Sam's dilapidated Escort rounding the bend.

I opened the door. Velvet scooted out from behind me and trotted up to the driver's window. Sam opened his door, unfolding his long frame out of the car. In one hand he held a bunch of daisies, in the other a small brown bag. Velvet sniffed this frantically.

"Hi!" he called, as he started towards the house.

"Hi back. Must have food in the bag."

He laughed as Velvet pranced along beside him, her nose reaching for the bag he held high in the air. "Gee, what's your first clue? It's a pig ear. Can I give it to her?"

"A little late to ask, don't you think? Besides the fact that they are disgusting and make me think too hard about what they used to be attached to, sure, go ahead."

He took the ear out of the bag. The sun shone through the dried skin. Yuuk. Velvet disagreed. Sam leaned down and told her to sit, then gave it to her. Surprisingly, she took it gently in her mouth and ran off to the porch to gnaw on it. Sam held up the daisies.

"And these are for the cook." He did that cute bowing thing again. I laughed.

"It's been a long time since anyone brought me flowers. What's the occasion?" I took them into the house. Sam followed me.

"I still feel badly about springing that on you about your Mum."

"Don't. It resulted in several very interesting conversations with Celeste and Paul, not to mention the discovery of a few mysteries."

"Like what?"

"You'll have to wait until my dear siblings arrive to find that out." I got a vase down, filled it with water and stuck the daisies in. I sort of fluffed them out, but beyond that I have no skills in flower arranging. Sam reached over, pulled and shifted the flowers, and all of a sudden they looked really artistic.

"How did you do that?" I took the flowers and put them in the middle of the dining room table. Sam followed me.

"Years of practice hanging out with my mother at church teas."

"You're kidding."

"I'm not. When we moved north, all the social life revolved around the church. Mom practically lived there. Until I was old enough for my brother to baby-sit me, I had to stay with her. Thus I learned flower arranging, the proper way to pour tea, and how to make fantastic cinnamon buns!"

I turned back towards the kitchen, Sam in my footsteps like a duck. "Mmm. I'll have to let you in my kitchen some other time, just to see if that's true."

"You're on. Can I help you with this?" He pointed to the bread. Was this man ever anything but helpful? The cynic in me started to wonder. The Pollyanna part of me thought it was nice.

"Sure, just put some butter in between the slices and sprinkle on some garlic powder. The foil is in the drawer to your right." I left the room to set the table. When I returned, I glanced with approval at the foil-wrapped bundle resting on the stove. Sam was washing his hands. I headed for the fridge. "Want a spring water?"

"Sure." He took the glass bottle from me, then pushed the door open to the deck. This time I did the following. As I sat down I started to laugh.

"What?"

"I was just thinking. We keep following each other from room to room. I flashed back to us as kids. We used to do the same thing."

Sam chuckled. "You're right. Whoever thought of the next thing to do was the leader of the moment. We didn't have very long attention spans then, did we?"

"Guess not. Hope that has changed enough to get the fence built."

Sam leaned back in his chair. "About the fence. It'll take one day to do the measurements, and then more than a day to actually build it. We have to dig post holes and all."

"We do?"

"You really are a product of the suburbs, aren't you?"

I nodded, feeling a bit sheepish. "But I can follow directions well."

He shook his head. Smiled that dynamite smile. "We'll get it measured tomorrow, then you can go and pick up the posts and wire next week. The rest we'll have to do in bits and pieces."

"Certainly sir, very well, sir." I saluted. His smile disappeared. A crease appeared between his eyebrows.

"Don't salute, please."

"Oh, did I step on some toes?"

He shook his head again, but I wasn't sure I believed him.

December 18, 1944
Still in Chabua

They certainly feed us information only a bit at a time. We have just learned that we are headed into Burma. It seems that the Burmese students at St John's did me a favor. It was my ease with the various Burmese dialects that convinced the powers that be to send this old man over here. I certainly have been enjoying getting to know the mountain soldiers while we wait, and helping the other men communicate with them. I have found out that my job will be to translate intelligence information that comes through from the mountain units, take over the radio when the chief radio operator can't, and help interpret for any enemy prisoners or Chinese we might encounter. However, I have also just been told that in order to do all this, I have to jump out of a damn plane tomorrow!

CHAPTER THIRTEEN

At that point the unmistakable sound of two cars broke through the tension floating in the air.

"How do they manage to be late at the same time?" I asked. That got Sam to laugh. He moved into the living room, letting me greet my siblings by myself. Paul arrived first, then Celeste's truck skidded in, kicking up dust in the face of Paul's polished sedan. As she was gathering up her things, Paul got out of the car and strode over to her.

"What? Don't you believe in stop signs?" Paul's hands rested on his hips.

"Hey, don't tell me if you had reached the intersection first, you wouldn't have scooted in ahead of me. Come on Paul, this isn't Minneapolis. There was no one around." She climbed down from the truck and shook out her white mane of curls.

"You don't know that." His hands stayed at his hips.

"Oh yes I do." Celeste patted him on the shoulder and swept

past him into the house. Paul stood, beet red, then breathed in deeply, letting his hands make the "what can you do gesture."

I laughed. "Ah, another memory assails me!"

"What?"

"How competitive you guys always have been. Come on, Paul, chill out. I did think of you. I bought beer."

He grinned and scrunched his nose up at me in that way he had. "You are a sweetie." We linked arms and followed Queen Celeste into the house. There we found her and Sam already settled on the two love seats in the living room with bottles of spring water in hand. They looked like old friends.

"Want to go out on the deck?" I asked.

Celeste looked up. "Maybe later. This is too comfortable to exchange for a deck chair. I've been on my feet most of the day." She stretched her tan legs out in front of her. Long shapely legs never seem to look old. I retreated to the kitchen. Paul crossed me with a beer already in hand and headed for the comfy chair in the corner.

"I helped myself."

"I see. I'll be right there. Just have to throw in the spaghetti and set the timer." After doing that, I grabbed another spring water and plopped down next to Celeste. I stretched my legs out too, but they only came up to where her calves were. Oh well. Sam reached over and picked up the picture of Dad and his buddies. He peered at it and turned it over. Then he replaced it.

"Was your dad in Burma during the war?"

"How do you know he was in Burma?" asked Celeste.

"It says so on the back of the photo," answered Sam, grinning. He picked up the photo again and handed it to Celeste, who turned it over.

"Oh," was all she managed. She put it back on the table.

"What did he do?" continued Sam.

"Some sort of translating, but we're not sure about the rest," added Paul.

"Which," I completed, "is one of the mysteries I was talking about."

"What's the other one?" Celeste asked. "You finally know about Mum's death."

"That's true, but when Paul and I were looking through her trunk earlier we discovered an interesting puzzle."

"Oh, come on kids, tell me already!" Celeste said.

Paul took over, a grin on his face indicating he was enjoying Celeste's curiosity. "There's a big space in Mum's trunk, as if something bulky was missing. The album there," he pointed to the table, "was resting on the top of her wedding dress along with baby shoes and stuff. But they all would have been lying underneath whatever is missing."

"Mum's fur coat," Celeste said. Paul's face fell. "That's not a mystery," Celeste continued. "I figured that out as soon as I had to tidy up the trunk after Hank went through the attic."

"Then why didn't you say anything?" asked Paul.

"In what conversation would that have been?" answered Celeste. "Your input has been notably absent for quite a while, Paul. I've been the one to take care of Hank, I'm the one who put him in the Veterans Administration hospital, I'm the one who called you both for your ideas about what to do with the house, which I will remind you, you still haven't found time to give me yet."

Paul wiggled in his chair at the tongue lashing. Sam watched them both as if he was at a tennis match. I wondered if Paul was going to say anything, but Celeste wasn't finished.

"Frankly my dears, I didn't really think about the coat once I searched Hank's stuff and found that he hadn't taken it. I figured Mum had probably removed it the day she was killed, and that the thief took off with it. Done deal. End of subject."

I braved a comment. "Did you ever wonder if the coat in the woods was Mum's?"

Celeste titled her head. "Yes. But, if it was, when was it put there? Like I told you the other night, when the cops went to investigate the tip on that old car and found the silverware, they would have seen the coat hanging there at that time if the thief had hung it on the tree."

I felt deflated and looked at Paul. "She's right. That answers our earlier question. Maybe it isn't hers. Just some old coat left by – "

"By who?" filled in Paul. "That's the thing. Don't you think it is just a bit too coincidental that some hobo wandered through and hung up a coat in our woods? A coat that at one time sure looked like our mother's?"

"A coat that you have now discovered is not in the place it rested for years?" Sam was getting right into this.

"But," suggested Celeste, "wouldn't Dad have taken it down and put it back in the trunk if it was hers?"

Sam said, "How come you never asked him about it when you were younger?"

It was Paul's turn. "We weren't exactly encouraged to have conversations on any topic related to the death of our mother."

"Where do you suppose all three of us learned the marvelous communication skills we have displayed with each other over the years?" Celeste leaned over and patted Paul on the knee, as if to apologize for her earlier outburst. He smiled at her.

"Pru was saying that there are still bits of the fur coat left, sticking out from the bark," Paul told Sam. Sam raised his eyebrows.

"As amazing as that seems," I said, "the tufts run pretty much all up and down the trunk." I turned to Paul and Celeste. "Also I noticed a flowery smell. It occurred to me after you left today Paul, that it smelled a bit like the scent of Mum's perfume we noticed in the trunk."

Paul answered first. "That's a pretty big stretch, Pip. Even if that coat was Mum's, there is no way the fur would still contain a scent after so many years out in the weather. Probably just the basswood flowers in bloom."

"Did you ever notice a smell or anything when you went in there, Cel?" I cocked my eyebrow at her.

Celeste answered a bit too quickly. "Nope. I think you're doing a bit of hallucinating without the drugs, Pip. I remember what Mum's toilet water smelled like. I used to have a bottle of it in my room that I would sniff every so often to help remember her. But I can't say I ever smelled it by the tree." She started twirling one of her white curls.

Something was off, but I couldn't figure out what. I pretended to agree. "Yeah, you're right. Probably just my imagination galloping away with me." Celeste relaxed. Sam looked at me with an odd expression.

Paul rubbed his hand over his bald pate. "If you are done discussing illusory scents," he said, "let's think of some ways that might actually be helpful in determining if the coat was Mum's."

"Maybe we could take a piece from what used to be the neck or the wrist," suggested Sam. "I wonder if a lab could pull up some DNA from it, if we found a piece that had been kept dry."

"Right," Celeste drawled. "Like that would happen."

"It's worth a try," argued Sam.

Celeste grunted. "You've been watching too much crime TV, Sam."

Before Sam could reply, Paul jumped in. "We could check with the Sheriff's Department and see if there was any mention of the coat in the old police report."

"That's one thing I admire about you, Paul. I can always count on you to be practical."

Paul looked at Celeste to see if this was actually a compliment or a dig. Then he relaxed a bit, as if deciding it was the former.

All of a sudden, I had a thought. "Jeez," I exclaimed. "I almost forgot! One of my old graduate school friends works at the Sheriff's Department."

"Who?"

"Donna Mertens. We spent a semester in one of those crossover classes – abnormal psych, I think it was. We had great debates, coming from different sides of the issues, and have kept up over the years. I was going to get in touch with her anyway. I'll give her a call on Monday, see what they've got." I stopped for a minute. "What about Hank, Celeste? Do you think he could shed some light on this?"

"I'm not sure Hank could shed light on anything, but I could try." It was obvious she was reluctant.

"Who's Hank?" Sam broke in.

"You know, the pig farmer who used to help out at Grandpa Dillen's," replied Paul.

"You forget I left here when I was six."

"Oh, right."

Celeste explained. "Hank returned from the war really changed. He was with the D-Day invasion, which was bad enough, but then after the farm incident that no one talked about, he became extremely peculiar."

"In what way?" Sam focused on Celeste. He sat very still, his eyes dark.

"He was more isolated than ever before. He just stayed in the barn apartment all the time. When Dad, Mum or I would drop food off, we had to whistle as we approached the door so he knew we were coming. He'd freak if we surprised him. It got so bad that Dad took him to the V.A. hospital for help. After that he seemed almost his old self for a while."

A memory tapped at me. "Was he the one who taught me magic tricks?"

"Yeah."

"I loved those tricks!"

"Hank could be a lot of fun," Celeste said. "He knew this place in and out. He loved the woods. He even showed me the old still once, although I wouldn't know how to find it now. After Mum died he got worse again. He wouldn't even walk the path from the farm to the house. Dad said he was afraid the guy who killed Mum might get him. Later, when Dad died and we moved Hank in here, he got even stranger. He obviously had his good periods, but as I told Pru earlier, these became fewer and fewer."

"Where is he living now?" Sam kept on.

"At the VA hospital in the old vets wing," provided Celeste. "It was finally the safest place for him. Recently when I've visited him, there have been times he hasn't known me at all, so I doubt he would be able to help us with our mystery."

"If you want, I could talk to him. I know my way around the VA a bit," Sam offered.

"You would? You do? Sure. Give it a try," said Celeste.

I sat there for a minute, wondering, then said, "Sam, why do you know your way around there? Was your Dad a vet?"

"No, I am," Sam answered. No other explanation.

There was a minute of silence while we all looked at him. I figured out that there was only one war he was the right age to have fought in. I mentally filed this information away. It would explain his odd reaction when I had saluted him earlier.

Bing! The timer intruded into my thoughts. I stood up. "Time to eat, guys." I moved into the kitchen hearing the shuffling of the troops behind me. When I brought the clam dish in, everyone else was already at the table.

"Need some help, Pru?" Sam looked up.

"Is it that obvious?" It was hard to keep the edge out of my voice. Glad someone had some manners. He followed me into the kitchen and took the salad and dressing. We returned to the dining area where Celeste and Paul were both oblivious of my little snit.

"So," Celeste was saying, "back to the other mystery Pru was talking about – the photo of Dad? I noticed it when I was tidying up the trunk, but I just figured it was the group he was with overseas. I was too busy with the rest of the mess up there to look closer."

Paul wound some spaghetti onto his fork. "Pru and I were wondering if the photo was connected to something odd I noticed when we were looking through the album."

"That you looked like a geek?" taunted Celeste with a twinkle in her eye.

"Like you were much better. Long gangly legs, wild child hair."

Oh, no. Here they went again. "Children! Stop bickering, and either get back on track or eat."

"Okay, eat first, "said Celeste. "Might improve my mood."

"Let's hope something does," muttered Paul under his breath.

"What?"

"Nothing."

My God, I thought, Jess and Adrian are easier to deal with than these two. I hadn't had much practice, but there certainly is something to that old adage that no matter how grown up you are, when you get back with your family of origin you take up the old place you occupied as a child. These two certainly had. As for me, I was too young then to be the peacemaker but that seemed to be my role now – my life's work spilling over onto my siblings. Lovely. There was a blessed silence for a while, broken only by the occasional request for more bread.

Finally Celeste sat back. "Aah, that's better. When I am hungry, my first instinct is to bite the ankle of the waitress."

"No kidding," I growled.

"Sorry, Pru. It was a good dinner. Paul, I apologize for my bratty behavior. You're not going to leave right away, are you?"

"Think you can chase me away, Cel? I told Pru I hadn't been jacked up for a while since the last time I saw you. It's got my blood running again." He paused. "And, I'm sorry I wasn't more help with Hank." He patted her on the shoulder then turned to Sam. "Quiet bunch, aren't we?"

Sam smiled. "I don't mind. I haven't seen my brother Lewis in such a long time I had almost forgotten what sibling bickering sounded like. Paul, go on about what struck you as funny about the album, because something struck me odd as well about your dad's photo."

"What?"

"No, you go first."

"Okay. What bothered me was that the family photos greatly decreased after our trip to Washington that year. There are very few of any of us after the war. No casual family pictures. Then, after Mum died, there are only a few of Dad and Mr. Barstow with a lot of other guys around, like a reunion or something."

"I looked at that picture after you left, Paul. Were those guys the same crew as in that photo?" I nodded towards the living room where the photo of Dad sat. "Also how did Barstow figure in with the others, and what *was* Dad doing over there?"

Sam smiled at my barrage of questions. "*One* of those was also my question. The picture on the table where they all have on a blue badge, that's definitely an official badge. And you can't tell me all those other guys are interpreters."

"So do you think Dad was involved in something else over there with the Army?" Paul asked. "I've been trying to figure out if those are uniforms, but they don't fit anything I remember when I was in the service."

"In the books I've read about World War II, several of them described the uniforms issued to the American GIs as pretty haphazard. The soldiers were lucky if theirs fit," responded Sam. "If your dad was in the Army, he wouldn't necessarily even have had a dress uniform to wear to receive that badge. Also, your dad wrote, 'Citation.' It was most likely a unit citation, which of course implies that he was part of some sort of unit." Sam smiled at his obvious statement.

"You are so enlightening. Thanks Sam." This of course from Celeste.

I decided to ignore her biting tone this time. "How can we find out what kind of unit?" I asked.

"Maybe we can find out if Mr. Barstow is still alive, see what he knows. He probably isn't as sinister as he seemed." Celeste decided to be helpful.

"That's what I suggested earlier," I said. "Then Paul told me he has all of Dad's old notebooks from the ham radio at home."

"You mean we're all actually on the same page for a change?" Celeste asked.

"Guess so, Big Sister. I can live with it, can you?" said Paul.

Celeste nodded and smiled at him in reply. "So," he continued, "I'll try looking up Barstow in the notebooks when I get back. Also I'm going to see what Annie can find on the Internet about Burma in World War Two."

"Good place to start, Bear." Celeste smiled at her overt compliment. Paul beamed. "As for the rest, I am done in for the night. I'm not sure there is any more we can do until we find out some of this other stuff."

"Celeste," I said. "You're usually the last one to bed."

"I told you I was working with that new horse all day. Days like this make me *know* I'm not forty any more."

"Okay, then. Sam and I will see what we can pull off the tree tomorrow when we go measure the fence line."

"If we get anything, I'll take it to the lab on Monday," added Sam.

"And I'll call Donna on Monday about the old police report and the coat," I finished.

"Not a bad evening's work," summarized Paul. "I have to go, too." He stood up. The rest of us followed suit and I ushered my brother and sister out, aware that Sam was gathering up the dishes behind me and taking them to the kitchen.

"Drive safely." I hugged Paul. He and Celeste exchanged hugs and cuffed each other on the head. Paul got into his car first, as it was blocking Celeste's. She didn't even object to being last out of the driveway. She *must* be tired. We waved at Paul and hugged each other. Then she climbed into her truck, turned around, and sedately for her, made her way home.

Velvet walked over to me. I scratched her ears. "Want to come in, girl? We'll walk you in a while." It was still fairly early. She and I went back into the house to find the dishes almost all done and filed away in the dishwasher.

"My, you are domesticated," I observed.

"Surprising the things you learn to do when you are the only one doing them."

"Do you want to stay for coffee?" I realized that sounded like a line from a thousand movies. "I mean, fill each other in on our intervening years," I added, feeling a bit awkward.

"It never occurred to me you meant anything else." I looked at him. No, he wasn't kidding.

"Good." I put on the kettle, poked in the cupboard for some decaf, pulled the two types of creamer out of the fridge, and saw the pie. "Oh. They left before the pie. Want some?"

"You mean I have to share it?" he twinkled.

"Half and half," I offered. I set the oven temperature and popped the pie in to warm up.

"Deal. Let's go out onto the deck. Will Velvet stay with us out there?"

"She will if we take her on a walk first while the kettle and pie are heating up. I'll show you where I want to start the fence." I gathered up Velvet's leash, clipped it on, and started out the door with Sam following me. As he shut it behind him, I decided to get the most obvious question over with. "So, you never married?"

December 19, 1944
Burma

I survived the parachute jump! It was very exciting, like mountain climbing only more intense. We've been assigned to the Mars Task Force and are on the go from sunup to sundown. Now that I'm in the midst of all the action, I realize the difference between myself and the twenty year olds. I hope I can keep up. Tonight, I am simply too tired to write any more.

CHAPTER FOURTEEN

By the time we circled back to the house, I learned that my childhood buddy was friendly, warm, and fun to hang out with as long as you avoided any topic that had to do with his adult life. I received a one word answer to my married question ("Once"), heard the same amount of words to the question about kids ("Nope"), and found out that the reason he had returned here was for "Stuff". When I asked him what branch he served with in Vietnam, his answer of "Army" followed by silence pretty much brought the whole conversation to a crashing halt.

Thank God for Velvet. She focused on a fat gray squirrel in a young oak tree who scolded her so loudly that Sam and I both started laughing. After reaching the edge of the area I had in mind for the fence, Sam held out his hand for the leash. Both man and dog seemed perfectly content with that arrangement and we walked back to the house with the silence sitting more easily between us. I wasn't sure he was going to stay for coffee and pie, but when I asked him if he still wanted dessert, he accepted readily.

"It will be much nicer for Velvet when we get that fence built," he commented.

"Did you ever have a dog, Sam? You seem really comfortable around Velvet."

"Once." Another one word answer. Sam took a breath. Maybe

not. "Her name was Happy. She was a collie and she was my best friend." He reached and took down two cups.

I pulled the pie out of the oven, cut it in half and put one half on a plate, which I took, and handed him the other half still in the pie plate.

He laughed. "No doubt about the portions this way, eh?"

"I don't believe you just put the 'eh' at the end of your sentence."

"I did live in Canada most of my life. I didn't even notice it."

"Sorry. Let's take our tiny dessert portions out to the deck and watch the sunset. Then you can tell me more about Happy." We wandered out to the deck. Velvet, smelling food, moved over to sit next to me, looking hopeful. I tossed her a bit of crust.

"You'll never train her not to beg if you do it on and off," Sam noticed.

"Yeah, I know. Strongest reinforcement for her begging behavior I could give her. As you get to know me you'll realize it's only one of my many inconsistencies."

"What are the others?"

Oh no, Buster, I thought. Two can play this game. I gave him a smile, slanted him a cocky look and said, "Stuff."

He stared at me. Oh God, I blew it. Then he broke into one of his lovely smiles, but this time graced by an odd dimple on his right cheek I hadn't seen before.

"Touché. Since neither of us is about to spill our guts to each other, how about we go back to where we left off? I'll finish telling you about Happy, and we can exchange childhood stories."

"From my point of view, that isn't much better. But I think I can make that deal." I wiped a blueberry-stained hand on my pants and shook hands with him.

"Okay, then. Happy looked after me as I explored the bush – woods to you – during the long summers. Together we picked blueberries and caught shiners to sell to the American fishermen who came up to fish in the lakes. She sat on the dock with me when I fished, lunging at the flopping fish whenever I caught one."

"Sounds pretty idyllic. Didn't you have any human friends?"

"Just Harry."

"Who was he?"

"A classmate who had such big ears, everyone called him Elephant Ears."

"Poor guy."

"He dealt with it pretty well. He was the best Boy Scout in the whole town, and knew where the prime fishing holes and blueberry bushes were. Once I found that out about him, I didn't even notice the ears, and we spent most of the summer days together. Harry figured out how to take some of our neighbor's fresh blueberry muffins off the back porch where they were cooling, and sneak them down to the lake to sell to the tourists. Between the muffins and the shiners, we made pretty good money for ten year olds. The second summer we had this business, my brother Lewis caught us and told Mother. That was the end to that."

"Jerk," I chimed in.

"He could be. Always had to be the fair-haired boy, especially with Mother. I was the screw-up."

"What did your dad do when you moved up there?"

"He continued to be a logger. Worked for a big logging company based in Winnipeg. He'd be gone for a week at a time." Sam looked a bit sad at this. I chanced a question.

"Did you miss him?"

"Yeah. Lewis was six years older than I was so he was able to go off with him sooner. I didn't think that was fair. The funny thing was, when I got old enough to go with Dad, I changed my mind after the first two times. I never seemed to be able to deal with the constant chainsaw noise."

"So you weren't necessarily the screw-up, just the sensitive one," I ventured.

Sam looked surprised. "Both Dad and Lewis used to give me grief about being sensitive, so I guess I became a screw-up to get back at them. Only then I'd have Mother on my case, who was usually my defender."

"If your activities were limited to stealing blueberry muffins, I don't think she had too much to worry about." I ate a chunk of pie. Sam took a sip of coffee.

"Well, my life in the woods sure prepared me for my current job."

"Which is?"

"Oh, I thought Celeste told you. I run an outfitting business on the same lake."

"How can you leave at the height of the season?"

Sam scooped up a big spoonful of pie. He chewed and swallowed. "Here's the good part. My partner is Harry." We both laughed and spent the next few minutes finishing our pie. "It's weird," Sam mused, looking off towards the far shore, his eyes fading. "My whole life has been spent in the bush in one way or another. I need to remember that it was only for two years that it wasn't so much fun."

I wondered if he knew he'd spoken out loud. He reached into his pocket and took something out that he popped in his mouth, then turned his head and refocused on me. Guess not. I tucked away any questions I had.

"So what about the childhood according to Pru?" Sam prompted. He finished up his coffee.

I wiped my mouth with my sleeve. "Well," I began, "obviously a bit more disrupted than yours."

Sam cocked his head gently from side to side in an "it depends" gesture.

I filled him in on Celeste's failure as a parent figure after Mum died, resulting in Dad hiring an older babysitter-housekeeper type to take care of me and the house during the day. "I wasn't very good with her either. I kept leaving little notes in different rooms that said, 'I hate Mrs. Bumbershoot'."

"Was that her real name?"

"No. I made that up. I've forgotten her name, I just remembered it had three syllables."

"So, did your Dad fire her?"

"Didn't have to. She quit due to my snotty behavior. Celeste told me the other day it was probably just my way of reacting to all the losses. So from then until Grandma Dillen died when I was ten, I pretty much lived at the farm. Her death was a blow to all of us. I think Mum dying was one thing, but we all thought Grandma Dillen would live forever."

"Is that why you went to live out East?"

"How did you know that?"

"Celeste told me a bit about where all of you had been over the years."

I bristled. "So you know all of this already? Why did you let me go on?"

He ducked his head. The dimple appeared on his cheek again. "Don't get in a bundle, Pru. I'm interested in hearing your life from your mouth, not Celeste's. It's like the difference between a headline and the full article."

Somewhat mollified, I said, "all right then. Where was I?"

"Being sent back East because no one here could handle you. How was that for you?"

"Pretty strange for a country kid. Uncle Hugh and Aunt Alice lived in Cambridge, Mass. Uncle Hugh was a doctor. Both he and Aunt Alice were upper-crust by birth and family connections, so it was a far different culture than I was used to. Their daughters had debutante parties and 'came out' – were presented in a huge ball-like thing called a cotillion – when they reached eighteen. Their sons went to Harvard because *everyone* went to Harvard for generations back. Just like some of the men Dad met at Yale. So, I was sent to dancing school once a week and learned to waltz, foxtrot, and even tango. It was the venue for parties, dances, dates, and the eventual debutante thing. But what mostly stays with me are the sweaty hands of my adolescent partners and having to dance too close to guys who had spinach caught in the braces on their teeth."

"Talk about different lives. Dancing for me meant being taught square dancing in gym class."

I chuckled, took the last gulp of my coffee, and ran my index finger around my dessert plate to get up the last bit of juice. "As I got older, I realized it was the kind of life all three of us kids would have lived had Yale not backed down on hiring Dad."

"Why did they?"

"Oh God, that is a *whole* different story. That's the one you can get from Celeste. She has more details on that part."

"Oh." Sam's face fell.

This talking about the past wasn't easy. I'd already told him more than my siblings knew. "Sorry, Sam, I didn't mean to snap."

"That's okay. This is probably as hard on you as the questions you asked were for me"

"Well, at least you were polite with your one word answers. I'll try to be less prickly."

"And I'll try for two words next time." We both smiled at the shared discomfort.

"Anyway. It wasn't that I couldn't fit in. Hell, I was a positive chameleon by then. I could look like I belonged in any environment. But when I went home it wasn't to *my* mother and dad. Aunt Alice and Uncle Hugh were great, but they didn't smell the same or laugh the same or hug the same as my own family."

"Did it help when you came back here in the summers?"

"Somewhat. Dad was probably at his best in the summers. I think he really tried to rally. Occasionally Celeste or Paul would visit and for a while it almost felt like we were a family. But then, they'd leave, and Dad would immerse himself in his work again or disappear back into the barn with his ham radio, and I didn't really have any friends left nearby."

"So what did you do?"

"I read a lot, rode my bike to the public beach hoping I'd know someone, learned to cook for Dad, and waited for him to come home."

"Did things finally get too bad to come home in the summers?"

"It's just that they never got any better, but I kept it up through school, for Dad. He died of cancer my senior year of high school."

I sat still, looking at the water, feeling the loneliness of that time. Sam let me be and took the plates and spoons inside. I stirred myself and followed him with the cups. He smiled in understanding as I came into the kitchen.

"This would be my clue that it's time to go home?"

"Yup." I managed a slight grin to take the sting out of my abruptness. I handed him the cups.

"But I get to wash these before I go?"

"What a master mind reader. I'll wipe up the counters. You put the plates in the dishwasher. After all, tomorrow comes early and you'll get to enjoy my vivacious company all over again while we measure and search for bits of fur that might say 'Adrienne' on them." We cleaned up in silence. Velvet and I then walked him out to his car.

Sam folded himself back into the driver's seat. Just as he was about to put the car in gear, he looked up at me, and offered a gift. "I was combat medic for the Green Berets in Vietnam." Then he drove off.

Wow. Way more than two words.

In the Jungle

Without the Kachins, the jungle tracks would be invisible, not to mention impassable. The long hikes leave my knees shaking at the end of the day. The only reward is emerging to breath-taking views of the mountain peaks stretched out before us. At times it is hard to realize that we are in the middle of a war. Then, reality intrudes as we descend once again to lay explosives at the next bend of the railroad leading North.

CHAPTER FIFTEEN

I drifted back into the house, Velvet at my side. As I finished tidying up the kitchen, I thought about what Sam had said. Funny, here I was a Baby Boomer, a member of the Vietnam generation, and I had never known anyone personally who had fought over there. Must have been the company I kept. In college I hung out with the protesters. David was rated 4F – unfit for military service – due to knee injuries from playing football in high school. I recalled the tough reception many soldiers received when they returned. They were often spat on and called "baby killers". I didn't agree with the war, but I thought that it wasn't the soldiers' fault. Hell, they were little more than kids themselves. I moved from the cushioned world of graduate school to the liberal Northwest. I knew there were still a slew of vets out in the woods in Washington, and that there was a vet center in Bellingham created to try to reach them. Occasionally I would work with a kid in school whose dad had fought in Vietnam, but Sam was the first real live vet I'd come face to face with. Sure blew most of my preconceptions out of the water. I wondered what else he'd eventually tell me. With the little information he had given me, I certainly wasn't going to ask him any time soon.

I walked into the living room, feeling again the loneliness I had dredged up from talking about those years of living – or rather *not* living – with Dad. I stood for a moment looking out at the lake. It was a lovely golden color from the sun hanging just above the trees. My eyes strayed to the photo of Dad with his fellow badge receivers, wondering what we would find out about that. My gaze moved to the old photo album Paul and I had found this morning. Was it just this morning? It always intrigued me that when you left the routine of your life and traveled to a different place, even a day seemed longer, with all the new stimuli – not to mention what I had stumbled on in the past four days. Was it still Saturday? Saturday. Oh damn!

I forgot to check to see if Jess had called back. I decided to remedy that and dug in my purse for my cell phone. Not there. Then I remembered I had plugged it in to recharge before going out to shop earlier. I checked my bedroom. Yup, she had called when I was out this afternoon. It was two hours earlier on the coast. I checked my watch. Still early enough to catch her before she went out. Good. I didn't want to wait until Sunday to talk to her. Talking to Jess was always good for the soul. I sat down on one of the love seats. Velvet jumped up and lay down with her head in my lap. I dialed and then stroked her soft ears. She sighed and turned on her back for a belly rub. I obliged while the phone rang.

"Hello?"

"Oh, Jess, I'm glad I caught you!"

"Mom! Have you disappeared into an alternate universe?"

"Close. You always are right on, Babe."

"Well, it's unlike you not to call back. I was worried."

I liked the sound of that. It doesn't hurt for them to worry about you for a change.

"Also," she continued, "Dad has been bugging me, wanting to know if I've heard from you. He sounded bummed that he hasn't been able to reach you."

Now, *that* was interesting, I thought. I said, "Sorry about that. I'll call him after I talk to you, so you don't have to be the middleman, or person," I added, bowing to Jess' instinctual sense of the politically correct.

"So, what's been going on?"

"An incredible amount of things for four days, Jess." I then filled her in roughly about Celeste, the fur coat, Paul, the album, the photo of my Dad, the reappearance of Sam, the mysteries and anomalies surrounding our family, and our plans to look into them.

"Whoa! Not exactly the boring visit to the homestead I had envisaged."

"Not quite."

"How much longer do you think you'll be there?"

Now that was another intriguing question. "I'm not entirely sure, Jess. I think I want to see this to whatever conclusion we come up with. I've got the summer anyway. I'll just have to see. Do you want to come out and join me?"

Jess laughed. "I'd love to. No one likes a mystery better than I, but Mom, some of us have to work for a living."

"Well, if I stay past the summer, I might have to find a way to live off Celeste for a while," I joked. "Maybe she'll hire me as a stable hand."

"In your worst nightmare. Hey, I was about to go out, but let me know if you need any help researching from here. Beats combing Los Angeles for identical apricot poodles for this show I've been working on for Animal Planet."

I laughed at the picture of Jess driving in a van with poodles sticking their heads out of the windows like in Gary Larson's cartoon, *Dogs Going to Work*. "I'll keep that in mind, Jess. *And* keep you in the loop. Sorry about the lapse."

"As long as you are okay. But call Dad."

"Will do. Love you, Jess"

"Love you too, Mom. Bye."

I hung up. Velvet pushed her paws at me wanting more tummy rub. I scratched her absentmindedly as I thought about what Jess said about David. What was that all about? I'm not around to take care of him, so suddenly he can't do without me, or was he really missing me? Wishful thinking? I sighed, stood up, and looked out

THE COAT IN THE WOODS

through the French doors at the lake. Velvet turned over and fell off the love seat. She shook her fur as if she had intended to do just that.

Still standing by the French doors, with phone in hand, I dialed home. It rang. Are you there David? It rang four more times. I was about to hang up when David answered, out of breath.

"Hello?"

"Jess said you wanted me to call," I answered without preamble.

"Pru, I'm glad to hear from you! I was out mowing the lawn, or I would have answered sooner."

I started chewing the inside of my cheek again. I thought, sure, in the dark? Then I immediately felt badly because I realized it was still light out there, and he did like mowing late when it wasn't so hot. I softened my tone at that thought. "What's up, David?"

"Not much. I was just worried I hadn't heard from you. For all I knew, you could have been plastered on the side of the road somewhere between here and there."

"You'd have heard if I had been in an accident. I have all the emergency information in my purse." Oops, back to sounding like a witch.

"Are you all right? You sound kind of rough." Damn the man. He could always sense what was underneath my voice. It was just that most of the time, he didn't seem to care enough to pursue it.

"Maybe a little." I flopped down into the easy chair. It was nice to be asked by someone who knew me so well. I gave in and told him most of the events of the last few days, even about my meltdown.

"Aw, Pip, I should be there for you. Do you want me to come out there?"

Why did he choose now to say the right thing? Part of me would love it if I could lean on him, talk to him as if he was the best friend I thought I had before his affairs started, and cuddle up to him to comfort the hollowness I'd been feeling. But the other part of me said that I'd only be setting myself up for the inevitable withdrawal that would follow as soon as the crisis was over and the next attractive grad assistant appeared. I stuck my tongue into my right cheek to get it away from my teeth. I took a breath and waffled. "Yeah, I sort of do, but I don't think it would be a good idea."

"I don't blame you, Pip. I know I've been a complete bastard," David responded to my hesitation.

God, I'd give anything to believe he meant that. I knew I had been hanging on to the unraveled threads of our marriage because I didn't have the courage to do anything else. His offer and admission made me hope that maybe I was wrong, that the threads weren't as worn as I'd thought. But I'd come out here partly to see if I could be on my own, and the emotional discoveries of the past few days hadn't changed that.

I was finally beginning to figure out that instead of leaning on David, or even Celeste and Paul, the person I needed to lean on the most was myself. This was my opportunity and I wasn't going to blow it, so I reined in my neediness and my ache for someone else to make me feel better. I decided to ignore his last statement for now. "You are sweet to offer, David, but I think this is something I need to do on my own. With everything else that's been going on between us, it would just add to the confusion here."

Silence. It went on so long I thought we had been cut off. Finally I heard him clearing his throat. Was he crying? David coughed. "Okay, I can respect that. It's just that I really miss you."

Dammit, David, I thought, please don't. I can barely keep from caving in as it is. It was my turn to start tearing up. I had to get off the phone before I gave myself away. Besides that, the inside of my mouth was a mess. Velvet sensed that something was going on with me, and crossed the room to put her paw on my knee. I stroked it. "David, I'm sorry, but I've got to go. I'll call you in a few days."

"Whatever you need, Pip. Take care. I love you." He finished softly and just as quietly hung up the phone.

I clicked off my cell. Loneliness swamped me, more than I'd felt even when living with David and his constant obsessions. Then, my anger had cushioned me somewhat, my detachment protected me. Now, with David's loving tone of voice flowing around me at a time when the phantoms of my solitary fourteen-year-old self were haunting me, I ached for his touch, for his warm body to curl up to in bed. I stood up. Velvet read my body language and headed up the stairs. I locked the doors and followed her. I found her already stretched out on the porch. I looked at my bed, not sure I could deal with the springs tonight. I contemplated my stuffed panda and decided it wasn't enough, not tonight. So I stripped the bed of the heavy quilt, spread it out on the balcony, pulled down another one from the closet, grabbed my pillow, and still in my clothes, lay down next to Velvet, my quilt gathered tightly around me and slept, my back next to her warm, furry body.

December 22, 1944

More trekking up and down. Our paths follow the edge of ravines so treacherous that today they claimed some of the large American pack mules brought in by the infantry. I'll never forget their terrified screams as they plunged to the streams below. Luckily the mules the Kachins have are smaller and more used to the steep trails. I just realized it is almost Christmas. I wonder where I'll be.

CHAPTER SIXTEEN

The next day announced itself at dawn with a wet dog tongue on my face. I pulled the quilt over my head. Velvet persisted, burrowing her nose under the quilt until I got up. Aah, a bit stiff. I decided sleeping on the hard deck with the dog would not be a regular habit. I let Velvet out and stood sleepily by the door while she did her stuff. I then took advantage of my still groggy state to stagger upstairs again and collapse on my bed. I was learning how to avoid the worst of the springs, so I slept hard for a couple of hours.

When I woke up again, the sun was over the house, shining on the lake. I checked my watch. Still only 8:30. Time to sit and enjoy breakfast and my tea without any company at all. Sam had agreed to wait until ten to help me measure the fence perimeter. I showered, dressed in a long-sleeved shirt and jeans to avoid poison ivy and other prickly plants later on, and descended to the kitchen. I poured a bowl of granola and cornflakes, steeped my tea, and wandered onto the deck. I sat with my tea, enjoying the warm breeze, the loon couple and the singing of the other birds. I mused if I ever returned to watercolors, the loons would be the first thing I'd paint. I had almost recaptured the peacefulness of that first morning here before learning of a whole new page in my family's history, when I heard the unmistakable sound of Sam's car. It signaled my need to put my guard back up. I decided not to share my evening's conversations with David and Jess or my pathetic efforts at self comfort. I didn't always have to explain myself to everyone I knew. Another new habit to develop. I hoisted myself out of the Adirondack chair to meet Sam.

"Hey, again," he called. "Sleep well?"

"Yup," I answered. Well, I had, eventually.

"Ah, one word answers this morning?" he asked.

"Yup," I answered back, but smiling this time.

"Is this any indication of how fun this project is going to be? No – don't say 'Yup' again," he said just as I was about to. So I changed my mind. Just to be ornery?

"Nope."

It was his turn to smile. For some reason, that was all I needed. Before I knew it I was doubled over with the giggles. I had to sit on the steps and hold my stomach it hurt so much. Sam stood looking at me with a bemused expression. Velvet was running back and forth between us, going, "Whooo!" I finally wound down. Sam sat on the step below mine. Velvet trotted over to him and gave him a big slurp. He threw his arm around her back and nuzzled her. She settled down, leaning against him.

"Sorry, Sam. I don't know what it is about this place. I was doing the same thing at Celeste's the other night."

"It's a good stress reliever."

He was probably right given the night before. "Yeah, well. Want some coffee?"

"I had a huge cup on my way over. I need to be on task this morning, as I still have tons to do at the store today, since tomorrow will be pretty busy with Dad in town."

"Fine with me. Let's do it." I went into the house, picked up the measuring tape I had bought, and pulled some baggies out of the drawer for the fur bits. I retrieved Velvet's leash and hooked it onto her. Sam had a pad of paper with a pen clipped to the top of it. Instead of heading towards the path to Celeste's, we pushed our way through the woods along the lakeshore. About 100 feet from the house I stopped.

I looked up from the lake back towards the path, catching sight of a big oak tree that stood out from the rest. "Let's head to that oak."

Sam handed me the tape, keeping the other end, and walked back as far as it would go. We then repeated the process, marking the places for fence poles. As we approached the oak tree, the brush became thicker. Sam disappeared into the bushes, only the tugging on the measure telling me he was at the end of it.

Suddenly I heard a crash of brush, the clattering of rocks falling against each other, and an unmistakable human exclamation.

"Damn!"

The measure whirred its way back to me, stopping at some mid-distance. Velvet started pulling me towards the sound, drawn by the distress in Sam's voice. I followed with my end of the tape in hand, winding through the undergrowth like the tail of a snake following its head. It was all I could do to release the measure from the bush where it had caught, before being dragged off again. Velvet was impervious to my efforts to leash her in. I called, "Are you all right, Sam?" No answer. More clunking of rocks. Now it sounded like they were being thrown. I broke through the last bit of shrub to find Velvet at the end of the leash standing at a distance from a hole in the ground surrounded by rocks. Every so often a rock would erupt from the hole as if it was being spewed from a volcano. I stood out of the way, then took advantage of a break in the shower of rocks to call again. "Sam! Are you all right?"

Muffled feet sounds. Sam's head poked out from the rocks, the rest of him swallowed by the hole – the *deep* hole I realized – if all I could see was his head. Brambles stuck out from his pony-tail and his glasses were thick with dust. He wiped them off, then looked vaguely around.

"Sam?" I questioned softly. He had the same look as last night on the deck when he was staring off at the lake.

"What?" He turned towards me, finally focused, and gave a weak smile.

"It's Pru. Are you okay?"

"Yes, I know who you are," he replied with uncharacteristic irritability. "And I'm not sure I am."

"What happened?"

"I was backing up with the measure, when bang! My foot got stuck in a hole, and the rocks fell away. All of a sudden my butt was following my foot and down I went."

"Lucky for you it happened that way. You could have broken your leg."

"Or been buried by the rocks." He gave a shudder. "*That's* a feeling I'd rather never experience again."

Remembering his comment earlier about small spaces, I wondered if it had to do with the war. I decided to risk it.

"Like the tunnels in Vietnam?"

Sam looked at me for a minute, and then laughed a joyless laugh. "Is that what you thought? Look at me, Pru. They didn't send men my size into the tunnels. I wouldn't have made it as far as my shoulders."

"I'm sorry," I answered. "I feel like an ignorant idiot. You had such a strange reaction, I just thought…"

"It's okay. You *are* a bit ignorant about that topic, but nowhere near an idiot. No, I flashed back to when I was a kid and a bunch of us made a cave in a sand pit. The other kids went home for lunch, but I wanted to stay and play. I decided to dig a little more when all of a sudden the roof of the cave collapsed."

"Did you get hurt?"

"No, just scared. Once I realized I could still stand up and it wasn't that thick, I was okay. But just for a few moments I was terrified. I was only eight."

"Thus, your dislike for small spaces."

This time his smile was back to normal. "See? Not such an idiot. So, no broken bones, I'm breathing air, and look at this place!" He started throwing some more rocks out from the hole then ducked back inside, and soon appeared, walking up a pair of steps on the other side. He motioned us towards him. Velvet and I obliged.

"What is it?" I asked.

"Your old still!" Now Sam was grinning from ear to ear like a kid who had just discovered his first frog.

"Is it safe? Will it cave in any more?"

"Jeez, Pru. Stop being a fussbudget! That was just the vent hole. The rest is solid concrete and wood. Come look."

I didn't like being called a fussbudget even if it was true. "I recall you told me the tree was safe too when we were five!"

"Yeah, but this isn't a tree, and we're a lot older than five. Come on."

Slowly I approached, keeping Velvet at my side as if she would protect me from whatever was threatening me from the hole. I noticed that bushes had grown over the steps and that the rocks Sam had stumbled into were on the top, where they had camouflaged the vent hole. Sam moved further in so I could join him.

I inched my way down. Velvet pushed past me and headed for Sam. He stood hunched over and scratched her ears. At the bottom of the steps I turned around and looked, my head just inches from the ceiling. I was in a chamber that was about twenty-five feet square. Concrete walls surrounded us on four sides. At the corners, four big timbers held up the ceiling. More timbers crisscrossed above. A gap showed where Sam had fallen through. As my eyes adjusted to the dim light, I saw a number of ceramic jugs lined up against the far wall. Sam moved over to them. He picked one up and turned it so the light would fall on it. It left a clean round spot on the floor that had been protected by its bulk.

"Boy, do we have a find here!" he exclaimed.

"Why?"

He shook the jug. "Not only is this full of a questionable fluid, God only knows how old, but this is an old Red Wing jug. Someone must have left these in here after the still wasn't used any more."

I peered more closely. Red Wing jugs were worth a lot when I was in college. They'd be collector's items now, and there were about ten of them lined up.

"Want to take them out?" I asked.

"Maybe one now. We can show Celeste and get the rest later. Your SUV is a four wheel, right?"

"Yep." I looked around again. There was another bit of light shining in opposite the steps. I moved towards it.

"What's this?"

"Must be the escape route in case the feds found them in the process of cooking."

At this point I was noticing Velvet. On the floor opposite the wall with the jugs, she had found a place worth sniffing to death.

"What do you think she smells here?" I directed Sam's attention away from the jugs. We moved closer. "Stuff that spilled from the long ago still?"

"I'm not sure," replied Sam. "But it certainly has her interest."

During this conversation, Velvet continued to sweep the marked area with her nose. Next, she folded her front legs and started rubbing the edge of her face and neck back and forth on the area. I jerked her up. "What the hell? She usually just does that with animal scents."

"Maybe a racoon found its way in here to sleep."

"Possibly," I answered, not convinced. "Let's take the jug and get out of here. We can mark how to get back here from the road when we get to it."

"Okay by me." Sam hefted the jug up and climbed the steps. I pulled Velvet who would have spent all day with her smell, and followed him out. After we finished measuring the fence line to the path, Sam put the jug down at the edge of the trail, somewhat hidden under a bush. "Who are you hiding that from?" I asked.

"You never can tell. Maybe the son of the hobo who left his fur coat in your woods." His eyes twinkled at the thought.

"Except that coat belonged to my mother," I insisted.

"You think." Sam raised an eyebrow at me.

"Okay, let's get to the next part of our task. I think the coat is just up this way, then we can come back here and measure the rest of the fence line."

"You're the boss."

I looked at him to see if he was giving me grief, but he had that absolute serious Sam face on. I had to get used to the fact that not everyone was brought up with biting humor. I found the branch I had broken, Velvet confirming it was the right place as she brushed past me, pulling me off to the left of the path again. After a few hundred yards, there we were once more at the weirdly furry basswood tree. The strong scent again wafted over me. Overhead a slight breeze rustled the leaves, stirring the aroma. Sam lifted his head, sniffing it like Velvet would.

"What is that smell?"

"The basswood flowers, I think. Go sniff them."

Sam moved over and stuck his nose in one of the grapelike clusters. He stood there. "Hmmm. Nice."

"Yeah." I stood in a semi-reverie with the breeze ruffling my hair until Velvet pulled to get closer to the tree.

"Guess she likes the smell too," offered Sam.

"But she's going for the tree, not the flowers, Sam. I think it's a different scent. I tried to tell that to Celeste and Paul."

As I was saying this, Velvet leaned into the tree and tried to rub her face and ruff on the pieces of fur at her level. She was so intent that she looked like a bear leaning against a scratching tree after a winter's hibernation.

"The other night when I found the tree again on the way over to Celeste's, she was doing the same thing. I had a hell of a time pulling her away."

"Maybe the same raccoon that slept in the still climbed the tree," suggested Sam.

"Possibly," I answered, putting aside my doubts. I pulled out two baggies from my pocket. "Here, while I hang on to Miss Sniffalot, will you pick a couple of fur bits off?"

Sam took the baggies. "I'll reach as high as I can get, assuming those would have been around the neck area, then maybe try one at the bottom. Sometimes that's where the labels are put inside."

I watched Sam stretch to reach an extra fluffy piece up at the top of the fur patches. There was a ripping sound. He held out a fur piece about four by four inches. Bark was attached to it. I peeled a bit of it back, noticing a smudge on the skin side of the fir. I took the piece. The scent was strong. I sniffed and held it out to Sam to smell. "Now, that is *not* the basswood flowers." Sam sniffed it, looking thoughtful. I put the fur piece, bark and all, in one of the baggies. "How about that one at the bottom?" I pointed to a piece that looked a bit more ragged than the rest, in a position to suggest the place where the edge of the hem and the front opening of the coat had joined. Sam bent down and plucked that one off the tree. He handed it to me. I checked the back of this one as well. Hard to tell if there was another smudge or just dampness from being attached to the tree. I slipped it into the second baggie. Velvet at this point seemed to have had her fill of the tree, and moved next to me, sniffing at the treasures in the baggies. I zipped them shut. The smell must have wafted away, as soon Velvet wandered off and watered a bush. Sam moved away and peered down at the ravine. The car was still there.

"I'd love to get down there and see if there is anything under that car. I think it's safe to approach as it doesn't seem to have moved in all these years." He sighed. "But we need to get the rest of the measuring done, so it will have to wait." Sam looked at his watch. "Our little detour at the still took up more time than I thought." At that, we headed out to the path and back to the oak tree. On the opposite side of the path from the tree, we made our way through the brush again towards the ravine, repeating our measuring routine until, following the cliff, we finally reached the driveway that led to the house.

There, parked next to our two vehicles was Celeste's truck. What was she doing here in the middle of the morning? She emerged from the house, tea cup in hand.

"Where have you guys been? I was about to call out the Mounties!"

Sam laughed. "Can't. This isn't Canada."

"Cel, what are you doing here?" I asked. "This time of day you're usually up to your elbows in horses."

"Paul called me with some tidbits Annie found on the Internet. I figured you'd want to know."

December 23, 1944

I certainly seem to be doing a lot of everything else except what I was brought here for. Because the Kachins discovered I am still a fast runner, as well as knowledgeable about explosives, I am the one setting them and running like hell. However good a front I put on, I am terrified each time that the charge might blow up as I'm setting it, or even worse, that it doesn't and I have to run back and set it again. We also have been shadowing the enemy for miles without them knowing it, only to pop out at unexpected times, forming a screen to keep the Japanese from realizing how many of us are following, as well as wreaking havoc with their morale because they never know from which direction we will appear.

CHAPTER SEVENTEEN

"Yes, I sure do," I replied. "You want to stay and hear this, Sam, or do you have to go?" As I asked this, I grabbed Velvet's water dish to fill up, Sam right behind me. I glanced back at him and we both laughed. Celeste stood and watched all this with a curious look on her face.

"I do have to go, but I wouldn't miss this for all the world." He put his pad and the measuring tape on the counter in the kitchen. I finished my task for Velvet and pulled the baggies out of my pocket, putting them on the top shelf in the fridge. Then I grabbed a bottle of water. I cocked my head at Sam who nodded, and pulled another one out for him.

Celeste was already on the deck, having decided not to stand around while we got organized. However, when we joined her, she couldn't keep from commenting, "You two have an interesting rhythm going on there," she said, eyeing me like she knew something I didn't.

"What?" I asked. "The following thing?" Celeste nodded.

"We started doing that last night at dinner and remembered we used to do that as kids. Not a biggie, Cel." My tone of voice told her to leave it alone. She raised her eyebrows, but kept her mouth shut for a change. I glanced at Sam. He was drinking his water and gazing out at the lake as if he hadn't heard her. Just as well. It was time to divert my sister's attention before she made something out of nothing.

"So, give. Tell us what Annie found out."

"When she looked up WWII with Burma, she got almost five thousand hits."

"Oh." The disappointment was obvious in my voice. "Did she go with any of them?" I asked.

"She started, then luckily Paul came upstairs after looking through Dad's ham radio stuff. He had found Ed Barstow's telephone number."

"Did he call it?" Sam came out of his reverie and turned to join us.

"Yep, and got the people who bought his house. Ed has moved. He's living in Los Angeles with his grandson."

"Does that mean we have a dead end?"

Celeste grinned. She loved holding onto information. She paused dramatically. "Nope," she exulted. "Annie found the grandson's number in a L.A. telephone book from the library. Paul called, and after a confused conversation, finally got Ed on the phone. Ed told him that Brian, his grandson, is very protective of him. Paul tried to make the conversation short, but Ed wanted to know how all of us were. Paul finally got around to telling him he found this photo in Mum's trunk and that we were trying to remember what Dad did in Burma. Ed's answer to the Burma question was, 'I thought you knew. I got him into the OSS!'"

"The OSS," commented Sam. "That was the forerunner of the CIA."

"According to Ed," countered Celeste, "the OSS was the combination of what we know now as the CIA and Special Forces. Dad served with something called Detachment 101 in Burma. He told Paul there was even a website on the Detachment. Paul said he sounded really spry."

I was totally nonplussed. Our father in the OSS? He just didn't seem like spy material to me.

"Once Annie had that information, she had no trouble finding the website."

"And what did *that* say?" I was getting frustrated at being fed all this piecemeal.

"It was pretty long. Annie and Paul are coming up this afternoon so we can all read and learn about it at the same time." Celeste sat back, having given her message, a Cheshire cat grin on her face.

"Well, that will be a whole lot better than waiting for you to feed us information drop by drop. You love the power, Cel."

"Yeah?" she responded. She leaned forward, ready to get into it with me.

"But it is *so* annoying."

"Pip, come on, stop pouting. The point is we'll have some of our questions answered."

"In that case, I think I'll take off now and return later," Sam piped up. In my irritation with Celeste I had almost forgotten he was still here. We both looked at him. He looked from one of us to the other. "That is, if it's okay with you two."

Celeste graced him with her best smile. "Of course, Sam. Paul and Annie should be here about four."

"Four it is. Now it's off to more sorting at the store. See you later, ladies." With that he gave Velvet a quick parting pat and almost bolted off the deck. I held on to Velvet who tried to follow him. Then I heard his rust-bucket start up and bump down the driveway. It sounded like a gorilla with intestinal problems.

Celeste twinkled, "Boy, he couldn't get out of here fast enough. Was it something I said?"

Of course I took the bait and answered seriously, "Not so much what you said, as *how* you said it. Not to mention me bickering back at you." Celeste laughed.

"Oh lighten up, Pru. He already said he didn't mind our arguing. Just maybe he had other things to do than stay glued to our family history." She looked at me. I looked away. Then I decided to follow her advice. I turned toward her and stuck my tongue out.

"Now, *that's* mature." We both laughed. We were on the verge of another giggle event when she stopped.

"God, I almost forgot the most important thing. Barstow said that Dad kept a journal from Burma and Paul asked if we could look for it. Come on Little Sister, Sam's not the only one with work to do." With that, she grabbed my hand and pulled me out of the chair.

I took my hand back. "There were several boxes spilling over with papers in the attic. I noticed them when Paul and I were up there yesterday."

"I was about to suggest that." Celeste grabbed me again and pushed me up the stairs.

At the attic steps, she opened the door, waited for me to go ahead, then closed it behind her. We climbed the steps, both ducking in the automatic bat reflex. I followed her past the dressmaker's dummy and the sewing machine to the back room. This time instead of aiming for the trunk, we moved towards the overflowing boxes. Celeste sat down on the floor with an "oof" in front of one box. I pulled another and overturned one of the hard suitcases to act as a seat.

"Why didn't I think of that?" groaned Celeste. She got up and followed my lead.

"I don't think you want me to answer that, do you?"

"Of course not," she replied. "Search, Pru. We don't have that much time."

I started sifting through the papers. Most of them were old lecture notes and various articles on languages in diplomatic situations. I found one folder marked, *Adrienne* which contained a number of architectural drawings. I put that aside on top of one of the suitcases. Further down I found a folder marked *Det 101 reunion, 1955*. I looked inside. "Hey, Cel, more pictures like the one in Mum's album. Dad and a bunch of other guys at dinner tables."

"Keep it, we can compare them. I found some folders of our old school records and pictures. And look." She held up a glamorous picture of herself.

"Your senior picture?"

"None other. At least he kept some things. Oh my, look at this. She turned to a large 5 × 7 picture of her and Sunrise, both dressed up for a show, with a very handsome man holding the reins.

"Wow. Who's that?"

Celeste looked at it. "That's Glen."

"Now *he* was handsome. For some reason I thought he was a whole lot older than you." I looked at my sister. She had a very different expression on her face than I had ever seen.

"He's only about eight years older. He had just started his stable when he began training me. This picture was taken later, at a local show, after I left the circuit. He was no longer my trainer." Something in her voice made me venture into dangerous territory – Celeste's personal life.

"But he was something else by that time?" Celeste's look told me I had hit the spot. "How come you never said anything?"

"Well, you were still an impressionable teenager and he was married." Celeste tucked her hair behind her ear.

"Oh." I didn't know who I felt worse for, Celeste or Glen's wife. After all I knew all too well how she must have felt.

"What happened?" I was ready for her to shut me down at any moment, but to my surprise she answered.

"What you expected. But it didn't happen until after I returned from treatment, when I was training for him. Then, when he ended it I went out on my own."

"Is he still in the area?"

"He lives in Sauk Rapids." She named a town north of St Cloud. "He runs a small stable and sends me horses every so often that are too much trouble for him."

"Is he still married?"

"Why, are you match-making?" She looked annoyed.

"No more than you are with me and Sam. And I am still married also, need I remind you."

"Fair enough. No, Glen and his wife divorced years ago."

"So then, how come you and he…?"

Celeste interrupted me. "Too much water over that particular dam, Pip. In fact a virtual flood. We do better as friends. Now, that is the end of that story. Let's keep looking for what we came up here for." Her words sounded firm, but as she put the photograph back, her face kept its wistful look.

However, I was beginning to learn when to leave things alone. I continued rummaging through my box, but found nothing more than academic-looking papers. I pushed that box aside and moved over to the last one. "Did you find anything that looks like a journal in your box, Cel?"

"Nope." She pushed hers aside as well. "But I'll get back to this one. It seems to have a few more personal things in it than we thought Dad kept. Just that one left?" She pointed to the last box.

"Unless there are more down in his study." I stopped for a minute. "Do you think Hank was looking for the journal?"

Celeste considered this for a minute. "It would be hard to tell, as these boxes have been in such disarray for ages, I never bothered with them."

"I reached down into the last box and felt something silky. "Aah, we might have hit pay dirt." I moved the papers aside, and brought up a notebook-shaped package wrapped in a thin silk-like material. "What do you think this is from?" I fingered the material.

Celeste looked over my shoulder. "Piece of a parachute?" she ventured.

"From where? That's another thing I can't picture Dad doing. Using a parachute." I unwrapped the material. Celeste kept her eyes on the package. Inside was an old school notebook. No label. I opened it. There was Dad's spiky handwriting. 'Arthur Dillen, Journal, Oct 6, 1944, Day One,' read the first entry. I closed it quickly.

"What are you doing? Let's read it." Celeste had her information-hungry look on.

"No, Cel. We need to wait and read this to everyone. This is one time you can't be first."

She sat back on her heels. "I'm impressed, Pip. Way to assert yourself with your older sister. I have to admit you're right, so you keep it. I don't trust myself, because I really want to know what's in it." She stood up and brushed her backside off. "In fact, I'll go back to the farm for a few hours so I won't be tempted. I'll be back at four." With that she hugged me and clambered down the stairs.

I tidied things up a bit and looked around the attic thinking I should bring Mum's portrait back down to the dining room some day, but left it there. Then, clutching the silky journal to my chest, I followed Celeste, closing the door firmly behind me.

Evening, December 24, 1944

The activity is becoming more intense. Yesterday something happened which, for all my training, I was completely unprepared. Our intelligence was inaccurate and a Japanese sentry guarded the part of the train track where I was supposed to set the charge. He came at me from behind and only my quick reaction kept him from cutting my throat. Then I froze – something I will never forget or forgive myself for. I simply could not reach for my knife, or lunge for my gun which had fallen to the ground. As the guard raised his knife again, I saw him as if in a dream, and only wondered how it was going to feel when his knife sliced through me. I didn't hear the sound of rifle fire until he fell to the ground. I looked around to see Naw Hpraw, one of my Kachin comrades, with his gun aimed. The noise brought the Japanese sentry's fellow patrol members out of hiding and I just had time to grab my rifle and run back towards the jungle as the Kachins covered me. I pointed my rifle along with the others, but I was so rattled I shot blindly, not aiming at anyone. Four of our Kachins were wounded, two of whom are at death's door. Naw Hpraw's cousin is one of them. He was standing next to me when he was hit and his blood sprayed all over me as he fell back. I can't even look Naw Hpraw in the face. What a Christmas Eve. I simply cannot write any more.

CHAPTER EIGHTEEN

By the time four o'clock rolled around, it had turned into an uncomfortably hot Minnesota day. The thermometer that was in the shade had climbed into the mid eighties. Velvet was sleeping on her back under a tree, spread-eagled to keep cool. The air was so humid that it would make a camel sweat. Luckily there was a bit of a breeze coming off the lake, so I opened all the windows to let the house air out.

    I decided it was a bit too warm for vegetable soup, so I made a taco salad. I had just returned everything to the fridge and wiped down the counters when I heard a car. Not Sam's. I looked out the window. It was Paul and Annie. I wiped my hands on the towel hanging from the oven handle and ran out to greet them.

Paul stepped out of the driver's seat with a bunch of papers under his arm. "Beware of Geeks bearing gifts!" he declared. I groaned, then immediately turned to the woman with dark salt and pepper hair curling around her face.

"Annie, it's *so* good to see you!" I moved into her wide-open arms.

"Likewise, Pip dear!" Her small, plump body took me in a vise-grip hug.

"What are you guys?" I exclaimed, "The hugging champions of Minnesota? You both give such good ones!"

"We enjoy the practice." Annie's blue Irish eyes danced. A dusting of freckles stood out on the bridge of her nose. Paul blushed.

"I think that's a bit more information than she wants, Annie," he said.

"Oh go on with you!" declared his wife. "We're all of age, are we not?" She turned her attention back to me. "Pip, you look younger than the last time we saw you out West, what, a couple of years ago?"

"Thanks," I answered, "considering I feel like I've lived a decade or two in the last week."

"God love you, it must be good for you," Annie stated.

"That's what I told her, too," added Paul. "Maybe she'll believe it if you tell her."

At this point, I was getting uncomfortable with the scrutiny. "Enough of that. Come on in. I even made a taco salad to feed everyone in case we get talking too long for you guys to make it back before dinner."

"You're an angel," exclaimed Annie. "It wouldn't have been me doing the cooking tonight, I can tell you. I would have probably dragged your brother through a fast food place on the way home instead."

Paul looked relieved. "Thank you, Pip. I can only eat that stuff about once a year." We all moved toward the house. Velvet got up long enough to sniff the newcomer and receive a pat, then flopped back down in the shade. "Where should I put these?" Paul indicated the papers.

"Are you reading all that to us? I should have made the beds as well."

Annie replied, "Ah, don't worry. I took advantage of the library's copying service so we could each have a copy. Will Sam be here?"

"Yep. He said he wouldn't miss it for the world. He has a secondhand shop he's trying to open in Avon this week, so he had to go back and do some more organizing."

"And Celeste?" Paul asked.

"I sent her packing. We did find a journal of Dad's. If she had stayed, she would have read it, rather than waiting for all of us to listen to it together."

Paul rolled his eyes. I thought, we sure do funny stuff with our eyes in this family. Is that a metaphor for something? He said, "Good call Pip. Maybe we'll let her do the reading. After all she has the most dramatic presentation of all of us." Annie elbowed him in the ribs. "Except for my lovely wife when she is doing poetry readings."

I looked at Annie. "You are? That's great! Where do you do them?"

Annie smiled at my enthusiasm. "After I took a poetry class, I linked up with some of the other students who all knew different venues. Sometimes we read at coffee houses, sometimes at the U. of M. Mostly just at gatherings of other poets."

"But she is one of the most sought-after readers." Paul looked as proud as Annie. Her face darkened.

"And how would you be knowing that? I think you've only made one out of the last ten I've attended." The silence dropped between her and Paul, and I could swear I heard it land with a thud on the porch. Paul inserted some words into it.

"Didn't I tell you Annie would have something to say about my overworking habits?"

"You mean you actually admitted to her that you do?" Annie

looked at me. "God love you, Pip. He usually isn't much for communicating his faults."

I felt like I needed to defend my brother. "It wasn't me, Annie. I think meandering down our family's paths has taken unexpected turns for all of us. And who knows what else is in store? Paul, I also found a folder of Mum's drawings. I left it on top of one of the suitcases in the attic if you want to delve into them."

"Oh, good," replied Paul. "Just what I need – a hobby."

"Didn't you say you used to draw houses and gardens before you decided on mechanical engineering?" asked Annie. "Looking at your Mum's stuff might get you going on that again."

Paul's face shut down. "That was years ago, Sweetie." We all stood there.

I broke the silence. "I made some iced tea. Let's get out of the heat. Sam and Celeste should be here any moment."

As I moved into the house, I heard Celeste's truck skid to a stop followed by Sam's car. I decided to leave them to greet each other while I sorted the papers into five different piles on the dining room table. I was drawn to the top page that was entitled: *Detachment 101, Office of Strategic Services, Burma – April 14, 1942 to July 12, 1945, The American-Kachin Rangers,* but I resisted looking further. I could never live it down if Celeste caught me reading it before the others. I returned to the kitchen and took down some tall glasses, fished a tray out of the cupboard, and pulled the iced tea from the fridge. I put the tray with the tea and glasses on the table next to the papers. As the others filed in, they each poured some tea, took a pile of papers and spread themselves around the living room.

Once settled, Celeste looked up at me and asked, "Can we start, teacher?" I glared at her. The others laughed.

Annie said, "As you can see, it's not too long. What year did you say your Dad was over there?"

"I think '44 to '45," Celeste answered.

"That's towards the back, but I think it's interesting to read the whole history of the Detachment."

"So you've read it already?" asked Celeste.

"Just bits and pieces," replied Annie.

"Which," I added pointedly to Celeste, "she has managed to keep to herself so far."

"Hey, guys," this from Sam. "A little quiet to read in?"

That settled all of us down. For the next half hour or so, all you could hear were shuffling papers and an occasional "hmm".

Finally, when the slowest reader, who was Sam, had finished, Paul spoke up.

"So, what do we know now that we didn't before?"

"For one thing," I said, nodding towards the photo on the table, "we know the citation badge that Dad and the other guys have in that picture was probably this 'Presidential Distinguished Unit Citation' given by Eisenhower that's mentioned here."

"I was interested in the fact that the Detachment 101 pioneered the art of unconventional warfare that we used in Vietnam," Sam added.

Jeez, and I thought he was just a medic.

It was Celeste's turn. "I was never really interested in history, but all of a sudden when it's connected to you it makes fascinating reading. Like the fact that the war began in the Far East as early as 1931, and that the Japanese controlled the coastline and pretty much isolated the Chinese and Allied troops in China north of Burma."

"Or that they also controlled the Burma Road from Rangoon, right after Pearl Harbor," Annie added.

"I'd heard of General Stillwell," said Paul. "He got caught in the politics between the U.S. and China later. Roosevelt had to work with Chiang Kai Shek, because the alternative was Mao and the Communists, but Stillwell knew Chiang was incompetent, and made the mistake of saying so."

"It looks like the Americans over in Burma didn't do the majority of the fighting. Just trained the Kachins – the Burmese mountain people – and then worked behind the lines to disrupt the Japanese." Sam looked thoughtful. "By the time your dad got over there, it was quite a huge organization. That guy Eifler who started it all must have been quite a wild cowboy."

"Just crazy enough to get the job done," added Paul.

"And you can see how Barstow convinced them to let Dad join up," I added. "Dad knew Burmese as well as Japanese and Chinese. The year he went, they were expanding the trained Kachins to 10,000 to help the Allied armies who were finally coming down the Burma Road from China."

"Also," Celeste added, leafing through the pages until she found the one she wanted. "It says that in addition to volunteers adept at languages, they had radio operators, and those skilled in logistics, engineering, explosives, and medicine, not to mention the pilots and those able to parachute. Dad knew a bit about explosives and engineering from the farm, and I bet his experience with the ham radio was an added bonus."

"As for parachutes," I said as I got up and retrieved the silk-wrapped journal from the hall closet where I had stored it earlier, "I still can't picture our father strapping himself into one and vaulting out of an airplane." I held out the package. Sam took it and slipped the silk off the cover.

"Yet, that's what this is, parachute silk."

"Someone could have given it to him," I countered.

"But," added Annie, "you notice it said the country was too dangerous to infiltrate by land and that all the agents had to drop in by parachute."

"Well," put in Celeste, "time to cut to the chase and find out just exactly what Dad did in this amazing group."

"Celeste, we decided you should be the reader," I offered.

Celeste looked at me to see if I was being irritating again. She must have decided I was for real, so she curtsied and said, "Aw, shucks, folks!" She reached for the journal, which Sam gave her while I regained my spot next to Celeste on the love seat.

"Go for it, Cel."

"Okay. Ladies and Gentlemen. Here we go."

* * *

By the time Celeste read the last entry about Dad freezing in combat, the only sound I could hear was the slight lapping of the water on the lake. I looked around. Everyone seemed lost in his or her own thoughts. I decided to breach the silence. "No wonder he had nightmares."

"Even men who didn't kill the enemy had reactions if they were involved in heavy fighting," Sam offered.

"Did that happen often?" asked Celeste. "I'd think the first instinct would be to tear the son of a bitch apart."

At this, Sam's eyes darkened, wandered to the photo of Dad, then stared into space. I noticed him reaching into his pocket again to pop something into his mouth.

Paul replied to Celeste, "Actually, Celeste, it did happen a lot. Most wars have had more non-firers than those who killed. In World War Two only about fifteen to twenty percent fired at the enemy at any given time."

"How did you know that, Paul?" I asked.

"I'm a History Channel buff." He sat back. "When you think of it, the experience Dad described must have been the thing that pushed him to work so hard after the war. Maybe he was trying to regain some of the self respect he felt he lost while in Burma."

"Makes more sense than trying to make up for getting drunk with the General Strike protesters back at Oxford and missing his exams," I said. Sam focused on me at this, silently interested again in the conversation.

Celeste changed the subject. "I was struck by how often he wrote about missing us and Mum. He used to tell me about the evening star thing when I went away to college. It's a touching picture of him sitting out and looking at it for some connection to us."

Annie's soft voice slid in. "He sure sounded lonely and was expressing doubts about being over there even before this last incident."

"And if he had a reaction to his combat, I bet he was also struggling about having encouraged Hank to sign up," Sam joined in again.

"Folks, we can run this around in circles, or I can read the next part. It is dated July 26, 1945, pretty close to the end of the Pacific war, so chances are it might give us some more clues to dear old Dad. It's only a few pages." Celeste leafed through the notebook. "Then there isn't anything else."

"Read on, then, Cel," Paul encouraged. Celeste began reading again.

CHAPTER NINETEEN

July 26, 1945

I'm on my way home. My work with the Kachins was completed at the beginning of July, but I was sent south for a couple of weeks, then it took time to sort things out and find out which ship I was supposed to take. This ship isn't as comfortable as the one that brought me out here. It is very crowded, we only get two meals a day, and there is hardly any room on deck. I have claimed a small space by the railing, as I still can't stand the smell below-deck, and the drone of the engines is especially aggravating. Also I find that I am very tired and feel a sense of loss at leaving my Kachin comrades behind.

I found this journal in my backpack, wrapped in an old piece of parachute silk. So much has happened since I started writing it seven months ago. I wonder about Adrienne and the children. I feel so far away from them. The last time I was on a ship returning to Adrienne, she was with me a hundred percent, much to my surprise. Will she still be that way? I've changed and maybe she has also. I wonder too, if Hank made it home.

However, I can brood about these things over which I have no control, or I can use the time I have left to jot down some more experiences before I get swept up into life back home.

The group I arrived with was sent to train the largest number of Kachins yet. But my participation was minor compared to the guys who were over there for the duration, many of whom are legends. One of them, "Skittles" had an ability with languages, especially the Burmese dialects, that makes me look like a Kindergarten student.

For myself, I have never encountered an environment like Burma, from my first parachute jump into the jungle to my last meal of leaf-wrapped rice, chicken, and monkey meat. The monsoon season challenged every bit of my claustrophobia. The fog prevented any sun from getting through the thick canopy of jungle to the extent that I started looking like something that had spent its life under a rock. Mosquitoes were the least of the insects that surrounded us. Although I avoided coming down with malaria, I had a bad case of dysentery that only responded to chewing opium. I was fairly useless for several days. I found also that the rice liquor we bought in bamboo shoots in the villages packed a wallop. It certainly did the trick to get to sleep after exhausting days that left me too keyed-up to relax.

We all did our part, but it was the Kachins who really won the war over there. Without their fierce nature combined with loyalty, dependability and courage, not to mention jungle skills, we would have lost many more men than we did. I certainly wouldn't be alive if it hadn't been for Naw Hpraw, something that shames me still.

An odd thing happened to me with Naw Hpraw. I was the one indebted to him, yet one day he handed me a pouch with something in it. "Duwa," he said in his mountain dialect meaning 'boss', "someone brought these from the mines at Mogok." I opened the pouch, and in it were six stones about the size of a peach pit. Four looked like red bottle glass, two were oddly bumpy, milky blue with a star shape on them. I wasn't sure what I was looking at. "Keep them," he said.

"I can't," I replied. "I almost cost your cousin his life."

"You are still my friend and comrade," he said as he put the stones in my hand, folding my fingers around them. "Besides, if they are worth what I suspect they are, you can bring my grandson to America."

I had heard stories about stones that might be precious, but most of the men laughed and threw them away. Something told me not to. So I told him I would keep the stones for him and at the proper time send for his grandson, since I had faith that Naw Hpraw would survive to return to his village to have one. With my short-wave radio at home, I plan to keep in touch with him and others. I keep the stones on me where no snooping fingers can find them. When I return, I will show them to Adrienne and we can find out their value. For now it is almost dark, so I will return to my bunk and try to get some sleep.

August 12, 1945

The war is over! Just as our ship reached the Persian Gulf, we received two radio flashes, first about an atomic bomb having been dropped on Hiroshima, and a couple of days later another one on Nagasaki. The ship is going bonkers! A few more days and we should be passing the Statue of Liberty. Then I will be just a train ride away from my dear family. I can only hope that our reunion will be a blessing and that I can make up for some of my war-time mistakes, bringing some of the dedication that I observed in Burma to my life at home. I must close now, as my shipmates are pestering me to come join in the celebration.

***

Celeste finished reading. The silence that followed settled among us like a thick blanket of snow after a winter storm.

Celeste sighed, "Opium, huh. Boy I would have been out of commission for a lot longer than that!"

"Yeah," added Sam. "I knew some guys who smoked it in 'Nam. Glad I stuck with pot."

"Well," added Paul, "he seemed to use it medicinally just that once, although the rice liquor sounded like a regular habit."

"Whoo," responded Celeste, "That reminded me of Greek Retsina."

"If it was anything like the rice wine in Vietnam, it would have been potent stuff," added Sam. "I went off-base once and drank some of that. I passed out on a rock while returning, and didn't make it back to base on time." He shook his head. "The MPs were not a happy lot. They were considering charging me with being AWOL. Instead, my C.O. had me burning grass for a day."

I was thinking this was turning into an interesting exchange, when Annie interrupted the alcoholic reminiscing to say, "I felt sorry for those poor mules."

"I'm glad Dad was as scared of jumping as I was," added Paul.

"Were you a paratrooper?" asked Sam.

"Yes. I was in Officer Candidate School, and it was the thing for the OCS guys to do. I found it a bit amusing, as I was rejected from the infantry because of my eyesight, but they decided I could jump out of airplanes as long as I put my glasses in my shirt pocket. Now what's wrong with that picture?"

We all laughed. Sam said, "No one ever accused the military of being logical."

"I don't know about you," said Celeste, "but I'll need to read this a few more times to let the details sink in. Do you mind if I take the journal home for a day or two?"

Paul shook his head.

"Okay by me," I said. "I lost concentration on the rest of it when Dad wrote about the stones that his Kachin friend gave him, and that he was going to consult Mum about finding out their value when he returned."

"That was a thought stopper. I don't remember either of them ever talking about anything like that," Paul said.

"And," Celeste added, "we didn't exactly live like kings, so maybe they weren't worth anything after all."

"Just one more brain teaser for you guys," added Sam. "I used to feel like my parents had secrets, but compared to what you've experienced, it was nothing."

"What secrets did your parents have?" I asked.

"Well," smiled Sam, "if I had known, they wouldn't have been secrets, now would they?"

"Duh, Pru." I hit my forehead with the palm of my hand.

Sam watched me and said, "Sorry about that crack. The comments you all throw around are starting to stick to me. To answer your question differently Pru, I always thought there was some unspoken reason why we left for Canada the same year your mother died. Then there was the fact that Mum and Dad weren't particularly close. She did the church, he worked in the bush. They didn't spend a whole lot of time together."

"Did you ever ask your Dad about it?" asked Celeste with her usual directness.

"No, but I was thinking about it the other day. All of this

mystery around how your Mum died has given me some incentive to do so."

"So where do we go from here?" I asked. "We've sort of solved the mystery of what Dad did in the war."

"And why he felt so responsible for Hank," added Sam.

"I wonder if Dad ever told him or Mum about the incident in Burma," said Paul.

"Or told her about the stones," offered Annie.

"Then of course we come back to why Dad left Mum's coat hanging in the woods and if the reason is connected to any of this." My comment caused everyone to look off into space. Paul brought us back.

"With all these questions, good thing Ed said he would talk to us again," said Paul.

"Kind of hard to do on the telephone though," countered Celeste.

"What about Jess?" I suggested.

"What do you mean?" asked Annie.

"When I talked to her on the phone, she said she was willing to do research if needed. We could ask her to visit Ed since they're in the same city. Maybe she could tape the conversation and express mail it to us."

"Good idea," said Paul. "Have her ask him if he knew anything else about Dad's tour over there, about the stones, about that promise Dad made to Naw Hpraw, whether he ever had a grandson…"

"And about Hank," Sam interrupted. "More about what he was like when he returned and how your dad dealt with him."

"And if Ed remembered anything about the farm accident," put in Celeste.

"And if he knew anything about the day your Mum died or what happened to her coat. After all, next to Hank, he seems to have been your father's best friend." Annie added the thought that was on my mind.

"Whoa! I will have to write this down while I remember. If you're hungry, want to take out the salad and other stuff so we can eat?"

I found Sam's pad of paper and sat in the living room to write down all the questions we had just thrown around. By the time I had finished, everyone else was sitting down at the table.

Maybe it was the hot weather or because we were all saturated with unfamiliar information, but dinner was surprisingly light and fun. Annie did imitations of some of the readers at the poetry get-togethers. Sam told stories about the American tourists who used his outfitting business. Celeste talked about the new horse she had received from Glen, and told the others how he sent not only the horse but his granddaughter as well to learn from Celeste. I had some more questions about Glen, but I figured they could wait. Paul told us more about his secret wish to be an architect and I reminded him about the folder of Mum's drawings I mentioned earlier. This time he responded more positively and said he might check it out. The only slightly uncomfortable note was brought on by me asking Sam about his earlier comment.

"Sam, are we really that sharp with each other?"

"You're kidding again, right?" answered Sam. The rest of my family looked at him intently.

"No, I am very serious." I replied.

Sam took a deep breath. "Yes, you are. Particularly you and Celeste."

Celeste turned to him and in her best Miss Piggy accent responded, "Moi?"

"I rest my case," said Sam.

"I think it must be a family trait from both sides," offered Paul. "It began as humor, trying to outwit each other. Somewhere along the line, the barbs became sharper and sharper until the only response was to be on your guard and sling them back at the other person. After a while you felt like a fish that has been caught and thrown back too many times."

"Not to mention, you never knew where the other person was coming from," added Celeste, now serious.

Which is exactly the point, I thought. I realized I did that even without Celeste, mostly with David or with colleagues I didn't trust, to protect myself.

"Good call, Paul." He smiled at my rhyme.

"Paul is rarely like that at home," said Annie, "but it sure is interesting to see how easily he drops back into it with you two."

"Thank you, Sam." Celeste gave him a wicked smile. He looked like he still couldn't tell if she was being serious or not. I couldn't either.

We then veered off into safer subjects, but I wondered about the brittle wit we all used. Maybe it was something else that could change. I was looking forward to talking with Jess. She and Adrian were two people I wasn't snide with. I wondered if they had learned it however, and whom in their lives they impaled with a sharp tongue.

After Celeste, Paul, and Annie left, I thanked Sam for bringing up the topic of our family communication style.

He said, "The first time I noticed it was when you and I were talking the other night. I would say something complimentary, and you would give me a funny look like you were wondering if I meant it. It started to bother me. Then when I was here earlier with you and Celeste, it really hit me. That's one reason I took off."

"I told Celeste, but she didn't think so."

"Even after all the years you've been apart, you and Celeste especially are so invested in being right with each other. It doesn't have to be that way, Pru. Sometimes it's okay if you just disagree."

This man was definitely direct when he wanted to be. "I think Cel and I started to work on that after the flashback about the day Mum died, but it is so ingrained it'll take some time."

"At least you're aware, now. That's the first step." Sam's smile revealed his infrequent dimple.

I nodded. "By the way," I said, changing the subject. "Would you mind if I rode to St Cloud with you and your dad tomorrow? You could drop me off at the Sheriff's Department while you take him to the doctor. Maybe you could see if they'll take the fur bits at the lab. After that, if you were planning to visit Hank, I would like to go with you."

There was silence, then, "Sure, that's fine. I mentioned visiting Hank to Dad. He wants to go too since they knew each other back in the old days. Dad would like to see you as well."

"Are you sure? You sound hesitant."

"Just have to readjust my thoughts on how many people I have to interact with at once tomorrow. I'll pick you up at ten, okay?"

After he left, I took Velvet for a short walk down the wood path before I called Jess. Then with the evening cooling off, Velvet and I sat on the deck while Jess and I talked. She was excited that she could help and wrote down the questions we wanted her to ask. Before she hung up, she told me that Adrian had called the other day and wanted to pass on a message for me to call him Monday when he would be back from a logging job in a remote part of Vancouver Island. She couldn't tell me anything more than that, so I would have to wait to find out from Adrian what was going on. Before I went to bed, I thought about calling David, but I was feeling pretty good and was looking forward to a half-way contented sleep in the bed as opposed to the deck. At this point I was afraid that contact with him would wreck that idea. Maybe I'd call him during the day which was less fraught with emotional shadows. With that, Velvet and I climbed upstairs, she to stretch out on the deck and I to finally indulge myself in the mystery novel I had brought but hadn't yet found time to read.

CHAPTER TWENTY

By morning, the temperature was still in the high 60s. Keeping the windows open the night before to the mild breeze from the lake had cooled it down barely enough to sleep comfortably. When I let Velvet out I realized I was looking forward to putting the fence up. It would give Velvet more freedom and me more security. That thought made me wonder for whom I was building the fence. Like many of my recent thoughts, I pushed it to the background. After showering and dressing in a sleeveless dress and sandals, I switched to the local weather station on the small TV in my father's study. Hot and staying that way – unless it got hotter. Conditions were ripe for tornadoes or heavy straight-line winds.

Good old Midwestern weather. Tornado touchdowns were the fear of everyone this time of year. Avon was near what they called Tornado Alley, a path that started in Sauk Centre, ran to Albany and Tower Hill, then swung North to Pine Lake and Two Rivers Lake, or South to Cold Spring. Most of the time the twisters skipped Avon, but it still received its share of strong straight-line winds. The 1958 tornado that tore the Zeimetz farm apart happened just before I was sent off East. Dad and I helped them clean up and Dad donated money to the local fund at the Credit Union. I even gave my monthly allowance of ten dollars. Thinking of this, another positive memory of Dad popped up – sitting with him on the deck and watching the lightning rip the sky apart above the lake ahead of the booming thunder. Dad would hold me tight so I'd feel safe. Of course, we had a portable radio on to tell us if a twister was coming our way.

I switched the TV off and turned back into the kitchen for breakfast. After eating, I sat in the shade with my tea and called the Sheriff's Department. I asked for Donna and was told that she was in a meeting, but would be available by 10:30 AM. I left my name and a message that I would be stopping by. *That* would surprise her. It had been five years since I had last seen Donna. Since graduate school, we often chose similar conferences to go to, as she was a designated specialist in crimes against children. We enjoyed our conference friendship and were known to ditch some of the sessions to hang out at the pool or explore the locale where the conference was held.

Right at ten, Sam bounced down the driveway. I gathered up my purse, water, and the baggies with the fur bits. I closed up the house to keep it from getting any warmer and left Velvet in. As I approached the car, I noticed that Sam had already picked up his dad who filled the seat next to him. Sam got out of his side to let me in the back seat. As I squeezed in, I noticed the car had been cleaned up. Only Sam's sleeping bag sat rolled up on the seat. I moved it over. When Sam got back in, I complimented him on his tidying job.

"I was impressed as well. You must rate as he sure doesn't clean it up for me!" Elias growled, then turned and grinned at me. He had Sam's smile, and a thatch of white hair that was thick and combed back. And he was big – broader than Sam and just as tall. The two of them looked quite comic wedged into this little car. But instead of Sam's soft brown eyes, Elias' were ice blue and looked right through me. His nose was hooked and dominated a large full-lipped mouth. He had raging Andy Rooney eyebrows and white tufts of hair growing out of his ears with abandon. He was a little intimidating.

"Nice to see you again sir," I replied. I smiled back and we shook hands over the seat.

"None of that 'sir' stuff, young lady. Just call me Elias." His hold on my hand belied his gruff tone.

"I'll do anything for someone who calls me "young lady", I answered.

"Ah, Sam," he addressed his son, but still looking over his shoulder at me, "she's a charmer just like her mother."

"That's nice Dad. Are you done holding hands with her? 'cause I can't see to back up."

"Yeah, yeah, yeah," he grumped.

I squeezed Elias' hand, and he let go. He turned back around.

"Yep," Elias continued, "you even look like her. Do you ever get told that?"

"Not recently. In my twenties when there were still some folks around who remembered her."

"Here's someone to confirm you still resemble her. Her hair had white streaks just like yours. Did you get yours early?"

"Yes. I had a skunk stripe down the right side when I was twenty-one."

"Beautiful woman, your mother." Elias seemed to drift off. I caught Sam's eye in the rear view mirror. He nodded as if making up his mind about something.

"Speaking of which, Dad, did you ever have a thing for Pru's Mom? I've always wondered."

"Why do you go and say something like that in front of Pru?" Elias avoided answering the question.

"It's okay, Elias," I reassured him. "I'm curious, too."

"It's just that I never quite figured out why we left Avon so quickly after Pru's Mum died," Sam went on.

There was a silence while Elias seemed to weigh something in his mind. When he finally spoke to Sam it sounded like a schoolmaster scolding a disappointing student. I wondered what a lifetime of that had been like for Sam.

"Samuel, Adrienne was beautiful, smart, and very kind, which was a knock-out combination." He paused. "Your mother often seemed more interested in the church than me, and Adrienne and I had our love of politics in common. We spent a considerable amount of time together. But," and here he sighed and dropped his voice, "she never had eyes for anyone but Arthur."

"Not even after the war when he was off doing all his consulting work?" I asked.

The schoolmaster was back. "That was a very difficult time for her, you must understand, Pru. I was happy to be her friend and soundin' board. But it wasn't like these days. You didn't just rush in and ruin a whole bunch of lives because of what you wanted.

No, I kept my distance." Another drop in his voice. "I don't think she ever knew how I really felt."

Sam kept at his Dad. "Was it because of how you felt about Pru's mom that we moved after she died?"

"You're pretty persistent today, Sam. Yes, if you must know. The reminders of Adrienne here were too painful for me, and I thought maybe a new place might give us all a fresh start."

"Did it work?" I asked, interested if someone else had succeeded in a geographical solution.

"To some extent." Elias combed his big gnarled hands through his hair. "Didn't change Sam's mother and me much, though. She was still bound to the church and I went off into the bush, but it gave the boys some stability."

"How come you never told me this before?" Sam glanced at his father.

"Never asked." The growl in Elias' voice told us the subject was closed. Sam heeded the message as he didn't follow up. However, I had a few questions.

"Why did you come back now? You're obviously in better health than many who live at assisted living places."

"Been to one of those places recently?" He looked over his shoulder at me, his eyebrows waggling.

I shook my head, thinking back to some I had visited about ten years ago.

"Didn't think so. They've changed. Lots more folks like me, who are tired of cuttin' the lawn and makin' our own dinners, who want some companionship our own age. Many of these places are more like a community center of condos than like the old fashioned nursin' homes."

"My apologies. I just assumed you had some health reasons for deciding to live there." I was thinking about Sam's earlier comment that his dad was getting a bit drifty. There I went, assuming again, and with a cantankerous old man who, come to think of it didn't seem drifty at all.

"No offense taken, Pru. You're just ignorant, and I don't take ignorance personally. After Sam's mother died, I decided I wanted to be among the memories of your mother. And after the explosion at the mine near where we lived, Sam needed to get down here to the Veterans Administration hospital, so..."

Sam nudged him with his elbow, and said through gritted teeth," Dad..."

"What? Oh, never mind, son. You're too sensitive about that."

"I don't care. Would you cut it out?" Sam's tone was now almost as gruff as his Dad's.

Elias must have heard something in it because he said, "All right, all right," then turned to look out the window.

Silence. Not only had I been called ignorant recently by both father and son, but I suddenly felt like I was in sixth grade when two friends started whispering in front of me and I was the only one who wasn't in on the secret. I sat back and glanced at Sam in the mirror. He avoided eye contact. It was clear he wasn't about to explain what just happened. After a bit I decided to return to the more distant past. That seemed to be a safer subject with these two. I leaned forward.

"Did you see my Mum any time before she died?"

"What?" Again, I had broken into some sort of reverie. I repeated myself.

"Yes," Elias answered. "I normally saw her every few weeks for Democratic committee meetin's. Just that mornin' I had given her a ride to and from one in St Cloud. She had to get back right after the meetin' to attend to some business before gettin' ready to go out East to see your grandparents. Was pretty closed-mouthed about what that was."

I took a deep breath and said, "Was she wearing her fur coat by any chance?" This time Sam slid his eyes in my direction in the mirror. I waited.

"You mean that big old fancy thing your father bought her? Wasn't wearin' it, but she had already pulled it out for her trip. That time of the year it was as likely to snow as to rain, here or out East."

"Do you remember what she did with it?"

"It was thrown over the newel post at the bottom of the stairs. I remember because I asked her if she was goin' to wear it to the meetin'. We knew it was goin' to be a meetin' full of posturin' and power plays, and your mother said that was the time to wear her jewels and furs. One of the few lessons she actually gave your grandmother credit for. But it was too warm that day, workin' up to a thunderstorm, so she left it at home."

"What time did you bring her back?" I asked.

"Good Lord, woman," he turned and gave me an eyeful again. "That was a long time ago!"

"Can you guess?" I persisted.

"You're just as bad as him." He cocked his head towards Sam. "You must have interestin' conversations. Does anyone get a word in edgewise?"

"Please, Elias, it's important."

"All right. Let me think. It was a breakfast meetin' about nine-ish. Went on for about an hour. I remember because they had to table some items since they didn't have a quorum that day. Adrienne was happy 'cause it meant she could get home earlier and not be so rushed. Then it took about twenty minutes to drive back to Avon." The old man paused. "Maybe around 10:30 or so? Oh, and I don't know if this means anythin' but, I think Arthur was comin' to pick her up as I left. As I pulled out of the driveway, I saw your father's car in my rearview mirror."

This time Sam and I definitely made eye contact. "I don't think that was Dad, Elias. He was still at the University at that time. When they couldn't reach Mum a little later that day when I fell from the tree, they tried Dad and they couldn't get him out of class to take me home, so Grandma Dillen had to come and get me."

"You mean the tree my son convinced you to climb?" His eyes twinkled for a change.

"The very one." I decided not to add the part about just recently remembering all that.

THE COAT IN THE WOODS

"Then why was Adrienne in such a hurry to get back to the house? She gave the definite impression that it was important she had to get back to take care of somethin' before she left. I just assumed it was with your father." Elias looked puzzled.

"Dad, did you ever tell the police all this?" It was Sam's turn to sound like the parent.

Elias looked at Sam, then back at me. He frowned. "Nope."

"How come?" I jumped in.

"Never asked." The growl was muted to a guttural whisper.

As we turned onto the highway leading to St Cloud, the only sounds were the hot wind whishing by the open windows and the cars passing us. Sam's car barely went the highway minimum speed. All of a sudden I thought of something.

"Elias, you knew Hank, right?"

"Hank Oink? A good man. Only someone with a sense of humor like his could have tolerated that nickname. Hope I get to chat with him later today. He and your father were like brothers. He was such a hard worker, did his old man proud with that farm. And that old crossed eyed pig of his!" Elias stopped to laugh at some memory. "Was the smartest creature on four legs. Reminded me of the pig in that old story about the spider."

"*Charlotte's Web*?" I offered.

"Yeah, that one. In the old days when your Grandpa was alive, we had some great times all workin' on the farm. Sometimes it seems as if those times were yesterday instead of the other way around." His tone was wistful.

"Could it have been Hank you saw when you were leaving?"

Elias didn't even hesitate on that. "Naw, Hank had a truck. The vehicle I saw was a see-dan, gray like your dad's. That's why I thought it was him. Besides Hank didn't visit much with folks. Just stayed on the farm. One of the things Adrienne used to talk about – Arthur worryin' about Hank."

"Do you know why he was let go as manager?" I decided to try another tack.

"Somethin' about your Grandma not bein' able to trust him anymore. He couldn't work the machinery like he used to, I think." He stopped, then started up again. "Too bad, though, he was a brave man. About my age. He didn't have to go to war but wanted to. Used to go off for war talk with your Dad and that fella who visited."

I followed a hunch. "Mr. Barstow?"

"Yeah, Ted..."

"Ed," I corrected.

"Right. Your mother used to tell me she felt left out of all that. Before the war when that Ed fellow visited, we'd all pass the time talkin' about farmin' or loggin' or such. But afterwards, the three of them just kinda kept to themselves. Never really trusted him."

"Why not?"

"Dunno. Was just kinda slippery. Never gave you a straight answer. I don't think I ever found out what he actually did for a livin'." At this, Elias seemed to run out of steam as he put his head back on the headrest and closed his eyes. A low snore rumbled from his throat. I leaned in towards Sam.

"Does he do that often?" I whispered.

"You don't have to whisper, he'll be out until we pull up to the Sheriff's Department. Happens mostly when he is riding in the car. I think it's left over from when he was off logging in the woods for days. When he finally got picked up, he'd crash."

"Oh, good. I was thinking he had narcolepsy or something. Otherwise he seemed pretty sharp to me. I thought you said his mind wandered."

Sam focused on the highway. "I know I did. It was because I didn't want to tell you why I really came back here."

"You mean for the VA hospital?"

"Yeah. Sorry, Pru."

"Don't be. You don't owe me any explanation." I decided to change the subject. "It'll be interesting to see your dad and Hank together. I wonder if Hank will remember him." Sam gave a 'we'll see' shrug then put his right blinker on, and we exited the highway at Crossroads, wending our way down Division towards downtown and the Law Enforcement Center. It was almost 10:30 AM when we pulled into the parking lot. Elias stirred and looked around.

Sam said, "I'll pick you up at noon, Pru. Dad's appointment is at eleven, but I don't know how long we'll have to wait for his lab work. Then I have to find out if I can give the lab our little fur samples." He held out his hand for the two baggies I had stuffed into my purse.

"I'd say I'd walk up to the clinic once I was done, but it is way too hot. If Donna can't take a break, I'll go over to Bravos to get a burrito and a cool drink." With all the pavement around us, the temperature felt like it was in the nineties. I hoped we could get our business done and retreat back to the country as quickly as possible. Sam got out of the car to let me out. I grabbed my purse and water, patted Elias on the shoulder and slipped out. Sam flopped back into the car, his hair already curling around his temples. He reached into the glove compartment to retrieve a blue bandanna which he folded and put around his head, native style, before driving off.

CHAPTER TWENTY ONE

As Sam drove off, I turned and started towards the Law Enforcement Center. It had been built several years ago to house the county jail as well as both the Stearns County Sheriff's Office and the St Cloud Police Department. It stood in Courthouse Square with the county office building on its left and the courthouse itself facing it. It was made of granite that some said came from abroad rather than the town of Cold Spring twenty miles away. An arched glass window soared above the main door. Inside, if you needed to visit anyone in the jail, you went up the center stairs. The reception desk on the left served the Police Department, while the one on the right led to the Sheriff's Department. I walked towards this one, gave my name to the officer there and told her I was here to see Donna Mertens. I gave her my license and another I.D. She wrote something down, and returned it to me. She then asked to search my purse. I was glad I didn't have my Swiss Army knife with me. Having decided I would pass, she told me to sit in one of the green plastic chairs against the wall and picked up the phone. She must have reached Donna, because no sooner had she put the receiver down than Donna came bursting through the locked door behind the reception desk.

"Girl! Why didn't you tell me you were coming to Minnesota?" Donna swept me into a surprisingly strong hug for a woman as petite as she. But then I'd seen her biceps. Her muscular torso always took me by surprise, especially after seeing her out of uniform and all dressed up. You would have thought she had just stepped off the pages of Vogue. She used to tell me her secret was a sister her size who was a banker and hated wearing outfits more than a few times. The only things of her sister's Donna couldn't wear were the more fitted shirts, blouses and jackets. Today, she was wearing a severe looking blue suit, softened by a cream-colored silk blouse. Short heeled pumps graced her slender legs. She had risen in the ranks to detective about six years ago, and said she was happy the day she shed the heavy utility belt that came along with the patrol uniform. I hugged her back then put her at arms length.

"You look great, Donna, as usual! I love your hair!" Today it was worn in loose curls softly curving towards her mocha face. Her beautiful brown eyes rose above an aristocratic nose that any African princess would have envied.

"Thanks," she replied. "I had to grow it out after the dreadlock stage. It grew back natural, so I decided to leave the color out." Her hair had gone from black to red and many shades in between in the time we had been friends. She looked me over. "You look – different."

Oh great, I thought. Out loud I said, "Bad different, or good different?"

"I'm not sure. Tell me why you're here and maybe that will help me figure it out." Donna ushered me to the locked door which buzzed as the officer let us in. I followed her to a functional but roomy office. She closed the door, brought her chair from behind the desk so it joined her visitor's chair, and sat down. She motioned me to the other chair and looked at me, her elbows on the arms of her chair, her chin resting on her steepled fingers. "So give," she commanded.

And give I did, including the argument with David that had catapulted me on the strange journey of the last two weeks. I told her about my gut- wrenching reactions to remembering past events, about meeting Sam again – her eyebrows raised at this part – and about the gathering of my siblings to figure out our "sordid family history". I described what was left of the fur coat in the woods, told her what I knew about how Mum had died, and then got to the point of my visit.

"We were wondering if you could check the old files to see if there was any mention of Mum's fur coat in the description of the crime scene."

"You mean the cold files?"

"I don't know. Is it considered such?" I hadn't thought of that.

Donna rolled her chair back to the desk and started tapping at her computer. She asked me for the year and date of Mum's death. I gave it to her. After about ten minutes, she stood up.

"Come on, it is a cold file. We get to take a trip across the street to the courthouse basement." With that, she strode out of her office, greeting a few people in the hall as she cruised by, me in her wake like a somewhat shabbier dinghy to her gleaming sailboat. Stepping back out into the heat took my breath away and I was puffing while trying to keep up with her as she climbed the courthouse steps. Soon we were back into marble coolness. We approached the elevator and took it down to the basement where we found a policeman at a desk who looked like he had taken one too many trips to the local donut shop. He was the sentinel to the room that held the cold files. Donna signed us both in. We entered a large space filled with rows of floor to ceiling shelves, holding hundreds of rectangular boxes, with names and dates written on the ends. My head reeled.

"Are all these cases unsolved?" I asked.

Donna nodded. "Sad, isn't it? We have a combined task force for cold cases, but it hardly makes a dent." I looked up and noticed we were in the "D's". Then I saw something that froze my heart: the date of my mother's death, and in black capital letters, DILLEN, ADRIENNE. I must have made a noise because Donna appeared from somewhere with a chair.

"Here, sit. You don't look too good. I'm sorry, Pru. I was so focused on helping I didn't even think about how this might affect you. I shouldn't have brought you down here."

I sat and stared at the box. "It makes it so real, Donna. I just learned a few days ago that she didn't just have a heart attack and here it is in black and white, literally. What's in the box or don't I want to know?"

"For one thing, I think it is too small for a fur coat if that answers any questions."

THE COAT IN THE WOODS 157

That made me laugh. "We have the coat. We just want to find out if it was Mum's. Go ahead, take the box down."

"Are you sure?" Donna asked even as she reached for it.

I nodded. She pulled the box down and put it on a table at the end of the row used for this purpose. I stayed in the chair while she opened the top. I wanted her to tell me what was in there first before I looked. She peered in.

"It's safe. It's just a file. She opened it and skimmed through it. "You want me to read it to you? The medical examiner's report is in here as well."

I thought of the forensic TV shows we had accused Sam of watching. "No, thanks. Can you just give me the gist of it?"

Donna nodded as she read. "She died from hitting the back of her head on the iron woodstove as she fell. There is some discussion here about why she fell, if she tripped on something, if she slipped, or if she was pushed."

I stared at the file. This was what my mother was reduced to. No essence left, no warmth of surrounding arms, no laughter, no smart comments, no thoughtful gestures. Just a box and a manila file. I wished I was back at the house or even better, in the woods where I could feel Mum's presence to some extent. But I had volunteered to find out what I could about the coat, so I wasn't going to turn back now.

"Is there any note about a full-length fur coat? Maybe that's what she slipped or tripped on. Any comment about that possibility?"

Donna continued to read. "Let's see. Here is the crime scene description. The doors to the sideboard were open along with a drawer above them. Both empty. It says the kitchen was surprisingly tidy. Two teacups along with a small cream pitcher were washed and turned upside down in the dish drainer. The kettle was empty of water, the partially empty cream bottle was back in the fridge, and the sugar bowl sat in the cupboard. The only odd thing they found was in the garbage. It had been emptied recently, but there were two paper napkins and three teabags."

"So, she had two visitors for tea?" I asked.

"Maybe," Donna replied. "It says that two of the teabags were twisted around each other, so maybe it was just one visitor who liked strong tea. No mention of a coat of any kind, much less a fur coat, which would be unique enough to comment on. There's an added note that the deputies later found the silver in that old car.

"Celeste told me that. Did they find the man who supposedly had been burglarizing the other houses back then?"

Donna skimmed some more. "Nope. They mention him because they thought it might be the same guy who was involved in your mother's death. But if so, he vanished into thin air."

"Like Jacob Wetterling," I said, referring to a kidnapping in the Eighties that had never been solved.

Donna nodded. Sadly, she had just joined the department back then. "You know, none of us who worked on the Wetterling case ever really put that behind us. I can't imagine learning this about my mother. I'm so sorry, Pru."

Donna put the file back into the box and bent down to give me a hug. I hugged her back and let the tears come. She dug into her pocket and came up with a nicely pressed white lace handkerchief which she handed to me. It was enough to jog me out of my sadness.

"God, Donna, I can't blow my nose into that." I handed it back to her. "Here. I have some wadded up tissue somewhere." I dug into my purse and came up with some thin tattered pieces. We both started to giggle. I wiped my nose and stood up. "Let's get out of here." I took the box top and put it back on my mother's file box. I patted the box gently and gave it to Donna to return to its place next to its companions, each representing someone's mother or daughter, father or son. I turned to her.

"We took some of the fur pieces off the tree, put them in baggies and Sam is taking them to the lab to find out about getting them tested."

"For what?" Donna asked.

"DNA, if there were any skin scrapings, or maybe blood type. One of the fur pieces had a brown blotch on the inside, like maybe she was wearing the coat when she fell, and it soaked up some of the blood from her wound."

"You're Hollywooding it, Pru. Those fur bits have been out in the weather for years. Besides, the local labs won't take that stuff. You have to send it to the state lab. And pay," she added.

"Oh, and here I was hoping Sam would have something when we met up later. Do you have the address for the state lab?"

"If you are determined, it's in my desk. Let's get some iced coffee and then head back. I'll catch you up on life according to Donna."

By this time, we had reached the desk outside the room. Donna signed out and after glancing at each other over the portly officer's head, we climbed the steps instead of taking the elevator. We strolled to one of the coffee stands that sprouted on the mall during the summer. After paying for two frozen lattes, we found a spot in the shade on the wall near Herberger's. Donna caught me up on life in St Cloud, which for a black woman still wasn't the easiest existence. Discrimination was still rampant on many levels.

"I can't think of anyone better to keep hammering at it than you," I commented.

"You're sweet, but sometimes I get tired is all. It sure would be nice if you decided to stay here. I have some black women friends but not too many white girlfriends with your spunk."

"I feel like I have about as much spunk as a bear that has been turned into a rug."

"Maybe that's why you're here, to renew that spunk – get the fur back up and growling." She "grred" at me. I chuckled.

"I forgot how much you made me laugh. Actually, even Celeste has made me laugh once we got through the mutual discomfort of our first evening."

"Ooh! You *must* be in bad shape!" exclaimed Donna, who had heard all about Celeste from my perspective. "But seriously, it's good that you two are on speaking terms again."

"I agree. I wish I felt clearer about the rest of my life." I told her about the loving phone call from David.

"Oh, Girl, that man can be so sweet when he wants something. What does he want this time?"

"Me?" I ventured.

"Hate to tell you, Child, but he's had you for years and it hasn't helped. You've been Charlie Brown to his Lucy for so long, you don't know any other game to play. Just when you think things are going well and start to trust that he'll hold on to the ball this time, whump, he pulls it away and you land flat on your butt again. If you want my opinion," she paused, "and even if you don't," she smiled, "I'd say the sweetness this time is because if you aren't on the field, it's harder for him to get you to play. Maybe there is part of him that isn't sure you will return. You're not the only one who doesn't know any other game." As usual Donna didn't tiptoe around the subject.

"I know you're right. Somewhere in the last few days I've figured out that I'm so scared to be left alone that I'll play the game by any rules he makes up. Maybe by the time we get some closure to this whole business with Mum and Dad I'll know what to do."

Donna's face softened. "Don't count on it, Sugar. Sooner or later you'll just have to make a decision. Either way it's going to hurt." Her face became clouded, perhaps remembering the man in her life who didn't get it until she changed the locks. She looked at me again. "But hey, that's what girlfriends are for, right?" She reached over and squeezed my hand. I squeezed back, looking down at our hands, so different, yet so much the same. I caught sight of my watch. Twelve fifteen. I jumped up.

"I've got to go. Sam was coming back at noon to pick me up. They'll be frying, waiting in the car." I grabbed my cup and started back, throwing it into a trash can on the corner. Donna quickly caught up with me.

"So, what is Sam like? Are you interested?" She nudged me in the ribs as we walked.

"Oh, please, Donna, I've known him for about four days. And

obviously I'm not exactly looking for romance." We turned the last corner, and I saw the parking lot next to the courthouse.

"Which isn't answering my question," she persisted.

I scanned the lot and the street. No elderly Escort. I slowed down. "They're not here yet. Want to wait outside with me?"

"If you answer my question," Donna said.

"Oh for heaven's sake. No, I'm not interested in him romantically, but he is easy to talk to. He's funny and very nice, if a little odd," I added.

"Odd, how?" Donna asked. "Odd's not always bad. Sometimes it's interesting."

"True. He was in Vietnam as a combat medic with Special Forces, and sometimes he has reacted a little weirdly to things – like getting stuck in that still we found, or me saluting him in fun, or when we were talking about my dad's war experience. Sam spaced out and seemed like he wasn't there."

"That's because he was probably somewhere else. You're the psychologist. You know about Post Traumatic Stress Disorder."

"Yeah, but most of my experiences have been with child abuse or rape victims. I've never known a vet. All of our friends resisted the draft. With all that has been happening I didn't connect the dots."

"I've worked alongside guys who were in 'Nam. A lot of them became cops when they returned. Sometimes things just trigger old memories. Lord, Pru, when you think about what you experienced all those years ago and buried until the last few days, you probably have a bit of it yourself. Think of how you have been feeling then magnify that."

There was something in what she said that rang true. I wasn't willing to go further than that for now, but I mused that it was funny how you can help someone else with a problem and not know you have one that is similar. As I thought about Sam and put what I knew professionally together with what I had observed in him, it all made sense and explained his father's comment about coming back to the VA hospital because of an explosion at the mine. I bet that was one mother of a trigger. I told Donna this.

"Now you're thinking, Pru. Sounds like it's just as well you aren't interested in Sam beyond friendship. You don't need someone with problems like that in your life on top of what you're already dealing with."

Although somewhere inside I had been feeling the same in spite of some sort of pull that Sam and I seemed to have, just Donna saying it made me feel like defending him. After all, he had been nothing but kind and friendly to me. Luckily at that point I spied his car turning the corner. "Here they are. Come meet him and his Dad."

"I'll be right there. I'll just run in and get that state lab address."

I walked towards the car. Elias' face was red, perspiration dotting his forehead. Sam's bandanna was damp. Elias was looking a bit grumpier than even before.

"We need to eat before we go to the VA," Sam informed me, "otherwise Dad'll have me for lunch."

"I heard that!" Elias barked.

Sam started to explain to me why he couldn't leave the fur off at the lab, when Donna re-emerged with the address she'd promised. I introduced them, then said to Sam, "Donna already told me. That's what she was getting, the address to the state lab where we have to send the fur. She said we're on a wild goose chase."

Donna nodded behind me. "But it never hurts to try, if you don't mind paying the fee," she put in.

"Maybe we can all pitch in a bit if it is really pricey," suggested Sam. "If we don't, we'll never know either way."

"It's worth it to me," I said.

"So where are you off to now?" asked Donna. "Heading home out of the heat?"

"I wish," I answered. "First eat lunch, then after we mail the fur samples off, we're going to the VA hospital to talk to Hank, Dad's old friend. They say he isn't always lucid but if we catch him on a good day maybe he might remember something about the coat. Celeste said he seemed to be looking for something when he was living at the house."

"Now that sounds like an interesting time." Donna turned me to her and hugged me. "Take care, Girl, and call me if I can do anything else. Call me anyway and don't leave here without telling me, you hear?" She waved to the men. "Nice meeting you!" With that, she turned and took her gorgeous legs back inside, while Sam slipped out and let me in the back seat.

"Where to, Dad?" Sam asked. "Lunch is next on the agenda."

"The Family Buffet, where else? And not a moment too soon!" Elias finally grinned.

CHAPTER TWENTY TWO

The Family Buffet is one of those bright and cheery all-you-can-eat-for-one-flat-rate places. It seems to attract mostly families who can feed a large brood for minimal cost and still call it going out, and retired folks like Elias who enjoy the atmosphere and the selection, giving themselves permission to stray into foods that are otherwise banned from their diet. I hadn't been in one of these restaurants since the kids were younger, but I remembered the overstuffed feeling that accompanied me as I waddled back out to the car with the odd taste of too much MSG and salt in my mouth. This time, I restrained myself and had a salad, some soup, and a soft ice cream butterscotch sundae. I noticed that the men showed no such moderation, each making a couple of trips back to renew their plates with their favorite foods. I smiled to myself as Sam complained of feeling too full when we left, and I wondered how long Elias would last until he started snoring in the front seat again. He was asleep before we left the parking lot.

However, it was good to be fortified because any way you looked at it, the upcoming visit with Hank was likely to be a bit of a strain.

First we had to mail our fur-filled baggies to the state lab. Sam made our way to the Post Office on Division Street. I bought a padded envelope and placed the baggies in it along with a piece of paper with Celeste's name, address and phone number. I also wrote a brief note about what tests we wanted – blood type, if any, off the two different pieces of fur and DNA, if possible. I sealed and addressed the envelope, took it to the counter, and paid for the postage.

As I reemerged from the building, I declared, "That part was cheap. Less than a dollar!" Sam let me back into the car. I added, "Wait 'til Celeste gets the statement from the lab. Should we tell her I put her address on it or just let her hit the ceiling when they bill her?"

Sam gave me an Elias look. Oops, there I went again. Be nice, Pru. "Sorry." I settled back for the short trip to the VA.

Sam navigated Division Street until we turned left onto 15th St., left onto 8th Ave., then right on 44th which curved past Apollo High School towards the VA. As we turned left into the VA driveway, a sign announced a 10 mph limit with speed bumps enforcing it. A pretty display of flowers spelled out the hospital's name. We turned right and headed towards the main building. The American flag flapped in the breeze along with a VA Administration flag and the somber black POW/MIA one, which flew out of respect for those who were prisoners of war or missing in action during the Vietnam War. As we approached, arrows pointed around to the left for the senior housing. Once on the grounds of the hospital, Sam started acting like a tour guide. Elias slept on. People were coming and going, mostly older and mostly men, but women were scattered here and there on their own as well as with their spouses. There also were a number of younger veterans, "the babies" Sam explained, mostly from the 1990 Gulf War. He said many of them had returned with physical and psychological problems from both combat and the chemicals used, although the latter hadn't been proved in any of the studies. He pointed out the multicolored vans with names of local veteran's organizations which transported vets from smaller towns around St Cloud and beyond, as the St Cloud VA specialized in chemical dependency treatment. I noticed that the older men tended to wear baseball-styled caps designed for each branch of the military. As we drove by one old guy, you could see the name of his ship and WWII printed on it. Sam said it was interesting to read the caps as they told a multitude of stories about where the men and women had served. He remembered one gentleman who had on his hat, "WWII, Korea, Vietnam". When Sam stopped him to thank him for serving, he tipped his hat to Sam and then, his eyes twinkling, tapped his forehead, saying, "Some of us never learn!"

This was a whole new world to me. An amazing microcosm

of people with often terrible experiences in common, but also a connection unlike any other. We followed the arrows to the left. Blissfully there was one spot available in the shade. We parked with our back to the building. Over to the right stretched the wide expanse of the golf course which Sam told me in the early days was a farm providing vegetables to the hospital. The veterans of the first two World Wars housed at the hospital used to maintain it, and the staff discovered the work had a therapeutic effect on them. Back then, the agonies those vets experienced were simply termed 'shell shock' or 'battle fatigue'. Sam said the term "Post Traumatic Stress Disorder" didn't evolve until the many Vietnam veterans brought the awareness of war stress to a whole new level.

Elias woke up with a grunt as Sam opened his door. Wide awake, he was looking forward to seeing Hank again. When he voiced my earlier question about whether Hank would know who he was, Sam told him not to count on it too much. We all got out of the warm oven of Sam's car. The light breeze that I noticed with the flags cooled us off a bit. After the stultifying heat of downtown it was a nice change, but part of my brain wondered if it was the beginning of the storm front the weatherman had mentioned. Elias and I followed Sam's lead. He was definitely the expert, looking comfortable and confident about where he was going. We approached the old building of red brick and soon found ourselves in a plain hallway, walls painted the light green color favored by colleges and other institutions that falls somewhere between lime and vomit. Plain linoleum floors led down the hallway to a desk. Elias and I stood back as Sam asked for Hank. He was directed to a day room occupied by seven or eight old men. Some sat in wheelchairs, some in vinyl covered armchairs. Two men were playing cards, one man was reading a book with the help of a large magnifying glass, and one was talking to the only other visitor. The rest just sat by the windows looking out. A faint smell of urine mixed with strong disinfectant hung in the air. A burley assistant in his mid-thirties saw us approach and intercepted us. He asked us who we were and what our business was. Sam started to answer but I piped up instead.

"We're here to visit Hank MacTavish. He's an old friend of my father's and our family," I explained. "I wanted to say hi and see how he was doing."

"Oh, is Celeste your sister?" He had a gap-tooth smile.

"Yes," I answered, wondering if Cel had cast her spell on one more helpless male, and this one young enough to be her son.

"Oh, then it's fine. She has been so nice to Hank. Visits him regularly. Of course, he doesn't always recognize her."

"Yes, she told us," I answered.

"So you realize he might not know you either," he offered.

"That's okay, we'll just say hi anyway." I was hoping Hank might be somewhat coherent as I was at a dead end about the coat and he was our last try.

As the assistant walked over to one of the men sitting by the window, I hung back letting Elias and Sam go first. I noticed that Sam and the other visitor exchanged smiles. "Hank, you've got some guests." The assistant spoke loudly and leaned down to try to get eye contact with him.

Hank looked up from his gaze out the window. He wore his white hair in a short brush cut and his freckles still danced across his nose, turning into brownish blotches on his cheeks. I didn't remember noticing in the old pictures, but he had the deepest brown eyes I've ever seen. He surveyed Elias and Sam and turned back to the assistant. "I may be old, young man, but I'm not deaf!"

Good, I thought. He seems feisty today. Elias stepped forward.

"My feelings exactly. I don't know if you remember me from back at the farm. I'm Elias Barrett. Used to do the loggin' for the Dillens?" He reached out and shook Hank's hand. Hank shook it back and looked at him blankly for a moment. Then his eyes cleared.

"Well, I'll be a pig's uncle! Which I was if you remember. Don't tell me you're in this old soldier's place too?"

"No, I didn't serve in the war like you and Arthur. I've been living in Canada all these years. Just came back here to live my last days out in the good old U.S. of A." He pushed Sam forward a bit. "This here's my son, Sam. He brought me. He's a vet, too. Vietnam."

Hank looked Sam over. "Is this that little guy that used to come with you?" Elias nodded. "Good Lord, he's even bigger than you were! Course you've shrunk some."

"Haven't we all," replied Elias.

Hank continued to stare at Sam. "Vietnam, huh? Now there's some crazy bastards. Run into some of them down in OT. You crazy, young man?"

Sam didn't seem to take offense like I would have. "Sometimes," he answered quietly.

"So what're you all doing visiting old Hank for? Where's old Celeste? Now, she turned out to be one fine woman!"

"She's working with her horses," Sam said. We came to see you and to ask you something about Adrienne."

At this, I moved a bit from behind Sam. Hank caught the movement out of the corner of his eye. He turned in his chair and looked at me. All of a sudden the color drained from his face, leaving his freckles and blotches looking strangely white – like skin that has been in the water too long. Hank's brown eyes grew darker as he rose and came towards me. He looked at me closely, then hugged me so hard it felt like my ribs would break. He whispered, "Adrienne, I don't understand."

I pulled away and told him as gently as I could, "I'm Pru, Adrienne's daughter, Hank. Adrienne is dead."

"Dead?" he asked. Hank looked at me again, then beyond me. His gaze surveyed the room. He pushed me away roughly and moved towards the men playing cards. "You there, Soldiers," he barked, sweeping the cards off the table. "You will be all dead if you don't get your ass out of here and run for the cliff. You can't help those poor bastards in the water, now go!" Hank turned and tramped around the rest of the room in an erratic manner, disturbing the other men.

THE COAT IN THE WOODS 169

This caught the attention of the assistant who walked over quietly. "What's going on, Hank?"

Hank pushed his shoulders back. "Sergeant to you, Corporal. Now follow orders."

The assistant eyed us and saluted Hank. "Yes, Sir. But I need you to check on something, Sir." He took Hank by the elbow and led him to the office, where a nurse appeared with a small paper cup. He handed it to Hank who tipped it into his mouth and accepted a glass of water from the assistant to wash down what he had taken. Hank then allowed the assistant to lead him into his room, still talking about his men and the bodies in the water. The assistant returned to us and looked at me. "What did you say to him?" he accused.

By this point I was shaking. "Nothing. As soon as he saw me, he hugged me hard, calling me my mother's name, Adrienne."

"Adrienne's your mother? We hear her name all the time when he has his bad days. Would you like to sit down? Have some water? These guys are used to all this. Happens daily to someone. It's kind of scary seeing it for the first time, though." He pulled a chair up for me without waiting for my answer.

I sat and looked around. The man who had been reading went back to his book and the guys playing cards had picked them up and resumed their game. In a minute it was as if the incident had never happened.

"Thanks," I said. "This is good. I don't need the water." The assistant nodded and went off to check on Hank. I looked for Elias. He was seated in the chair Hank had leapt up from. Sam was leaning over him.

"You okay, Dad?"

"Yep. Got the old pumper goin', though." He looked up at Sam then squinted at him. "What about you, Son? You don't look so good." He turned towards the other visitor across the room. "Hey, there! Wanna come over here?"

The man walked over to the window.

"How're you doing, Sam?" He looked up at Sam. He only came up to his shoulder.

"You know my son?" Elias asked.

"Yessir," the man answered. "I'm a vet just like he is. Met him in group."

Sam looked down at him. "I'm fine, Alan." Then he glanced over at me and he didn't look fine. His eyes were vague and distant. He was looking at me, but I wasn't sure it was me he was seeing. It was like the other occasions he had spaced out, only this time Sam had definitely left the building.

"Do you have your meds with you?" the man named Alan asked.

"What?" Sam answered. "Does Hank need them?" He started moving towards Hank's room.

"No, Sam," Alan said firmly, stopping him with his voice. "It's okay. Hank's going be okay. *Your* meds, your *pills*."

Sam just stood there looking around.

"Can I check your pockets, Sam?"

Sam looked at Alan as if wondering why he was asking him this.

"No, I'll do it." Sam finally reached into his pocket and brought out a small pill bottle. He handed it to Alan who opened it, shook out three small white pills, closed the bottle up and gave it back to him. Sam placed it back in his pocket. In this gesture something clicked about the times Sam had done this before, but surreptitiously. Alan gave him the pills. Sam looked at them, then put them in his mouth. He took a seat next to Elias by the window.

I got up and went over to him. Elias was patting his son's knee. After a few minutes the only sounds in the room were the guys calling out their hands in cards. Sam looked up at me, his eyes focused a bit more.

"I'm sorry about that," I said. "Cel told me Hank sometimes acted very odd. I should have warned you."

"You didn't know you would set him off."

"It's 'cause you're the spittin' image of Adrienne," Elias noted.

"You can't ever predict what will set us vets off," Alan added.

Sam stood up. "We have to go. I've got to get Dad back to his place."

I looked outside. The small breeze was picking up, the oak branches starting to click against each other.

Alan looked at me. "I don't think Sam should drive just now. I handed him a triple dose of his Lorazepam."

"I'm fine," Sam insisted, but his speech was beginning to slow down.

"That's okay, Sam," I said, trying to help him save face. "I've been dying to drive your car since I first saw it. Come on. Elias will show me how to get to his place."

Sam looked at Alan then at me. He shrugged. "All right. Guess I know when I'm over-ruled."

"See you at group, then?" Alan asked.

Sam patted him on the shoulder as he passed. "Yeah, maybe." Then he led us somewhat unsteadily down the hall to the staircase.

As I followed, Alan stopped me and pressed a small piece of paper into my hand.

"The on-call emergency number," he explained. "In case he gets worse."

I tried to tell him Sam didn't live with me, that we were just friends, but he had already turned away. "What the hell," I thought. I pocketed the paper as I hurried out after my old friend and his dad into what was starting to look like a gathering storm.

CHAPTER TWENTY THREE

As we exited the building, I noticed that in addition to increasing winds, the sky no longer looked pale gray, but was darkening in patches. I wondered if we would get home before the storm hit. As we neared the car, Sam handed me his keys. He climbed into the rear seat, and adjusting his rolled sleeping bag under his head, lay on his back with his knees bent. His eyes were closed even before Elias and I got in. As soon as Elias sat down, he too leaned back in his seat. As I pulled out of the parking lot and headed back out to Division to catch West 94 to Avon, I was the only one awake in the car. Both father and son slept with their mouths open, low snuffling sounds accompanying their breaths.

After turning onto the highway, I went into highway meditation zone with one eye out for the weather and ditches we could dive into if a twister decided to cross our path. I was still shaken by the scene at the VA. Poor Hank. It made my occasional glimpses of flashing red and white lights throughout the years seem like a drop in the large sea of his traumatic experiences. I thought about the coat, about the mysterious twisted tea bags, about Hank's reaction to me-as-my-mother. What was that all about? All these questions whirled through my brain, questions that might never have any answers, since no one seemed to know Hank that well and he very likely would never be in any shape to answer them himself.

Maybe Mr. Barstow would be able to fill us in. At that thought I realized Jess hadn't called back to let us know when the tape would arrive. I groped in my bag with my right hand as I kept the left on the steering wheel. After several minutes of searching, I realized that I had left my cell phone on the kitchen counter. No wonder I hadn't heard from her. Poor Jess. This was the second time she might have called and I'd left my phone behind.

Then there was Sam. What was I going to do about him? Would he be able to drive back to his store after sleeping on the way home, or would he need to bunk down at the house? I scanned the sky again. My thoughts and feelings were as heavy and wind-tossed as the dark clouds above me. I decided I would try to call David when I got home. After all, he had been sweet the other night in spite of what Donna thought. In an odd way he was still my anchor, the only thing about this last week that felt at all familiar. A dose of his familiarity might help me absorb all the old emotions and fears, not to mention the new realizations, understandings, and experiences that were flooding me.

As I turned off the highway at the St Joseph exit and took the back way to Avon, I could hear faint rumbles of thunder in the distance. Sam had said that Elias's apartment complex was at the edge of town between the farm and the highway overpass. I nudged Elias awake as I passed the turn-off to our house.

"Whaa?"

"Elias," I whispered, "I think we're near your place. Can you show me the way?"

Elias stretched and looked around. He directed me and soon I turned into a nicely-kept apartment complex. The grass was green around the buildings and a number of fenced-in garden plots flourished out back. A small pond stood off to one side, with benches placed around it and oak trees shading the benches.

"This is nice," I said. "Do you have one of those garden plots?"

"Nope. Came too late for one this year. Hope to get on the list for next." Elias pointed out the entrance to his section. I stopped outside the door and glanced back at Sam. Elias turned to look at him too. He was still fast asleep.

"What about him?" I gestured with my head.

"Mostly when this happens, he just needs to sleep," Elias answered.

"Will he wake up enough to drop him off at the store?"

"Not on his own, what with the combination of the event at the VA and the pills he took. If it's all right with you, could he sleep on your couch or somethin'? He has resisted stayin' with me, but your place might feel more comfortable for him, bein' bigger, you know. I worry if he wakes up and no one is around. He doesn't always know where he is at first after one of these bouts. Plus, if this storm hits, that may throw him a bit." Elias looked at me.

"Err, sure. I can probably get him into my Dad's study. It's on the ground floor."

"Thank you m'dear. You needn't worry. He may be a bit vague when he wakes up, but if you're there, he'll recognize you and that'll help orient him." Elias gave me a rough hug and got out of the car.

I waved him into his complex and took off towards home. With the weather worsening, I was starting to be concerned about Velvet. She did not like thunder. As I turned onto the deserted two-lane road that led to our driveway, I floored it and went as fast as the Escort could go. I whipped into the driveway and then was forced to slow down over the rolling bumps. The Escort was lower than my SUV, and probably twice as rusty. I didn't want to take Sam's muffler out.

Finally, I pulled up by the house and got out of the car. I could hear Velvet jumping against the door on the inside. I called to her, "It's okay, Velvet, I'm back." When I opened the door, Velvet jumped up on me and raced around. Finally, she sat down, her bushy white tail wagging back and forth, sweeping the ground behind her. I scratched her ruff, patted her back and stroked her ears. She gradually quieted then sniffed around and moved towards the Escort, her nose telling her there was still someone in the car. I headed towards the kitchen and plunked my purse down on the counter. My phone was just where I had left it. I looked at it briefly. Two calls again: Jess and David. Then I remembered that I had forgotten to call Adrian. I hesitated, then figured I should get Sam settled first in case he woke up in the car and decided to drive it away. I checked in Dad's study to see if the afghan that used to drape over the sofa back was still in the closet. I pulled it down and folded it over the desk chair. I was ready to try to engineer the Sam transfer. I envisioned little five-foot-four me trying to hold up six-foot-four him as I tried to maneuver him in.

It turned out to be easier than I had thought. Sort of. When I walked back out to the car, Velvet was lying down by the driver's door. I leaned in the window and called, "Sam." No response. "Sam!" a little louder. He stirred. I went around to the passenger door, leaned in, and tapped him on the shoulder. "Sam, time to wake up!"

"Whaat!!!??" He sat up like a bolt of lightning had seared his backside, hit his head on the ceiling of the car, and bumped his knees on the back of the front seat as he turned to see where the voice was coming from.

Oh my God, what did I just do? "Sam, it's just me, Pru. I'm sorry. I was just trying to wake you up. We're at my house. Your Dad said I should let you sleep here for a while." He looked up at me, confused. I repeated. "Pru? Your old tree climbing buddy?" He focused a bit and looked around. Velvet had joined me on the passenger side when she heard Sam yelling. She was big enough to stick her head in the window without her paws leaving the ground. Sam reached out and stroked her ears. She licked his hand. That seemed to help. Finally he put his hands to his head and sat up.

"I got it." He said, sounding fuzzy, "but don' ev' touch me again without first tellin' me you're there. Okay?"

I felt duly chastised. I thought, Duh! Startle response is extreme in those with PTSD. I've read it millions of times. Too bad books don't always prepare you for real life. I felt like a real dork. I didn't want to be the person to add to his stress, yet here I was. Okay, move on, Pru. Get him inside so he can rest.

"I'm really sorry, Sam. It won't happen again. Want to come in and snooze on the sofa in the study?"

"Jus' til these damn meds wear off." He pushed the seat forward. Velvet and I moved out of the way, and he slowly emerged from the back.

"Do you want your sleeping bag?"

"Nah. Won't be here long enough. Jus' a little nap." He stood up, then wobbled a bit and leaned against the car.

"Here, put your arm around me. We'll go in together just like when we used to try to walk through the woods, scooting around the trees so we didn't get broken apart."

Sam gave me a sleepy grin. "Yeah, I 'member that. Let's do it." He reached around me, his arm coming almost all the way around to my stomach, while mine stretched just to the middle of his back. I just hoped it was enough to keep him steady. We slowly made our way to the house. Curiously, although I was the one helping him, his hold on me felt warm and comforting. We managed the doorway with me turning sideways and going in first. Sam followed. "Just like th' woods," he mumbled. Oh God, was he going to crash before we reached the sofa?

"Stay with me, Sam. We're almost there." We navigated the hallway to the study. I did my doorway twist again, Sam behind me. When we were at the sofa, I turned to let Sam sit down. He did so with a thump, falling onto his side, his head landing right on the pillow nestled at one end. Almost immediately he started snoring again. I picked his legs up one at a time and folded them onto the rest of the couch. Still talking to him, I took his shoes off and covered him with the afghan. "There you go. I'll be in the other room. I'll see you later." I wasn't sure he even heard me, but his snoring suddenly stopped and he slurred, "Shee ya laaider."

He turned with his back to the room, and curled up, pulling the afghan up to his chin. Velvet, who had been right at our heels the whole journey from the car, plunked herself down next to the couch and put her head on her paws. Her amber eyes looked up at me.

"Oh, it's that way, huh?" I patted her and left the room. I listened to my messages. David's was short, just asking me to call. Jess's message told me she really enjoyed the interview with Ed, and that she found a twenty-four hour place, so the tape should be here by today or tomorrow. I hoped the storm didn't change that.

I glanced out at the lake. The wind was westerly, coming right at the house. Definitely cooling everything off. I went into the living room and opened the front windows a bit the way they tell you to do in case of tornadoes to keep the windows from blowing out. I checked upstairs and did the same on both sides of the house. I started back down, deciding to make some tea and sit in the front room to call Adrian and David. In the kitchen, I put the kettle on, took a cup down and hung a teabag in it. Earl Grey for the afternoon. I dialed Adrian. His roommate answered. "Ryan, this is Pru Daniels. Is Adrian around? Jess said he would be back Monday."

"Oh, hi, Mrs. D. Didn't you already talk to him?"

"No, I was out and left my cell behind."

"Oh. He must have talked to Jess, then. Anyway, after he talked to her, he took a shower, checked the airlines, packed his bag, and said he was heading out to see you at the old homestead. Bellingham, right?"

"Ah, no. The really old homestead is in Minnesota."

"You're kidding! Well, then, that's where he's heading. Left here this morning. Should be due there sometime tonight or tomorrow, depending on his luck with ferries and planes."

Great, with a storm coming. However, Ryan didn't need to know that. "Thanks, Ryan, I guess I'll see him when he shows up!"

"Sure thing, Mrs. D!" Ryan hung up. Cheerful guy. Are all Canadians that friendly? Reminded me of Minnesotans. So, two out of three accounted for, although who knows when Adrian would get here. I'd check the weather station later and see how far this storm system reached. Maybe it was just local.

I decided to try David next. Two o'clock. He'd still be at the office. I settled on the love seat and dialed. It rang and rang. I got his voice mail.

"You have reached the office of David Daniels. I'm not available now, but please leave your name and number, and I'll get back to you as soon as I can."

I tried David's cell. No luck there. I hung up before that message came on. I was starting to get a sickening feeling in my stomach. My last resort was to call his secretary. Betty had worked for the psychology department for years and liked her job enough to put up with the idiosyncrasies of the various professors. She did have her way of getting back at the ones of whom she disapproved and David was one of those. She and I had lunch occasionally, and one day she finally got around to the subject of David and his "assistants". She was talking around the subject so long that I finally told her that I knew what he was up to, but had so far chosen to live with it. She gave me a strange look, but asked me if I wanted her to tell me when he was currently involved. I debated internally with myself that day, but decided I would rather know. Nothing like showing up at your husband's office and walking in on him and some sweet young thing. Until the day I found him on the boat, Betty had kept me in the know enough to help me avoid total humiliation. I dialed Betty's direct number.

"Psychology Department, Betty speaking."

"Betty, it's me, Pru Daniels. I'm trying to reach David with no luck so far in his office or on his cell."

Betty paused. "Pru, you might say that at this moment he is *intensely* busy" – her code word for hanky-panky in the office. My heart thudded. I started getting light-headed. The tell-tale sweat trickled down between my breasts. My teeth found my cheeks. Betty lowered her voice. "I'm so sorry, Pru. When are you going to dump the weasel?"

"It's okay, Betty. Sooner than you think maybe. I've got to go." I hung up, sat there, and started to do my deep breathing to avoid the anxiety attack that was barreling it's way through my body. I stood up and looked at the lake.

What a messed-up life I led. What the hell was the matter with me? I had friends, I had the kids, I had a good profession, siblings I was actually starting to enjoy. Why was I hanging on to David? I looked in on Sam in the study. For a minute I flashed on Dad sleeping there. All the old feelings of loneliness and helplessness swamped me. No matter what I did, I could never make Dad happy after Mum died. Yet, he went on. After reading his journal about the war, I realized Dad had done the best he could. So had Sam, and God knows what he had endured, was still enduring.

So what was I doing with a man who cheated on me whenever my back was turned? Was being alone that awful? Maybe it would be, but I was beginning to feel like there was a huge difference between being alone and being lonely. Better late than never. Screw him, I decided, as I moved back into the kitchen. He could call until he was blue in the face. I would not talk to him until whatever had brought me here was finished. I had a feeling that when it was done, whatever it was, I would be ready to finally assert myself with David, even if it was to cut the anchor loose for good. I looked at the stove. Oops, the teakettle was almost dry. I took it off, poured more water into it and set it back on the stove, this time turning the burner on low.

That was when the rain started.

CHAPTER TWENTY FOUR

The rain began softly, reminding me of the beginning of a game we used to play when I worked as a counselor at a summer camp in Maine. We'd have the campers make a rainstorm with their hands. The first part was rubbing their palms together in a swishing sound, which is what I heard as the first drops hit the oak leaves. However, just like in the game, I knew what would follow. I turned on the radio to check the local weather station. The forecast confirmed my fears, saying that a cell of lightning, thunder, and hail was moving in from the west. No reports of wind yet, but you never knew. I glanced out of the window. Dark, but none of the scary greenish color that precedes a tornado.

I decided to be prepared. Remembering there used to be flashlights in the cupboard over the fridge, I dragged a chair from the living room and climbed up. I found one big flashlight and one smaller one. I pulled them out of the cupboard, climbed down again, and checked both of them.

One worked, one didn't. Luckily the one that didn't was the smaller one, and I had some double A's with me somewhere that I kept for my portable tape player. I returned the chair to the dining room and left the flashlights on the counter. I decided to fill the bathtub upstairs in case the power went out and we were left without any water. I also washed out a couple of gallon water jugs left under the sink, filled them and stuck them in the fridge.

The rain was increasing, sounding now like the snapping of many fingers. I looked outside to make sure the car windows were up and noticed I had left the passenger one open on Sam's. I threw a jacket over my head and ran outside again. As I was opening the passenger door, I saw a large flat box labeled First Aid Kit just behind the seat that had been pushed forward when Sam got out. We might need that. I picked it up, pushed the seat back into position, rolled up the window, and ran back into the house, kit under my arm. I didn't think Sam would mind. I'd just have to remember to give it back to him when he left. I shook out my jacket and hung it up on a hook by the door. I took the kit into the kitchen and opened it up on the counter. It had the usual things – iodine, band aids, benydryl for wasp bites, Caladryl for poison ivy, and tweezers. But it also contained items I didn't associate with your typical car first aid kit like Betadine, antiseptic lotion, surgical clamps, compress bandages, a tourniquet, a pen and a small razor knife, needles and dental floss, and a whole bunch of tampons. Tampons. What were they for? Emergency supply for girl friends?

I thought Sam's medical experience had been years ago. Obviously I was mistaken. Otherwise, why would he have all this stuff? I closed up the kit and stuck it by the wall under the coat hooks. I looked out at the lake and noticed the rain was starting to come down in sheets. This would be the point at which the campers slapped their thighs with the palms of their hands to imitate the rainstorm peaking. However, I knew there was one more stage – the thunder part that neither Velvet nor I did very well, and maybe one of Minnesota's famous hailstorms. I looked in on Sam. Velvet looked up at me and whined. I moved quietly over to her and stroked her ears. Her eyes told me she was getting stressed, but she wasn't moving from her self-appointed spot. All of a sudden, the rain changed, sounding like the campers were dropping marbles all over the roof. Sam stirred. Velvet licked his hand, and the hail continued. I stood up and looked out. Thick little ice balls fell to the ground and almost immediately started melting. Then in the midst of the hail pelting the house, thunder grumbled in the distance. As it approached, it rolled over us, sounding like hundreds of pairs of campers feet pounding the floor. The lightning rode ahead of it, flashing every few seconds. My nerves flashed with it as my mind revisited the newfound memory of the storm the day Grandma brought me home after I had fallen out of the tree. Maybe I had always needed Dad to hold me during thunderstorms because I associated them with a day that changed my life.

Whatever the reason, it was fast becoming obvious that I wasn't the only one reacting to it. Velvet began panting, and Sam, at the next quick burst of hail, sat straight up, eyes wide open.

"Ambush!" he yelled. He jumped up and looked wildly around him. "My weapon! Where's my weapon?!"

Velvet jumped out of his way and crawled to safety under my father's desk. I just stood there, shaking. I wanted to go sit on the basement stairs, where I used to feel safe when Dad wasn't around during storms, but I didn't know what Sam would do if I moved. Finally his gaze settled on me.

"Get down, get down!" he screamed. Then before I could move, I felt the full weight of his body tackle me and fling me to the floor, just missing the edge of Dad's desk. My nose was pressed to the carpet. I could hardly breathe as he covered my body with his.

"I told you to get down! How many are there? Where's my weapon?"

In his floundering around, I managed to turn my head to get a breath and found myself looking right into Velvet's eyes as she lay under the desk, her head on her paws. And people said she wouldn't be a wuss if I were threatened. Right. If only they could see her now. I looked at her then I realized that Sam had quieted on top of me. I wiggled.

"Sam?" I ventured.

"What?" Another bolt of lightning. Baroom! Another barrage of thunder. The house shook. "Incoming!" Sam was shouting in my ear.

"Sam!" I tried again, this time with a bit more volume, to match the storm. "Sam! Sam! It's Pru! You are at my house. It's just a storm. Just thunder and lightning! It's all right! There is no ambush!" I decided to use his words. "You don't need a weapon. There are no incoming! There is just me and Velvet, and *you are squishing the hell out of me!*" I wiggled some more. Something must have gotten through as he looked down, not at me but at Velvet. Thank God they didn't have malamutes in Vietnam. She seemed to be grounding for him. Maybe that is why she didn't rush to my defense. Maybe she realized he wouldn't hurt me. Sorry, Velvet, I misjudged you.

All of a sudden, Sam pushed himself off me with his strong arms.

He sat back on his heels and looked at me. It was still lightning out, but the hail had died down, and the thunder was more distant. It was just raining again, back to the clapping hands sound. Sam looked out the window and around the room. He seemed to be back in the present. He reached out a hand to me. I rolled on my back, sat up, and took his hand as he helped me stand.

"Are you hurt?" he asked.

"I don't think so." Other than rug burns on my knees and bowels that felt like they were on the verge of letting go big time. "Are *you* okay?"

He shook his head. "I don't know. I haven't done anything like that since the explosion up home that started this up all over again." He reached into his pocket for his pills. He took the cap off, and shook one out. It was the last one. He stared at the pill bottle, then at the storm outside. "Damn. I meant to pick up more at the VA today, but when all that happened with Hank I forgot."

"Will you be okay without them?" I remembered Elias saying he usually just needed to sleep after one of these episodes, like when we came home from the VA. But he had taken the pills then. Would he be able to sleep without them? I envisioned the whole night ahead of me with him in and out of whatever he was fighting. The thought frankly scared me.

"I don't know that either." He sat back down on the couch, his head in his hands. "I'm so sorry if I hurt you, Pru."

"You were trying to help me. It's okay. However, hang on a minute, 'cause I have to go to the bathroom." The deluge that was threatening pushed my wobbly legs into a run. I slammed the bathroom door and made it just in time.

A few minutes and several flushes later I opened the bathroom window then reappeared in the hallway. I looked into the study. Sam was still sitting there, Velvet by his side again. His hand absently stroked her head, but he was constantly scanning the room and outside the windows. God, I didn't think I was up to this. Then I remembered the card in my pocket that Sam's friend had given me. I picked up my cell and dialed. What I got ended up not being that helpful, just a recorded message saying that the hospital was closed for the day, and if this was an emergency, to call 911. I closed my cell. Was it an emergency, or was I just feeling overwhelmed? With the amount of rain and hail we'd had, I was sure there were far more pressing needs out there than those of a woman with a burnt-out war vet who was trying to protect her from the thunderstorm. The only thing was I didn't feel like a woman, or even a grown-up. Just as the storm had thrown Sam back into his nightmares, it had left me feeling like a little girl again. The one who knew in her heart she would never have her mother back to hug her and make her feel better. So I did the next best thing. I called Celeste.

CHAPTER TWENTY FIVE

As I dialed, I noticed the rain had decreased to the snapping fingers level. Maybe the worst was over. I didn't reach Celeste, but got Josie again. She told me the horses were going nuts with the combined noise of the hail and thunder, not to mention the lightning. In dealing with Sam, I had completely forgotten how it might be over at the farm. Not that different, I guessed. Josie ran off to see if Celeste could get free now that the storm was calming down. I waited for a few minutes, deciding if she didn't come soon, I would just leave it. She had enough to look after. However, when Celeste came on the phone, breathing hard, I was really glad I hadn't hung up.

"You okay, Pip? Josie said you sounded a bit stressed out!"

Observant woman. "Just a tad, Cel. Sam is here, and I don't know what to do." I filled her in on Hank's episode at the VA, on Sam's reaction, and on the activity since the storm. I told her about the pills and my fear about Sam not being able to sleep without them.

"Cel, what I know about PTSD victims, is that if they don't get a break from the stress, it just gets worse. I'm not afraid of Sam in the present, but after being tackled in the study, I'm not at all sure what will happen if he stays in the past. I hate to ask, but is there any chance you can get away and come over for the night?"

"Hey, Pip. At least you did. Much better than trying to take it all on yourself. I'm pooped. That horse we were working with was almost ready to be shipped over to Glen for further training. The vet had even prescribed him some tranquilizers for the trip over, but the storm squelched that idea. He'll need days to recover from this before he's ready again."

"Hey, if you're too tired, I'll figure something out." My stomach started cramping again.

"Cut it out. You didn't let me finish. Ollie and Josie can take it from here. I could use a break. Probably get more sleep over there anyway. I'll throw some clothes in a bag and drive over. Hang on."

I felt a wave of relief wash over me. There was something about having a big sister. I jokingly added. "And bring some of that tranquilizer for Sam." There was a pause.

"I don't think so. Way different stuff. What was he taking, anyway?"

"Lorazapam."

"Hmmm. I might be able to help. Diazepam, which is in the same family, was my favorite, and like many a former pill-head, I still have about six in a bottle just to prove I don't need them any more. They should work to get Sam to sleep."

"Is that legal?" The ethical professional in me asked.

"At this point, does it matter? I don't think this is the time to be Miss Goody Two Shoes, Pip."

"Got it, Cel. Thanks."

She hung up. I stared at the phone and closed it, feeling relieved. I returned to the study to check on Sam. He and Velvet were still sitting there. I decided to turn the TV on to the weather station to see if it might help re-orient Sam. As it came on, his gaze did switch to it and his eyes cleared.

"Can I get you anything?"

He looked up. "Maybe some tea?"

I nodded and went back into the kitchen. Good old tea. Comfort drink for generations.

As I pulled out the teabags and cups, I listened to the TV weather woman in the other room say that the storm was traveling through quickly, but there was still a chance of heavy winds, possibly tornadoes, to follow. Oh, great. I wondered what a windstorm would sound like to Sam in his current condition. While I was in the kitchen, Velvet was hanging around my knees, a sure sign that it was time to feed her. I looked at my watch. Almost five. Amazing how time flies when you are being tackled by a former Green Beret. I scooped some dry food into Velvet's dish, then looked in the freezer to see what I had to feed the three of us. A package of chicken breasts. I had some salsa, mozzarella cheese, rice, and enough stuff left over for a salad. That would do. No dessert, but hell, we were in a storm. Why was I worrying about being the perfect cook? They were lucky they weren't getting boxed macaroni and cheese. I threw the chicken in the microwave to defrost. After pouring the water in for the tea, I carried the cups to the study. Poking my head in the door, I asked Sam if he wanted to drink it in the living room.

"No, thanks. This is fine." He seemed to feel safer in the study.

I handed Sam his tea. "Okay. I'll be in there if you need anything." Sam nodded, then smiled a little. I felt badly deserting him, but I didn't really know what to say to him, afraid that anything could serve as a trigger. I was having some flashbacks of my own involving the times when I would tiptoe around the house when Dad tried to nap after having a bad night. I sat down on one of the love seats. Velvet in her infinite wisdom decided it was my turn to receive comfort and plopped at my feet. I picked up my whodunit, trying for some quiet distraction until Celeste arrived, but I kept reading the same sentence over and over.

In about half an hour, Celeste blew in the door along with the residue of rain.

"Whoosh! Is it nasty out there! Some of the lower points on the road are flooded. Glad I drive a truck!" She shrugged off her raincoat and hung it on a hook next to mine. Velvet trotted over and sniffed her from thigh to toe. Celeste leaned down and patted her.

"Yes, I've been with horses and dogs." She stood still patiently for a few minutes. "Are you done?" Celeste then moved into the living room. We both sat on the love seat. She turned and looked at me closely. "You're looking worse than the situation calls for, Pip." She narrowed her eyes. "Anything else going on?"

I tried black humor. "You mean besides being taken down by a six foot-four combat vet who was sure the bullets were winging through the house?"

She just kept looking at me. I started shaking, then crying softly. Celeste leaned forward and enveloped me. I leaned into her and let go. She patiently held me and handed me Kleenex from her cavern. I finally sat up.

"I've been doing this alot to you recently. You must be almost out of tissues down there." I pointed to her breasts. She chuckled.

"It's a bottomless pit, Pru, an endless supply." It was my turn to laugh.

"You know, Celeste, in the last few days I've been thinking of how you used to come to my rescue, take care of me, or tell me to get my head out of my butt, whichever it was I needed. I'm a fool to have let so much time go by without you in my life."

"Glad you finally realized it, Pip." I gave her a hug and she sat back with her foot on one knee. "So," she said, digging something out of her pants pocket, "where is our spooked friend?" I nodded towards the study. She got up and poked her head in. Sam was lying back down on the couch, looking at the ceiling. She came back. "I see part of your problem. His posture sure is familiar." Celeste had taken her turns with Dad. "Now give with the rest."

I told her about Jess's message, my call to Adrian's place and my conversation with David's secretary. At this last bit all she said was, "Aah."

I was thankful that she left it at that.

"So, when do you think Adrian will get here?"

"Who knows? Depends on what the storm is like in the Cities. Maybe tonight or tomorrow. I hope he calls when he gets in. Jess' package is also up to the weather gods. I've got some chicken and salad I'll make in the meantime."

Celeste handed me the pill bottle. "Sounds good to me. I'll go up and make the bed in Mum and Dad's room and get another quilt out for Sam, then we'll feed him some food and the pills, wait for him to go to sleep and call it a day."

"A little early don't you think?" I usually had a set bedtime no matter what. My inner clock wouldn't wind down until about ten. I put the bottle in my pocket.

"Not for me after today. And I suspect Sam will be grateful for whenever he gets to sleep. You can do what you want. That is," she added, "after you feed us." With that she headed up the stairs.

I prepared the chicken breasts and started them browning. I

THE COAT IN THE WOODS   189

then added some salsa, covered the pan and turned the heat down a bit. It was kind of weird not having Sam in the kitchen helping and talking with me. When I finished making the salad, I wandered into the study. This time I called to him twice from the doorway. He looked up, then sat up. He looked so sad and tired.

"Sam?" I asked.

"What's up, Pru?"

He knew who I was. This was encouraging. "Celeste is here for the night."

"Oh?"

"And she brought you some pills that might help you sleep. Same sort of stuff as your Lorazapam." I handed the bottle to him. He looked at it.

"Diazapam," he read. "What is she doing with this? I thought she was clean."

"She is. She said she kept this bottle for years to prove she didn't need it."

"Oh," was all he said. Sam opened the bottle, tapped out three pills, and put them on the table by the couch. He closed the bottle and sat it next to the pills. "Looks like these'll work. Sure beats rummaging around for any leftover booze you might have."

I looked at him. "You serious?"

"Very. I would have done anything to get to sleep. Never thought I'd be saying this, but I'm glad your sister was a druggy."

"Me, too," piped up Celeste from behind my back. I jumped. She moved past me and handed Sam the quilt. She gestured towards the pills. "So do you want to take those before we eat or after?"

Sam didn't even seem embarrassed. Must be an AA fellowship thing. "I think after. What's for dinner?"

"Chicken and rice with a salad," I answered. "Sorry, no dessert." Damn, there I went again. Martha frigging Stewart.

"No dessert! I always have dessert after I freak out!" Sam's dimple appeared again.

"Your sense of humor is back," I replied.

He grinned as he stretched and got up. "Want me to take Velvet out?"

"Sure, if you think you'll be all right." I said.

"Stop worrying, Pru. The storm is mostly over both inside and out. I'll be fine after I sleep."

"Okay." He must not have heard the part on the TV about the wind coming. And I wasn't going to be the one to remind him. If he knew about it, he might have trouble relaxing enough to let the pills work. I wanted him to sleep as much for my sake as his.

As Sam walked Velvet, Celeste helped me with the plates and utensils. By the time dog and man returned, we were ready to eat. There was little conversation but a comfortable sense of companionship among the three of us. Sam even rallied enough to help clean up. He then said goodnight and retired to the study, pushing the door mostly shut. I heard him turn the TV to the History Channel. Would he have it on all night? I needed to stop worrying. Who cared if he did, as long as it helped him sleep?

Celeste gave me a hug and said goodnight. It was only eight o'clock, but the sky was darker than usual and I was really tired. I climbed up to my room, Velvet behind me, and felt comforted by the nesting sounds of Celeste next door to me. As it turned out, I stayed awake long enough to sneak back down and put my ear to the study door. Hearing snoring sounds, I peeked in. Sam was curled up under both afghan and quilt with the television softly murmuring in the background. I closed the door, and remembering to take the flashlight upstairs just in case, went back up to my room. I think I was asleep way before ten. It had been a *very* long day.

CHAPTER TWENTY SIX

The sound of Velvet's howling woke me even before I heard the wind. There is something about her breed's howl that cuts through even the soundest sleep. Must be her wolf ancestors. Once Velvet had my attention, she shoved her nose into my face. I patted the covers next to me. She hopped up and lay panting. I reached over to turn on the bedside light. Damn, no electricity. I listened for sounds next door. I couldn't really hear anything over the wind, so I scuttled out of bed and listened at Celeste's door. Snuffling sounds. Maybe she only woke up if she heard horses neighing. I remembered the big flashlight I had brought upstairs last night. I switched it on and looked at my watch. Four A.M. Great. The wind was whipping through the balcony door and the temperature felt like it had dropped down into the fifties. I pushed myself out against the wind and looked up at the sky. Not raining any more, clear in fact. The blazing stars were an odd contrast to the wild windstorm. Before I pushed the door closed, I listened for a moment more and heard our little lake sounding like the big fierce ocean with waves crashing onto the shore.

I glanced back at Velvet. She wasn't about to go back to sleep, and neither was I. I closed the sliding door all the way, then slipped on some sweatpants, a hooded sweatshirt and a pair of socks to counteract the chill in the house. Clutching my flashlight, I tiptoed downstairs to see how Sam was doing. Velvet, deciding I was not going to leave her sight, followed me, her toenails tapping on the steps. Once downstairs, all I heard was the wind, and an occasional distant crraack! I wondered what the woods were going to look like when this was over. I glanced into the study, half expecting to find Sam where Velvet had found shelter last night – under the desk. He was still sound asleep. How did that happen? One minute he was hyper-alert, the next so sound sleep he was impervious to a windstorm such as this. I glanced at the pill bottle Celeste had given him. I tiptoed in and picked it up.

Empty. He had taken the other three as well. If I took that many I would sleep for a week.

At least I didn't have to worry about Sam for the moment. I decided to start a fire in the woodstove to warm the house up a bit and to boil some water for tea. Luckily, the good camper instinct in our family had resulted in a supply of newspaper, kindling and a few logs left by the stove. The rest I could fetch from the shed later if it stayed cool. The fire started right away. I dug an old camping pot from the bottom cupboards and filled it with the water I had put in the fridge earlier. I found some candles and put them on saucers. I spread them around the kitchen and living room and lit them. I also tried the radio. Nope. The batteries were dead. I guess if the big one hit, I wasn't going to find out about it. With the fire crackling merrily, and the pot of water heating up, I curled up on the love seat closest to the stove. The candlelight created soft shadows around the room, counteracting the fierce storm outside. Velvet stood in front of me with her liquid eyes focused on me.

"Oh, all right." I patted the seat next to me. She curled up, nose to tail, her bulk warming my feet. Gradually the star-splattered sky turned to dawn, rosy streaks stretching across the top of the house to erase all but the brightest stars. I watched the black outlines of the trees on either side of the lake do a frenzied dance. As it grew light, I could see waves splashing up onto the deck, even spraying far enough to reach the front windows. For some reason I wasn't afraid, but comforted, as if Dad's arms were still wrapped around me. I would feel better, however, if I knew we weren't in for any tornadoes.

I heard a thud. I jumped. So did Velvet. I peered through the french doors. A tree from the left of the house had landed on the roof. I ran two flights upstairs to the attic to check the roof. Velvet followed me as far as the attic door, but wouldn't venture any further. I didn't blame her. The noise of the wind was spooky up there, but I didn't see any holes. Hoping it was just a small fixable dent,

I realized I couldn't do anything about it now anyway, so I skittered back down the stairs and closed the door firmly against any bats that might have found shelter in the storm. I paused outside Celeste's room. Still pretty quiet. I peeked in just to make sure she was all right. She slept with a pillow over her head, little snorts emanating from the space between the two pillows. I tiptoed back downstairs and checked the pot to see if it was boiling. A hot teacup between my hands would be soothing just about now.

Little tiny bubbles. Soon. I blew out the candles and scanned the sky above the lake to see if there were signs of a tornado sky. Nope, clear. The winds seemed to be straight-line ones. Suddenly I had an idea. Since it was light, I could use the batteries from the flashlight for the radio. I made the switch and turned the radio on to the local station I had tuned in yesterday. Ah, Pru, you should have been a weatherperson. Straight-line winds topping at fifty miles per hour. No tornado touchdowns. Should be on its way out of here by midday. I turned it off and heard another crack further away. I checked out by the cars. They were okay. One thing to be said for clearing trees around your house. The only ones near were the oaks, and they were too big and deeply rooted to be vulnerable. I wondered about the basswood tree where the coat grew. I checked the water again. Ready to go. I took it into the kitchen and made some of my Lapsang Souchong tea, heavy with cream and sugar. I replaced the water in the pot and put it back on the stove for whenever Sam and Celeste emerged. Then I sat on the love seat again and watched the storm over the lake.

After finishing my tea, I noticed that the wind had calmed down enough to venture outside. I put my raincoat on, grabbed Velvet's leash, and together we pushed our way out through the side door. We walked around the front first, as I wanted to look at the tree that had landed on the house. The wind was still gusting on and off, and I put my hood up to avoid the splashes from the lake. Velvet shook the water off her fur and onto my legs.

"Thanks, Babe." Velvet wagged her tail, and then pulled me off to smell the base of the tree that had fallen. A smallish white pine.

Luckily it had landed on the gutter that ran across the front of the porch roof. However, it had put quite a dent in it. The tree branches lay on the roof, the denseness of the needles providing a pillow-like soft landing on the surface. However, the tree was short enough that if it shifted again, it might fall and hit the windows below. I hoped Celeste had a chainsaw at the farm.

Since we were out, I decided to try to get to the coat tree. We circled the house. I looked down the path to the farm where I could just barely make out the trail amongst all the trees that crisscrossed the lane. But there was just enough room for Velvet and me to climb over or duck under each tree. Some were big, but most of them were small ones that had grown too tall too soon, searching for light amid the canopy created by the bigger trees. I couldn't even tell where to go to find the basswood tree any more.

But Velvet could. All of a sudden, she put her nose in the air and veered off to my left. I reeled her in so she didn't leave me hanging up on some downed tree. I pushed some branches aside and stepped around others.

Finally Velvet led me to the clearing. Trees were down all over the place. I had to crawl over one that had been uprooted and had fallen down the ravine, as if ready for someone to carve a big slide in it to go wooshing down into the stream below. I looked around to see if a similar fate had befallen the coat tree. It had not, because there was the basswood, on the other side of the downed tree, standing tall, shining in the morning sun, its tufts of fur shifting like feathers in the remaining wind. Velvet pulled me over the big tree and leaned into the basswood, her ruff rubbing against the fur again. What was it about that fur that she liked so much? Maybe it was just the smell that wafted up from the ground where many of the flowers had fallen around the base of the tree in the rain. But that didn't explain the other stronger smell that came directly from the fur itself. Mum's lavender smell. I was sure of it this time. I stopped and said out loud, "Mum, are you there?" The wind blew harder around the tufts. Mum's scent seemed to surround me. A warmth spread through me. What was going on? Was I sensing something real or just what I needed to? I reached out and patted a tuft. A bit wet still. Then I turned around to check the old car. Finally, after so many years, the car had been pushed over by the top of the fallen tree and was now upside down against some trees right at the edge of the stream below. The tree that had moved the automobile bridged a big dugout space left when the car had turned over. Now this would be a place to return to with a chainsaw. Buck the tree up and follow Sam's urge to see if there was anything left under the car.

With that in mind, I decided to turn back. As I pushed my way through the last of the thick brush back to the path, I noticed Velvet's hackles were up. Before I could wonder why, I ran straight into a strong arm that reached out to grab me.

"Huuh!" I cried. What the hell? My next split second thought was that once again, Velvet was useless as a protector. I looked down at her. She was actually wagging her tail. I looked from the arm to the face, not sure what I would find, and stared right into the twinkling blue eyes and goofy grin of Ollie, Celeste's manager.

"What are you doing out here, Pru? Are you nuts? The trees are still dangerous!"

"Jesus, Ollie, you scared the *crap* out of me!"

He looked around and sniffed. "Not so as you'd notice," he remarked.

"Ohh! You know what I mean. What are you doing up so early? I was sure I had met Freddy if not Jason!"

"I've got the chainsaw. That would be Jason." He indicated the saw that lay at his feet. "Anyway, I wasn't sure how things were over here, so I decided to check on you all. I figured the woods might look something like this, and I wasn't sure about your parents' house. Then I heard a noise and decided to take a look."

"I was hoping someone would show up with a saw. This just isn't the way I had imagined it. We have one tree down on the roof, not to mention all of these, and I have no idea what the driveway looks like. The thing is, Sam and Celeste are still asleep, so we should wait on the sawing, but come with me. We'll check the driveway, and I'll make you some tea."

"Is your power on? Ours is off."

"Ours is too. I put a pot of water on the woodstove."

"Sounds great, if you make that coffee instead."

"Just instant."

"As long as it's strong enough to take the paint off a tractor. Now let's get out of here." Ollie handed me the coil of rope he had been carrying. I swung it up onto my shoulder while he took the bucket that contained a small gas can, chain oil and tools for the saw. Holding the saw in the other hand, Ollie led the way. Velvet jumped ahead of me, pulling at the very end of her leash to follow him, looking back at me as if to reprimand me again for doubting her instincts when it came to taking care of me.

"Yeah, Yeah, Yeah," I muttered as we slowly climbed and ducked our way back to the house. Before going inside, we walked down the driveway and found one tree across it.

"When we start, let's cut this one first. I'm hoping to have something delivered today."

"That is, assuming they can get as far as here," Ollie added.

"Good point." I looked at my watch. "I have a battery-powered radio. It's almost eight o'clock. Maybe there's more news about what the rest of the area looks like."

Back by the house, the wind was still noticeable but weaker. I handed Ollie the rope and Velvet and I went inside. As I opened the door, I was greeted by both Sam and Celeste sitting at either end of the love seat closest to the fire. Both pairs of hands were curled around steaming cups. They were either in the midst of a very serious conversation or were staring out at the lake thinking their own thoughts. It was hard to tell. Both of them looked exhausted, Sam for the obvious reasons. As for Celeste, I started to worry that the level of activity she embraced was beginning to wear on her. But my first concern was that there wouldn't be enough hot water for me and Ollie. Celeste read my mind.

"Not to worry, Pru. I was a good girl and filled the pot back up.

It should be hot again by now." She turned at a noise out front and saw Ollie wiggling the tree. "I see Ollie made it over."

"He almost gave me a heart attack in the process," I said. I told them about finding the coat tree still standing and about the tree that had rolled the car over. I decided to leave out my little supernatural experience. Sam sat up and looked almost alive for the first time since we had visited Hank at the VA.

"So the ground that used to be under the car is exposed now?"

"Right out of your dreams, Sam," I answered. "As soon as someone volunteers to buck up the tree which is sitting on almost a 45 degree angle slope."

"Sounds just up my alley," replied Sam.

"I thought you hated chainsaws. Anyway, should you do that much right after last night?"

"What about last night? I was just tired, is all. I'm fit as a fiddle now."

Celeste and I exchanged glances. She said, "Sam and I were just talking, and he doesn't remember the storm last night. Says he slept through it." Her eyes told me not to question this.

"Yep, I can't believe I missed all the excitement. By the way, have you seen my pills? I was looking for them this morning, but all I found was a bottle with Celeste's name on it. What's that all about, Cel? Back on the downers?"

He obviously hadn't remembered that conversation either.

"You don't have to drag me to a meeting, Sam. It was from my old stash. Pru told me you were out of your medication, so I thought it might help you get to sleep."

"I guess it did." Sam looked thoughtful for a moment, then he ventured, "I think I was supposed to get my meds at the VA yesterday. Must have forgotten. Don't usually do that." He looked first at Celeste and then me.

"It was a bit chaotic after Hank saw me and got upset," I said, seeing if he remembered that.

"Oh, right. We had to get Dad home because it sort of disturbed him. Is he all right?"

Celeste and I flicked eyes back and forth again.

I reassured Sam. "He's okay. We took him home, then drove here because of the storm instead of trying to go to your store. You can use my cell to call him if you want, or we can drop off to see him if I give you a ride later to pick up your meds."

"Yeah. I might stop off on the way to the VA. I'll just go myself."

Was he in major denial or did he actually not remember? It would be nice to know. If he really didn't remember anything past the VA visit yesterday, how could I be sure he could remember how to get to the VA and back today? The answer was I couldn't. Hell, I had driven off in terrible shape from his place the day he told me about Mum, and I'm sure he wasn't comfortable with that. I could help him through this without getting out the flannel blanket. He's probably found his way out of more hairy situations than I've ever dreamed of.

"Whatever works for you, Sam. Obviously we're going to need your help with a tree that's across the driveway before anyone goes anywhere."

Sam looked a bit puzzled. "Oh, right." Again, Celeste and I exchanged glances.

At that point, Ollie literally blew in through the front door.

CHAPTER TWENTY SEVEN

"Whew!" Ollie exclaimed as the door snapped shut behind him. "Wild, but getting better. So, where's my coffee?" He looked around, blue eyes dancing, clearly loving this kind of action. I took off into the kitchen to grant his wish. When I returned, I handed Ollie his cup and sat on the other love seat. Ollie plopped down in the corner chair. Velvet had already staked out her place by Sam. He was absently stroking her ears. He seemed to waver between being focused and off somewhere again.

With Ollie's lead and our occasional input, we planned our clearing jobs. First, the driveway and then the tree on the roof.

"What about the tree in the gorge?" Sam suggested.

Celeste took over. "That will wait, Sam. These need to be done first. Then remember, you have to go to town."

"Town?" he asked, his brown eyes vague again. He thought for a minute. "Oh. The VA. Got it."

Was this the same man who sat on the deck with me trading childhood reminiscences and tromped through the woods giving me advice on fencing? How does war do this to people so many years later? Better question might be how does it not? In any case, it seemed that in the current situation, the best thing was to stay matter of fact and keep Sam oriented in the present, which in this case meant it was time to go to work. The others already had on their raincoats and were on their way back outside. I grabbed my coat and slammed the door behind me.

I walked quickly to catch up with the others. Celeste led the way, followed by Ollie carrying the saw, and Sam with the rope and the bucket. As we came to the downed tree, Ollie fired up the saw and began cutting. Sam had thrown the rope down as it wasn't needed, and we concentrated on removing the branches and carrying the logs back to the house as they were bucked up. I graciously gave Celeste the light ones, while Sam and I hefted the medium-sized ones.

"Nice of you, Pru, considering years ago my seniority would have earned me a place beside the stove, cooking for you all rather than out here doing the grunt work."

"Be my guest," I yelled over my shoulder.

"You forget. The power is out. I'm not about to cook over a wood stove, thank you very much. Give me some more branches. I'll soldier on."

Sam was ahead of us and was on the way back to get more logs as Celeste and I dropped our armloads by the woodshed. The saw was still going strong. We'd have to use Celeste's truck to move the rest of the logs, as we were getting down to the wider part of the trunk. On our way back to Ollie we passed Sam again, loaded up with wood. He smiled over his armful. I smiled back. He seemed to be doing okay with the saw, so far. When Celeste and I arrived at the downed tree once more, Ollie had finished clearing the driveway and had moved the rest of the logs to the side of the road. He motioned over our heads to a large limb that had broken off but was caught on another tree. If the wind changed or increased, there was a chance it would land right on the driveway, maybe on someone's car or head.

Ollie turned off the saw. "Want me to take that one down?"

Celeste and I looked up. "A widow maker, Grandpa used to call those," she said. "Yeah, please do. This is going faster than I thought. We have plenty of time to do this and the one on the house before either of us needs to get back to the farm."

"Right on, Boss." Ollie grabbed the coil of rope and trod into the woods a ways. It looked like he was going to take down the tree that had the other one hung on it.

He was already climbing the bigger tree as I picked up the last few reasonably sized logs, and as I was walking, I heard the chainsaw rip away behind me. Then there was a crack and a THUNK! The ground shook as part of the tree fell. Ahead of me at the shed, I noticed Sam standing still while he let the logs fall from his arms, not even jumping back to avoid them rolling on his toes.

I walked towards him as quickly as I could, given the load I had. Unencumbered with wood, Celeste ran past me

"Sam!" she yelled. "Are you all right?"

He slowly turned our way. "What?"

There was another crack, another THUNK! God, even I felt that. Ollie, aren't you almost done? I moved closer, dropped my log on the pile and followed Celeste's lead, this time about a foot away from Sam.

"Are you all right?" I yelled at him. The saw stopped.

"What? I can't hear you. It's like you're talking to me under water!"

I looked at Celeste. Not good. Not good at all. I felt helpless. I had no idea what to do. But fortunately, Celeste did.

"Come on Sam." She reached for him, took his arm and wrapped it around her waist. I followed suit and took his other arm, tucking my shoulder under it. Together we walked Sam to the house. Velvet greeted us by stretching and then licking Sam's hand. Sam looked at Velvet and moved his hand to pat her. Celeste and I manoeuvred him onto one of the love seats. Celeste stayed with him.

I went to the kitchen to get some more tea bags. As I moved around collecting a pan and the ingredients to make eggs and toast on the woodstove, I heard Celeste murmuring to Sam, keeping up a low soft tone, talking about what, I couldn't hear. Well, I thought, if you don't have your meds, the next best thing would be to have access to a horse whisperer.

By the time I returned to the living room, Celeste had stopped talking to Sam. He was sitting back on the love seat, his eyes closed, breathing calmly. No new chainsaw noise, Thank God. A light thump on the porch announced Ollie's return. He took in the scene and nodded his head towards Sam. I motioned him into the kitchen.

"He all right?" he asked.

"Doesn't like chainsaws," I answered.

"A lot of folks don't."

"And he's a war vet. I think the tree shaking the ground when it fell got to him." I wasn't sure I should tell him that, but he would see soon enough that there was more going on here than chainsaw phobia.

Ollie looked out the window. "That makes more sense." I had underestimated him. "My uncle was in 'Nam, and my cousin was in Desert Storm. Fucked 'em both up pretty bad, if you'll excuse my language."

"Seems like this is one of those times when that word fits pretty well, Ollie."

"Yep, don't know too many folks who aren't affected by some war or other, either them, or their families."

I thought about Dad, about Hank, even about the elusive Mr. Barstow, and about Mum. "Isn't that the truth, Ollie. There's an old saying that the only people who make war are those who haven't been in one."

"If so, given how widespread war has been, there should hardly be anyone left to wage any more of them."

"You'd think," I answered. "Want some breakfast before we tackle the last tree?" That seemed to change the energy a bit.

"Sure thing. What can I bring in?" I showed him where the plates and utensils were, and he set the table, while I did my best imitation of Laura Ingalls Wilder on the woodstove.

Sam didn't wake up enough to eat, so I put his share on the stove and covered it with another plate. Ollie turned on the radio and found out that the local damage amounted to trees down here and there and some minor flooding, but that the power should be on by the evening. The storm had skirted the Twin Cities.

"Good," I commented. "There's a good chance Adrian as well as Jess' package might get here some time today."

"The tape?" Celeste asked. I nodded. She continued, "Hey, let's call Paul and Annie to come help clean up the place. That way we'll all be here when the tape arrives."

"If it arrives," I cautioned.

"It will. Here, hand me your cell phone and I'll give them a call, see if they can get away. They can call it a family emergency." I gave her a look as I pointed to the phone on the counter. "Well, it is – sort of." She grabbed the phone and walked into the study.

I prepared to join Ollie back outside. He had already set up the ladder from the woodshed against the house. Sam raised his head just as I opened the front door. He looked at me.

"I'm going out front to help Ollie get the tree off the roof. Will you be okay?"

"Just need to rest," he mumbled.

"The chainsaw will be going again," I warned him.

"Too tired to bother me. I'll just nap." Sam's head lolled back onto the love seat again, his long legs stretched out in front of him. His hair was loose, his grey pony tail askew. His glasses had fallen down onto the tip of his nose. Half of his shirttail was untucked. I waited for a minute to see if there was anything more, then went out the door. Velvet settled back down beside Sam.

Outside, Ollie climbed the ladder to the roof. He tied the long rope to the middle of the tree, just between some of the smaller branches. He instructed me to station myself on the other side of the house. He would throw the rope over the house and I was to anchor it to a tree there, so that once the larger branches keeping the tree on the roof were cut, the whole tree wouldn't slip off and hit the windows. Since following directions and doing the right thing was one of my talents, I did just that. I caught the rope and tied it to one of the big oak trees at the rear of the house. I walked around to the front.

"What's next?" I called.

"I have to start the saw up again," Ollie apologized.

"I know, I told him. I'm not sure he'll hear it at this point anyway."

"I'll need you to move out of the way as I throw the smaller branches down. Then you can drag them off."

"Aye Aye!" I saluted, then stopped for a moment, remembering Sam's earlier reaction to the same gesture. However, Ollie wasn't Sam. He saluted back with a big grin and started up the saw.

Celeste reappeared from the house, closing the door quickly to muffle the sound to the inside. "Paul says he and Annie can get here about three or so."

"It'll give us time to put them to work while it's still light even if the tape doesn't get here today," I answered.

"Yeah. Since they're coming later we can take a break in a bit. I'll have to go back to the farm when Ollie is done and check on things there. Maybe you can persuade Sam to let you take him to get his meds."

"Oh, thanks. Give me the easy job!"

"You can do it, Pru. He might let you take him to his dad's for a bit so he gets away from the saw noise."

"It depends. You've noticed he doesn't seem to think anything's wrong."

"He *says* he doesn't. But I get the feeling he's aware of it on another level."

"Ah, my metaphysical sister." A branch flew over my head. "Oops, flying trees! Want to go back inside and keep an eye on Sam while I help out here?" Celeste was already gone.

For the next half hour I got into the swing of dodging and dragging the smaller limbs as Ollie chucked them off the roof. I checked the rope on the tree at the back. My sailor's knot was holding. Just as I was rounding the corner to the front of the house again, I heard a snarl, like the saw had caught on something besides wood, then a howl of pain that stood the hairs up on the back of my neck. I ran.

"Ollie! Ollie! Are you all right?" The chainsaw growled again and stopped. I ducked just in time to see it hurling down not two feet from me.

"Ollie!" I climbed up the ladder, at the same time yelling for Celeste.

"Cel! Come quick! I think Ollie's hurt!" My eyes were even with the edge of the roof. Sitting up above the tree, which was the only thing keeping him from following the flight of the chainsaw, sat Ollie holding his left calf. His hands and jeans were dripping with blood.

"Oh my God, Ollie! Can you move?"

"I'm afraid to. I don't know how deep it went. I'm afraid to let go of my leg."

Below I heard a door slam, then one of the car doors, then, "Where the HELL is my first aid kit!?" Sam?

Celeste called up. "Sam heard Ollie cry out. Jumped up and went to get his first aid kit."

"I brought it into the house! It's by the coat rack!" Celeste disappeared.

The next minute Sam was at the bottom of the ladder. Awake, alert, and all business.

"Pru, climb down! Let me up there!"

"Should I call 911?"

"Not yet. Wait until I assess the situation."

Geez. Was this the guy I just left mumbling into his mustache a while ago? Never mind, I told myself as I scrabbled down the ladder as fast as I could. "It's his left calf. He's afraid to let go of it long enough to come down. It's bleeding badly." I was trembling. I don't do blood and guts very well.

Sam climbed up quickly, his first aid kit banging against the side of the ladder. In a heartbeat I could hear him talking to Ollie. Cool, calm, and extremely collected. A whole other Sam. I could hear his voice sounding like he was the horse whisperer this time.

"Okay. Ollie, I'll take care of it. Here, let me see it. Let go. It's okay. I'm going to put a tourniquet on your leg above the cut to stop the bleeding. You hit a tibial artery. No, don't panic. It's not that bad, just looks like it. There. Good. There we go. It's slowing down already. Now I'm just going to stuff a couple of these babies in."

"Tampons?" I heard Ollie gasp.

"Don't worry, never been used." If he was trying to distract Ollie he did a good job, because I heard a slight chuckle. Celeste joined me under the ladder just in time for that last comment. She raised her eyebrows.

I told her, "I was wondering why he had tampons in his first aid kit."

"Guess they're doing the job they were made for," she cracked.

"Okay, Ollie, I'm going to wrap this around the stuffing, then I'll help you down. We'll get you to the hospital, you'll be fine. Helluva scar, but definitely in working order."

"It'll match the one on the other leg I got from skateboarding when I was fourteen."

I looked at Celeste. "He'll be fine," she said.

"Pru," Sam called. "The bleeding's under control. We can get him to the hospital faster than if we call 911. We'll have to take him in your car. Mine isn't big enough to keep his leg stretched out and elevated. I'm bringing him down now." Celeste moved to hold the ladder as I hurried off to make the car ready. When I returned, Ollie was sitting on the deck leaning against Sam, his cut leg propped up on one of the porch posts. Sam leaned forward every few minutes to release the tourniquet.

"Will the tree stay that way until we get back?" I asked.

Ollie looked up, a bit greenish in color. "Was your knot good?" he asked weakly. I nodded. "Well, there's your answer."

Sam helped Ollie stand up on his good leg and lean on the deck post. He then stood in front of Ollie to drape him over his shoulders, and carried him in a fireman's carry to the car. I rushed ahead to open the door. Celeste followed with the afghan and a pillow from the study.

"Good thinking," I told her. "Let me get my purse. Will you keep Velvet with you?"

"Definitely. I'll take her with me to the farm and let her play with my guys. I'll bring her back around three or so. Call if you get hung up at the hospital." She looked at Sam who was fussing over Ollie in the car, making sure his leg was high enough over the seat back. She motioned for me to follow her to the house. "What do you think about Sam?" she asked.

I finally let my professional self use what it knew. "He'll be fine until we get Ollie to the hospital, but with all that has happened in the last two days and now this, when his adrenaline levels out he will crash, big time. I'll drop by the VA on the way back for him to get his meds. By that time he may need more than that. I'll see if I can get someone there to talk to him."

"That was my thought, too."

"So why did you ask?"

"I wasn't *entirely* sure," she rejoined. I elbowed her in the ribs. We climbed the porch steps into the house. I grabbed my purse, patted Velvet, and rushed out the door again to ambulance duty.

CHAPTER TWENTY EIGHT

As it turned out, there weren't many obstacles between the house and the hospital. On the back roads, the car splashed through water in a couple of low spots. Some trees had fallen down in the woods beyond, but because much of the area was farm land cleared years ago, there was only one place where a couple of trees had blown down across the road. Most of these had already been bucked up and rolled to the side by the time we drove by, with the neighbors out to make sure the traffic went around what was left.

I stopped long enough to find out how the neighbors had fared, which was just about how we had. With Sam clucking at me to get going, I told them we had an injury in the back seat and had to go. The rest of the way was a piece of cake. Sam kept talking to Ollie, checking his pulse and the tourniquet frequently, and monitoring the bleeding. I kept the heat on high which was making me sweat, but which Sam demanded to offset the shock Ollie was beginning to demonstrate.

We arrived at the Emergency Door to the St. Cloud hospital in under a half hour – which I never could have done on a regular day when traffic was normal. Sam hopped out, went in and immediately reappeared with a nurse and a gurney. Between him and the nurse, they eased Ollie out of the car onto the flat surface and rolled him in. I looked for a parking place and followed them. After locating the cubical where they had put Ollie, I sat in the waiting area. I was close enough to hear the nurse chuckle about the dressing in Ollie's leg as she unwound the gauze to assess the wound. She and Sam talked a bit and then Sam materialized, his once bloodied hands clean.

"They're going to sew him up and admit him for observation. We'll call later to see how he is."

"Should I go say goodbye?"

"They already gave him a sedative so he's pretty out of it."

"Okay, then. The next stop is the VA to get you taken care of."

"What do you mean? I'm fine," he said as he climbed into the passenger side.

"Right. You did a great job with Ollie, Sam."

"Did what I had to do," he answered. Then in a gesture reminiscent of Elias, he put his head back on the seat, his eyes already closing.

"I'll wake you up when we get there." No answer to that one. Just his signature snuffle. I put the SUV in gear and nosed out of the parking lot. Oh boy, what was I going to do when we got to the VA? As I was driving down Division back to the VA turnoff, I remembered Sam pointing out the direction to the Pharmacy and the Mental Health Unit. Where to go first? Sam needed his meds but I knew he might not be making enough sense to pick them up without someone from the Mental Health Unit helping him. That decided me. I turned onto the grounds, slowed my speed for the speed bumps, and turned right this time around to the back of the hospital instead of left when we had visited Hank. I followed the signs for the Mental Health Unit and looked for parking. I found a space under a hickory tree. Here goes.

"Sam," I called somewhat loudly given that he was sitting a foot away from me.

No response.

"Sam!" Louder this time. A stirring. I knew how I could wake him up for sure but I wasn't going to touch him. Not after last time. I tried one more time.

"SAM!!" I yelled. He started twitching and mumbling.

"Yessir! Did my bes' Sir, think I got 'im set up. Dunno. Can't find it. When are the choppers...?" He reached out as if to work something with his hands.

"Sam! It's okay. You're just having a dream. It's Pru. We're at the VA. Got to get your meds."

"S'right. Be right there." He settled down again, snoring once more.

At this point I realized he wasn't going anywhere, so it was time to go into the hospital and get help. I took the sidewalk up to the brick building. The inside was concrete with the same greenish paint on the walls I had seen yesterday. A few couples were sitting in the waiting room. I approached the receptionist, a fifty-something woman with red henna doing its best to hide her emerging white hairs. She had a pair of turquoise reading glasses perched on her nose.

"Can I help you?"

"Er, my friend is a Vietnam vet, and he just had an episode with chainsaws. I can't get him to wake up. I think he needs help."

"Ma'am, the Emergency room is two buildings down. You need to get him there quickly!"

It took me a minute to figure out what she was talking about.

"Oh, no, he isn't hurt. It was the noise, and helping another guy whose leg was cut. He used to be a medic. I think he sees someone here."

"Oh, well. Last name?"

"Barrett."

"Last four?"

"What?"

She sighed. "Last four digits of his social security number."

"I have no clue. We were friends as kids. We just met up again. I don't know a whole lot about his personal life."

She must have sensed the anxiety starting to creep into my voice. After all, if she worked here she must have some skills with the clients.

"Oh, then. Let's see what I can find with just the name. First name?"

"Samuel"

Her fingers flew over the keys. She then hit the Enter key several times.

"Ah, here we are. Samuel Barrett. From Ontario? Local Address: 11 Sunnyside Acres?"

"Ah, yeah." He must have given his Dad's address. "Does it say who his counselor is?"

She scrolled down a bit more. "I'm not at liberty to give you that information. All I can tell you is that he is in our database."

"Well, is there *some*one who can help me wake him up to get him in here?" I was starting to lose it. It had been a trying couple of days.

"Do you need some help, Belinda?" From behind me appeared a small man with fuzzy grey hair fluffed out around his head like a halo, a bushy beard, and heavy horn- rimmed glasses. He wasn't much taller than I and wore crinkled up khakis and a Mr. Rogers sweater over a white button-down shirt.

"I think so, Dr. Len." She then explained my request. "And the thing is I don't know what to tell her as she isn't family or his spouse."

He turned to me. "I'm Len Slovak, Sam's doctor. She can't tell you that, but I can. Where is he? What happened?" He steered me into an intake room, and closed the door against the curious ears of the other waiting patients. I sat on the vinyl chair on one side of the table. He took the chair on the other side and leaned on the table as I introduced myself. I told him my connection to Sam and explained, as succinctly as I could, the events of the last two days starting with our visit to Hank. As the doctor listened to me, I noticed his eyes – grey with yellow flecks reminding me of a compassionate owl. They made me want to tell him my life story and problems.

"So it was you who caused all that activity in the retirement wing."

"How did you know that?"

"News travels fast in the mental health community." He paused. "All without any identifying characteristics of course."

"Ironic, isn't it, given the confidential nature of the profession." I told him what I did for a living. He gave me a wry smile.

"Then you know how it is. Now, back to Sam. He had a negative reaction to your friend's reliving his war trauma, followed by the storm and the chainsaw noises. He has been having periods where he has drifted off, forgotten parts of the day, slept heavily at times yet couldn't get to sleep at night without the medication your sister offered him. In the middle of one of his sleeping spells he was immediately alert to your friend's cry of pain and demonstrated skill and good judgment in administering him first aid."

"That just about sums it up," I said.

"It must have been a difficult twenty four hours."

"More for him than for me," I protested.

"You're a good friend for Sam to have," offered Dr. Slovak.

"I'm not sure I've really helped at all," I replied.

"He's here isn't he?" His wise eyes blinked at me.

"I guess."

"So let's go out and see what we can do for him now."

I jumped up. "But how will we get him in, you and I?"

"Because between the two of us we are just about his size?" Dr. Slovak's eyes twinkled behind his glasses. "We use our heads!"

Dr. Slovak led the way out of the building back to the car. I looked in. I called Sam's name before I opened the car door. Dr. Slovak did the same. Maybe Sam had been able to sleep it off a bit, or maybe it was the addition of the good doctor's voice, but this time Sam responded.

"Huh? Where are we? That you, Doc?"

"Certainly is, Sam. Missed you the last few weeks."

Sam sat up, ran his hands through his hair until he came to his snarled ponytail. He pulled the rubber band out and shook his hair. He looked at Dr. Slovak with a sheepish grin. "Been working on getting around to it."

"Maybe now would be a good time. I'm free. What about you?" The gray eyes twinkled again.

Sam looked at me then said," Dr. Len is the main reason I came back here. He put me back together the first time when I returned from 'Nam. But I haven't exactly been a regular. He looked at the doc. "Hey, I went to group. I was going to come back to see you."

"Oh, you mean I'm more than just a prescription pad?" I thought Dr. Slovak was being a little rough on Sam, but he didn't seem to mind.

"You knew you'd have another chance at me when my present one ran out." Sam graced him with his dimpled smile. He stretched. "But, okay, if Pru doesn't mind waiting a bit." He looked at me.

God, no. I was so relieved. "Not at all. I carry a book in my purse for situations just as these. You guys go and do your thing."

Sam nodded. Dr. Slovak stood up from leaning in the car window and stretched his back. Sam got out of the car, tucked his shirt in, and together they walked back to the building, another pair of Mutt and Jeffs.

CHAPTER TWENTY NINE

I must have dozed off, because the next thing I knew, Sam was calling my name for a change. I noticed he didn't tap me on the shoulder. I was grateful for that.

"You mind coming in for a minute? Dr. Len wants to talk to you about something."

Great. The only time that happens is when I've done something wrong. My thought must have shown on my face because Sam said, "Don't panic, Pru. It's not about you. It's me."

"Oh then, I'm already there!" I smiled at him, closed my book and picked up my purse. "Did you get your meds already?"

"Not yet. So you might want to bring your book. Everything at the VA takes a while."

I grabbed the book and stuffed it in my purse, then rolled the windows up and locked the car. Back in the building, the receptionist smiled at me this time. I had obviously gained status as I followed the official veteran down the hall to Dr. Slovak's office. The room had high windows, comfortable stuffed armchairs, and an old oak desk with a rolling oak chair made softer by matching quilted blue and green cushions. A variegated spider plant draped its leaves from the top of a tall bookcase stuffed with psychological and war-related tomes. Perched on top of a nearby standing lamp was a baseball cap with the words, "Honey, I shrunk the Vets!" embroidered on the front. Dr. Slovak noticed my chuckle as I saw that.

"My son's addition."

"Cute. But how do the vets react to it?"

"Sam?" Dr. Slovak let Sam answer that one.

"Just 'cause we're a little nuts doesn't mean we don't have a sense of humor, Pru."

"I knew that. It's been a tough few days. Mine has disappeared a bit."

"That's fine. I feel badly that I've put you through all this."

"It's not like you had a whole lot of choice."

"Well, that's what the doc and I have been talking about. You know the group I talked about? I only went once." I remembered the guy at the retirement unit mentioning something about that. "And I not only forgot to get one of the prescriptions filled, I also cancelled a couple of appointments with Dr. Len. Told the secretary I had to get my store going."

"When the veterans experience war triggers," Dr. Slovak intervened, "short-term memory is affected and denial is very strong. There aren't many people who are really excited to relive all the chaos again, but if they don't start talking about what's going on and how it relates to what they went through, while letting the medications help, many just get worse. It's kind of a 'Catch 22'."

"So, if I had been a good boy I might not have had such severe reactions to the events of the past two days, which," he added, "I admit I still don't remember much about. Dr. Len wanted to know if you would repeat what you told him earlier so I can listen to it while he's here."

I was beginning to feel anxious about getting back to the house. I was wondering about Adrian, and remembered Paul and Annie would be arriving in a few hours. But if it was going to help Sam, I would make the time. As a result, I spent the next forty-five minutes or so in my first therapy session with a war veteran. Of all the information, the one that upset Sam the most was my description of him taking me down during the storm.

"I could have really hurt you."

"But you didn't. You were trying to save me, or so you thought."

"Don't you see? That's the crazy part of it. I think you're in danger, because I'm fucked up, then I do something that actually *puts* you in danger." He shook his head and ran his fingers through his hair.

"Sam," Dr. Slovak said, "that is something we can keep working on." He looked at his appointment book. "I can make some time for you Thursday if you're serious about coming again." Sam nodded. "In the meantime don't forget to pick up *all* of your prescriptions, and Pru," Dr. Slovak turned to me, "is it all right if he stays at your house until Thursday?"

"We've got family coming, and there may be more noise as we have to clear the woods near the house, but if you think he'll be okay, sure. We're all getting kind of used to him."

"I think the doc doesn't trust I'll show up on Thursday," Sam said.

"That's part of it, to be frank. Also, Sam, at this point you're not stable enough to be on your own at that store. So it's set?" He looked at both of us. I nodded. Sam also, a bit reluctantly.

"Good, so get out of here so you have a chance of picking up your meds sometime in the next millennium." He referred to his computer. "I added a different anti-anxiety medication that will help with the noise of the next two days, Sam, but won't make you so sleepy. You can report its effectiveness when I see you Thursday." With that, he shook hands with both of us then turned back to his computer. We were dismissed.

CHAPTER THIRTY

I thought Sam and Dr. Slovak were kidding about the wait at the pharmacy, but by the time we had waited long enough to take a side trip to the cafeteria (franchises are alive and well in the VA hospitals) I was concerned about getting back on time for Annie and Paul. I looked at my watch. It had only been an hour, it just seemed like two. Finally, the harried-looking clerk called Sam's name, checked his VA card, and made him sign for a small brown paper bag with his name and social security number on the front. Sam retrieved the medication and refill slip and gave the slip as well as the bag back to the clerk. I raised my eyebrows in a silent question.

"This way I make sure I don't forget and throw it in some wastebasket where some identity thief can have a great time with my social security number."

"I never thought of that."

"Sometimes it pays to be mildly paranoid."

By this time we were at the car. After I unlocked it, I offered Sam the keys but he shook his head and slipped in the passenger side. He took one of the pill bottles out of his pocket, tapped two tablets out, and popped them into his mouth. I wondered if he was going to fall asleep again once he got settled, but he was awake and basically back to the Sam I was beginning to know before all the events of the past two days. We proceeded at the leisurely pace provided by the speed bumps until we left the grounds, then hooked a left so we could get back on 15th again and access Division.

"Do you mind if we stop off at Home Depot on the way back?" Sam asked.

I checked my watch again. "I think we have time. As long as we aren't picking up fencing material."

"On a different day that would be a good idea as it is probably cheaper than the Lumber One in Avon, but I wasn't thinking of that. I want to pick up a pair of ear mufflers. When we get back to your place, I want to go down and see if there is anything stashed under that old car. If I use the head gear with these new meds, maybe I won't have such an intense reaction to the chainsaw."

I nodded, then decided to ask him something that had been on my mind since talking with Dr. Slovak.

"Sam, do you think what the doctor was saying happened to Hank?"

"What do you mean?"

"That maybe he was never able to talk to anybody about his experiences and feelings, so his PTSD just got worse."

Sam thought a minute. "Possibly. In World War Two, because the guys went over as a unit and returned as a unit, not to mention returning home to parades and hugs and kisses and gratitude, most of the veterans adjusted pretty well." He paused. "But for the same reason, the ones who didn't, never really talked to anyone about it. So, yeah, it might have been what happened."

"Are you going to follow up with Dr. Slovak?"

"I haven't decided yet."

I was silent.

"Yeah, yeah, I know what I told him. I probably will. Obviously it's not my favorite way to spend my time."

"But it might help you get back to your life."

"Speaking of which, what progress are you making in your effort to move on with yours?"

"We weren't talking about me."

"Now we are."

Oh, I guess the other conversation was over. "I keep waiting for that next thing to happen to tell me in what direction to go."

"What next thing would that be?"

"Currently, to see what Jess found out in her interview with Mr. Barstow."

"Which will help you how?"

"There you go again, better at asking the questions than answering them, old friend."

"Pru, it's got to be a two way street. Friends do that, you know."

"I know it works that way with my women friends. I'm just not very good at trusting that process with men."

Sam let that one go. Instead he repeated, "How will what Mr. Barstow says help you?"

I signaled to go right into the Home Depot parking lot. "I keep thinking that we'll somehow find the answer to Mum's death, and why the coat was hanging in the woods, not to mention how Hank and Mr. Barstow were involved. I'm hoping that I'll learn why Dad kept the coat there if it was Mum's and if there was something more than his war experiences that kept him from sleeping. Maybe then I'll be able to see where I fit in the picture and figure out what to do next."

We parked and sat for a few minutes. Sam replied, "You've lived all of your life until this last week not knowing any of the answers to those questions, and you've lived a pretty functional life."

I laughed. "Depends on your definition of 'functional'."

"Good point. My view of that word may be a bit off the mainstream."

"A bit?" I tossed him a glance. He responded by getting out of the car. I followed him and we went in search of ear protectors for him.

It was 3:30 PM by the time I turned into my driveway. It is impossible to go to Home Depot and not wander the aisles. We avoided buying anything else, but we had to price the lumber and the fencing. Sam was right. It was cheaper than Avon, but when you added the delivery fee that was waived at Lumber One because you were buying it locally, it came out to about the same thing. We agreed to support the small guy.

As I rounded the corner to the house, I saw Paul and Annie's car, Celeste's truck, and then recognized a familiar figure carrying branches from the front of the house to the woodshed, Velvet trotting happily alongside him. I pulled the car up, slammed it into park, and was out the door before even turning off the ignition, hoping Sam might do that. I called as I ran, "Adrian, you made it! I am *so* glad to see you!" With that, I hurled myself into his just empty arms and was encompassed by a bear hug that rivaled that of his Uncle Paul. I returned the hug and stood back to look at him. "You look great!" Adrian was taller than Paul, but not quite Sam's height. His dishwater blond hair was worn just over his collar and pushed back off his forehead. His jeans were starting to tear at one knee. Dad's strong nose and square chin, combined with David's soft, light blue eyes, made him seem like a study in contrasts when he was really about the least convoluted person I knew. He looked me over.

"And you, Mum, look a helluva lot better than I thought given Jess' description of your recent experiences. I expected a wraith, and here you are, sunburned, bouncy, with the old snap back in your eyes!"

I looked around. "Where's everyone else?"

"Paul and Annie tramped off down the path to the farm to see how bad the woods were, and Aunt Celeste is out front helping me with that tree that was hanging on your roof. I was pretty confused when I first got here and there was no one in sight, but there was half a tree suspended from a rope on your roof. I could hear the TV going inside but I couldn't see anyone. For a moment I freaked that something had happened to you, but then Aunt Celeste arrived and told me – 'the *rest* of the story'." He looked behind me and extended his hand. "And you must be Sam. I'm Adrian." Sam reached out and they shook.

"And a good thing he was here!" Celeste called from the corner of the house, joining us. "How is Ollie? What's the news?"

Sam filled her in, telling her she could probably call later on to see how Ollie was doing and when they would let him leave. I turned and greeted Velvet then back-tracked and grabbed my stuff from the car. Just as well, since it was still running. Way to go, Sam. Maybe not as tuned in as I thought. I turned the car off and ran into the house, Velvet prancing alongside. She needed water, so I attended to that. As I passed the kitchen counter on the way to the sink, I saw a brown paper package. A quick look at it told me it was from Jess. I ran to the door.

"When did this come?" I called. Adrian looked up.

"With me. I got a ride from the highway with the FedEx guy delivering it"

"Someone go find Paul and Annie. Let's listen to it."

"Down, girl," called Celeste. "I'm sure as hell not going to drag my ass through the woods to track them down. They'll be back. There's plenty of time."

"Guys?" I looked at Adrian and Sam beseechingly. Adrian shrugged his shoulders. "We've got to finish lowering that tree, Ma."

"Don't look at me. I'm with Adrian." Sam crossed to the car to get his package.

I retreated into the house, pouting. I tore the package open and was pleased to find a note from Jess folded up around the cassette.

"Mom," it read. "Thanks for letting me do this. I really enjoyed Mr. Barstow, not to mention his grandson who is sweet and really hot!" Oh yeah? The note continued. "I tried to ask your questions, but I also ended up doing some follow-up ones of my own. Let me know what you think and how it fits with everything else. I love you, Mom. You're the greatest. Jess."

Well, I thought. At least *someone* else was excited about this. I looked out of the kitchen window. They had all scattered. Adrian was probably on the other side of the house, untying the rope that kept the rest of the tree on the roof, while I could hear Sam and Celeste out front, waiting for it to be lowered. There was no sign of my brother and Annie. So, since Adrian's comment about hearing the TV told me the power was back on, I did what I do best when I'm in a situation I can't control. I cleaned.

CHAPTER THIRTY ONE

I started upstairs, where I vacuumed the accumulated dust-bunnies out of the corners and from under the beds, and then did a quick once-over in the bathroom. I made up the bed in Paul's old room for Sam and the one in Celeste's room for Adrian. If Annie and Paul decided to stay, they could have Mum and Dad's room.

Back downstairs, I dragged the vacuum cleaner into the study. As I was dusting off the desk, it occurred to me that I hadn't really explored it yet. I decided to start with the center drawer. When I pulled it out, all I saw were a couple of pens in the tray and some paper clips. As I pushed the drawer back in, there was a jiggling noise further back. I pulled it all the way out and in the back corner found a small key, the kind that fits into a padlock. I pocketed it and finished my cleaning. By that time I heard people talking on the porch, and the next moment Celeste and Adrian burst through the door followed by Paul, Annie, Sam and Velvet.

"Phew!" "The tree is finally down," announced Celeste. "All we have to do is buck it up at some point."

"And you'll have tons of firewood if we cut up the trees that were blown down between here and the farm," added Paul.

"Except you have to share those," reminded Celeste.

"It's a mess out there," cried Annie.

"Yeah, I know," I said. "I went out earlier to check on the coat tree with Velvet."

"We couldn't find the way into it", said Paul.

"It's okay," I replied, "Velvet can." Adrian looked at us, questions written all over his face.

"Something to do with the smell," Sam explained.

"So are you guys ready to listen to the tape Jess sent?"

"Did it come?" asked Paul. Why didn't someone come and get us?"

I made a face at Celeste, Adrian, and Sam.

Paul noticed and grinned. "Am I missing something?"

"Not really. I asked these guys if someone would get you about an hour ago, and received no enthusiasm whatsoever."

"Hey, Mom, we were busy," protested Adrian.

"Okay, okay, I give up." I started laughing. "So, do you all want to get some tea, and we'll get to it?" There was a general hubbub of agreement and a flurry of activity as everyone did a little to haul out tea, sugar, cream, and make some cinnamon toast to go with it. The latter was Adrian's contribution.

"Gotta have cinnamon toast with afternoon tea," he declared. I smiled at him. It had been a Sunday tradition when he and Jess were growing up.

Finally we assembled in the living room. I thought we could use my cassette player until Adrian mentioned the small fact that it had no external speakers. Sam remembered seeing a small combination radio and tape player on Dad's desk. How had I missed that? I went into the study, and there it was in plain sight, pushed up against the wall at the back of the desk. It reminded me of the key. As I reentered the living room, I took it out of my pocket and held it up for all to see.

"Hey folks, I almost forgot. Look what I found way in the back of Dad's center desk drawer. What do you suppose it goes to?"

Celeste frowned. "Oh great, another loose end. What next?"

"Maybe it'll lead to the big ball of twine." This from Annie.

"What twine?" Paul asked.

"I think she is speaking metaphorically, aren't you, Aunt Annie?" Annie winked at Adrian. Paul looked at her.

"Oh," was all he said.

"Maybe we'll have more of an idea about the key after we listen to Mr. Barstow's interview," Sam suggested.

"So, shall we? I said. I put the tape in the machine and pushed "Play".

* * *

Jess's voice: *"Hi Mom, everybody. I am at Mr. Barstow's house. Brian, his grandson is also here. Mr. Barstow, are you ready to start?"*

A low voice replied, *"Ready when you are, Ms. Jess."*

Jess again. "Okay. My Mom and Aunt Celeste and Uncle Paul wanted me to ask you some questions about my granddad's service in World War Two."

"In the OSS. Right."

"But, first, if you don't mind, would you tell me how you and Granddad met? Mum didn't go into a lot of detail about that part."

"Sure. We met at Yale. I was studying pre-law and government. Your grandfather was in graduate school in Far Eastern Languages. We met in an upper level policy class we both needed. We knew by the end of the first class that our minds ran along the same track. We started studying together, to challenge each other. Everyone called us Mutt and Jeff due to our size difference. As for me, I guess I was stuck up enough to be amazed that someone like your grandfather could have come out of the Middle West."

"Where did you grow up?"

"New York City, like your great uncle and grandmother. Your great uncle Hugh was an old friend of mine. I introduced your granddad to him, which is how Arthur met your grandmother."

"Oh, that's news to me. What happened with you and Grandad?" asked Jess.

"I went on to law school and your granddad finished his program and went over to England on that scholarship." Ed paused. "Are you aware of the events during that time?"

"You mean how he blew his exams because he was out protesting? Yep, that's pretty much part of the family history."

"I was one of the few people who knew how much that hurt him, and how badly he felt that he wasn't able to provide your grandmother with the kind of life she expected to live."

"From all accounts, she seemed to do fine in Minnesota."

"Be that as it may, your grandfather was undeterred in his thinking that he had not lived up to his potential and had failed your grandmother."

"So how did joining up for a war thousands of miles away when he was over-age anyway make up for that?" Jess was getting into this interviewing thing.

"I'm not sure someone from your generation would understand, since the wars that are more familiar to you are Vietnam and the Gulf War, which were very different from WWII."

"In what ways are you thinking?"

"In terms of wanting to participate in a higher purpose, I guess. Men lined up for blocks to sign up for the armed services. Women volunteered where they could. Unless they were old enough to have fought in WWI, those too old to enlist felt they were letting their country down."

"So, that's how Granddad felt?"

"In a nutshell."

"So you helped him sign up?"

"Yes."

"How did you do that?"

"I was working for the government when William Donovan was assigned to pull together America's first coordinated intelligence organization."

"The CIA?"

"It's precursor. The OSS."

"So you joined up?"

"Yes, I was fascinated at the dual objectives of gathering facts and statistics that would help our armed forces, and planning sabotage and guerrilla operations that would hurt the enemy."

"So you were in the think tank part of it?" Jess asked.

I was getting annoyed with Jess beginning every sentence with "so".

"If you want to call it that, yes I suppose I was."

"Did Granddad know what you were doing?"

That's better, I thought.

"Not until I recruited him for Detachment 101 in Burma. Each time we got together during the early part of the war, he questioned me about what I was doing and what the opportunities were for someone like him. He knew by the fact that I avoided telling him what I did that it was clandestine. So when the final build-up was on in Burma and they were looking for more people proficient in

Chinese, Japanese and Burmese, Arthur came to mind. His years of working on the farm and operating your great granddad's ham radio didn't hurt either."

"Is that why they overlooked his age?"

"Probably. Of course they might have decided against him if he was some overweight bureaucrat who had been sitting on his behind all these years, but your granddad was active and in great shape for his age."

"My Mom and Aunt Celeste found a journal he wrote on the way over and back. They had some questions about some of his experiences."

"Ah, yes, the parachute journal."

Oh, so Dad didn't keep that a secret.

"What kind of experience did he have over there?"

Sam leaned forward, listening intently to the next part.

"Working with the Kachins was fulfilling for your grandfather, since their culture was one he had studied for many years. In my conversations with the other Det 101 guys, most of them reported feeling energized and fully alive from their experience. It was a very close group.

"Did he tell you about the incident when he froze?"

"He what?"

"He couldn't react to a threatening Japanese sentry and his friend Naw Hpraw had to save him."

Silence. "No, he never told me about that."

Oh, so Dad had kept *that* part a secret.

"Why don't you think he told you?"

"I can only conclude out of shame and embarrassment. He must have felt so distant from his comrades. No wonder."

"No wonder what?"

Ah, my persistent Jess. Reminded me of the days when she tried to persuade us to let her go to rock concerts alone with her friends when she was thirteen.

"Well, most of the guys from Det 101 went on to pretty high-powered lives after the war."

"Like what?"

"Let's see. There was a three star general, a U.S. ambassador, a U.S. Representative, not to mention lawyers, doctors, inventors, editors, engineers, artists, business men..."

"Whew! I get the picture."

"Yeah, pretty impressive company. Your grandad was known for his diplomatic and translating skills from Minnesota all the way to the East Coast and beyond. If Arthur was ashamed enough of how he comported himself in Burma, no wonder he dove into his postwar career to such an extent when he returned. Poor Arthur, trying to prove himself all over again."

"Do you think he ever told Grandmum?"

Now that's the sixty-four thousand dollar question.

"Hard to tell. The energy he put into his career after the war negatively affected his relationship with Adrienne, which might not have been the case if she had understood why he was so driven."

I looked at Celeste and Paul. It was their turn to lean forward to hear better.

"What happened between them when he came back?"

"First, Adrienne had missed him, and I think had felt a bit abandoned by him when he left for Burma. Secondly, he wasn't allowed to share any of his experiences with her until the mission was finally declassified, which didn't help, and then with all his renewed energy going into his career, they spent much less time together than before his service."

"Were they going to get divorced?"

Celeste and Paul looked at each other in surprise.

"I don't think that was an option in those days, for them at least. I think your grandmother dealt with the estrangement by getting involved in her work and in politics."

I looked at Sam. I was wondering if there had been more between Elias and Mum than Elias was admitting. Sam looked back at me with an expression of "who knows?"

"It's weird to think of your grandparents as real people with relationship problems."

It's hard enough when they are your parents, I thought.

"*I'm sure it is. They must have come to some agreement in the summer of '49. Arthur said that he and Adrienne were looking at working on some project together.*" Barstow paused. "*But then Pru's birth changed all that.*"

It was my turn to raise my eyebrows.

"How?"

"*Well, as you know, your grandmother was a pretty assertive woman. As much as she loved Pru, a baby at this time in her life and career was a big surprise. It took some adjusting to and Adrienne was very clear that she wasn't going to be the only one adjusting. However, for a while Adrienne was left alone with Paul and the baby on many occasions as Arthur continued traveling to lecture and consult. In addition, when Arthur was absent, Adrienne had to deal with Hank, who was having more and more problems. It was a very stressful time for your grandmother.*"

"No doubt," said Jess.

No doubt indeed, I thought.

"Were they still having problems when Grandmum died? Do you know what was going on the day she died? Did you visit her that day? What was the deal about Hank anyway?"

"Slow down, young lady!" Ed was laughing. "*I'm an old man. I can only go so fast. Let's take a break. Brian, can you get us some tea?*"

I punched the "stop" button. "Anyone here want to take a break?" I stretched and got up to get some more tea. Sam and Celeste disappeared in opposite directions. Velvet thought the activity meant she was going to get a walk. Paul was heading outside, so I asked him if he would take her around the house. Annie and Adrian chatted. In about ten minutes everyone was reassembled.

Paul said, "I noticed lots of nonverbals going around as we were listening. Anyone have any comments?"

"Tons," replied Celeste, "but I want to wait until we've heard the entire interview." She looked around. We all nodded.

"At the risk of sounding like Jess, So then, here we go." Chuckles from the peanut gallery. I punched the play button and sat back again. Ed's voice started this time.

"Ms. Jess, I will try to answer your questions, but because I am cantankerous from all those years of working in intelligence, I will address the last one first. You knew that Hank had landed on Omaha Beach on D Day."

"Yes. Mum filled me in. She said he drank a lot when he first came back but then seemed to be all right for a while."

"Exactly. Even the men who saw terrible things returned with the support of their troops and families and communities. But I fear that the positive aspects of that support at times kept the more damaged veterans from being able to talk about their experiences, which over time could result in more emotional difficulties for them. Some of them dealt with it by drinking. Hank was one of them."

Sam looked at me as if to affirm my question earlier about Hank.

"How did that get better?"

"Mostly because of your grandfather and grandmother. Arthur listened and they both welcomed Hank as the member of the family he always seemed to be, which motivated him to try to keep the drinking under control. Your great-grandmother Dillen believed in Hank and supported him in returning to his job as farm manager. But then not surprisingly, it was the death of Dirk the pig that began Hank's downward slide. That and a bad thresher accident at the farm."

I looked at Sam who nodded as if that made perfect sense. Paul, Celeste, and Annie noticed. Adrian was focused on the tape.

"Was that when he started wandering in the woods or just staying in his apartment?"

"Yes. Your great grandmother had to replace him as manager, but she didn't have the heart to kick him out of the barn apartment."

"And Grandmum had to spend a lot of time with him 'cause Granddad was gone so much?"

"Right. Hank took almost more care than the new baby. That's when Adrienne finally sat Arthur down and read him the riot act."

"Did it work?"

"Funnily enough, I think it was beginning to. Arthur was staying closer to home, declining some of the national forums to which he was invited. He might have finally told Adrienne his war secret, because he had avoided the Det 101 reunions until then, but Adrienne encouraged him to attend, and supported him by going too. At the reunion I attended with them the summer before your grandmum died, your grandfather indicated things were going better. He told me he had finally heard what Adrienne was saying and was trying to come to terms with his overworking habits."

"And then she died. How sad."

"Indeed."

There were a few moments of silence. I felt that sadness to my toes. It was my sadness, too. Luckily the talking began again.

"The day I visited her though, I don't think she was very happy with him, but it was because of some of Arthur's behavior that was a holdover from the earlier days."

"Was that the day she died? Elias, Grandmum's political friend, thought he saw a car coming down the road after he dropped her off that day."

"Yes, that was me. I noticed his car, too. Adrienne told me she had just returned from a political meeting in St. Cloud."

"Did she have her fur coat on?"

"Oh, dear, let me see. Good thing I was trained to notice details, otherwise my old brain would be useless to you, Ms. Jess. No. It was hung over the newel post of the stairs."

"Mr. Barstow," Jess said, her voice slowing down. "Was she alive when you left her?"

Absolute dead silence both on the tape and in the living room. Then a splutter.

"You think I…? Oh, my dear, NO! I adored your grandmother and grandfather. I would never have done anything to hurt them! Oh, no, no, no!"

"I'm sorry, Mr. Barstow, but my aunt and uncle said you were always so mysterious, that they just didn't know, and you said you were present so close to the time she died. Now that you say you didn't know about grandad's war secret, maybe grandmum did and blamed you for it."

"And because I was a slippery CIA guy of questionable character, I eliminated her?"

"Well..." said Jess.

"I think you've seen too many spy movies, my dear. My job was never that exciting. But to answer your question, she was alive when I left. I had to leave quickly to drive back to the cities before the storm hit. My dear, a day doesn't go by that I don't wonder about whether I could have prevented Adrienne's death if I hadn't been in such a hurry. I did look into it, you can be sure of that, after the police finished their investigation. But Arthur persuaded me to let it go, that it was probably just a terrible accident and that it wasn't worth trying to find the guy. However, it has stayed with me all these years and I have felt so badly that my last memory of her was her cleaning up my messy entwined teabags and dumping them in the garbage."

Well, that answers that question.

"Jess, I think Grandpa has had enough." A new voice that must have been Brian's interrupted.

"I'm almost done, Brian, I just have one more question."

"Stop fussing, Brian. I'm a bit tired, but also strangely energized. I am so happy that Adrienne's family is looking into this after all these years. What's your question, young lady?"

"I was wondering why you were there that day, and what was Grandmum not happy with Granddad about."

"Aha! Yes, I did leave that piece hanging, didn't I?"

"Sort of."

"All right. I had come to Minneapolis for a meeting at the U. of M. I intended to get together with your grandfather to return some things he had lent me, but between his schedule and mine we weren't able to meet. So Arthur asked me to stop by the house and give the articles to Adrienne. What she wasn't happy about was that he had lent these to me several years before to help me overcome a debt – during the period of time I mentioned when they were somewhat estranged – and he hadn't told your grandmother about the loan."

"What were you returning?"

"Oh, I thought you knew. Two of the stones Arthur had brought back from Burma. The star sapphires."

I had a feeling he was going to say that. A glance at my siblings told me they were thinking the same thing. Sam looked intrigued and Adrian totally nonplussed.

"What star sapphires? No one told me about those. What did Grandmum do with them?"

"Put them in the pocket of that fur coat of hers that was on the newel post."

"Do you have any idea what happened to the stones after that?" asked Jess.

"All I know is that your father did get them. Just before he died he used them and some rubies he also had to send for Naw Hpraw's grandson to attend college in the U.S."

So much for any dreams about unlimited wealth.

"Wait until I tell Mum and Aunt Celeste and Uncle Paul!"

"My dear, if they are listening to this, I believe we just did."

I could hear a low chuckle, a louder guffaw in the background and Jess's embarrassed giggle.

"Duh!" was all she said.

"Now, my dear, I think it is time to heed Brian's advice. I need to rest. Thank you so much for this opportunity, and Pru, Celeste, and Paul, if you find out anything more about the mystery of Adrienne's death, I need to be the first to know. After all, I don't know how much longer I'll be around and I would dearly love to know before I die."

"Oh Grandpa!"

"You can count on it, Mr. Barstow. Mum, everyone. This is Jess signing off."

CHAPTER THIRTY TWO

Before I could even push the "stop" button once again, Celeste burst out, "I think the bastard is lying through his teeth!"

"Gee, Cel, don't be bashful. Tell us what you really think!"

"I'm serious, Paul."

"Okay, but why do you think Barstow's lying?"

"Because he's spent his life doing that – lying, obfuscating, giving disinformation, whatever you call it. No wonder his wife finally divorced him. How could you trust anything he has to say?"

"I agree he was probably more than he makes out, but his history with Dad and the family seems to support his assertion that he really cared about Mum and Dad," I countered.

Celeste made a noise that sounded like one of her thoroughbreds snorting. "Yeah, a caring spook with an uncontrollable temper."

"What about the rest of you?" I asked, the conciliator in me rising to the occasion.

Paul said, "I want to believe him, but he had a few too many easy answers."

"Like what, Uncle Paul?" asked Adrian.

"In the first place, he is still the only person we know of who was with Mum just hours before she died."

"Which he pretty much confirmed by saying he was the source of the double-twisted teabags that Donna and I found mentioned in the police report," I added.

"You didn't tell us that, Pru," chastised Paul.

"I really haven't had the chance. It's not as if I was trying to keep it from you. In the police report it was the only thing that seemed unusual – beside the silver being gone."

"But then, they found the silver later," reminded Celeste. "Almost too easily. The teabags pretty much shoot the robber-in-the-storm theory. Then there's the bit about Barstow mentioning that Dad wanted him to stop trying to find out what happened, because it was just a tragic accident. Do we really buy that? Why would Dad have said that when he told all of us it was a robbery gone bad."

"Not everyone," I murmured, but nobody heard me.

"Then there is the fact that Barstow is probably the only one who was in contact with your Mum who would have had the expertise to set the scene up to look like a robbery or an accident," said Sam.

"Except for Dad," I added. All five faces turned to look at me, their expressions horrified. "Maybe there was a reason he was the one who called the police, supposedly the first one to find her." My anger at all of the lies was revving me up. "You're not going to tell me I'm the only one who has thought about that," I kept on, "especially with all the stuff Barstow was saying about how Mum and Dad were having problems."

"Maybe that was part of the disinformation he was feeding us," Celeste added.

"No, Cel. That part *was* true. I remember their arguments about Dad not being around to go to my games, take me fishing, or whatever," Paul protested.

"And Cel, you told me the same thing just the other day when I remembered sitting on the stairs listening to them as a little kid. You headed for the barn when their arguments heated up. Did you forget?"

"No, but I was trying not to go where you just led us, Pru. I convinced myself years ago that the arguments weren't a big deal."

"Yeah, left me and Pru in the middle of them," reprimanded Paul.

"All right, my dears!" Annie broke in. "This is getting us off the topic. As for your dad, do any of you really think he could have ever hurt your mum? Now, really!"

We were all quiet for a while. One by one, Paul, Celeste, and I shook our heads.

"I'm sorry I brought it up," I said. "I was so afraid of that possibility I had to say it out loud."

"All right," said Annie. "Now let's get back to the tape. I for one believe Mr. Barstow. I don't think he was responsible for your Mum's death."

"Why?" asked Celeste.

"Intuition, the sound of his voice."

"Leprechauns," added Paul.

"If you will, Darlin'," Annie smiled at him.

"I believe him too, Aunt Annie."

"Adrian, he makes his living trying to convince people of one thing when the other is right in their face," I challenged him.

"Yes, Mum, but maybe he doesn't do that with the people he cares about. Maybe he just does it in his job when he needs to." Adrian gave me a stern look. I felt my cheeks go red. I wondered if anyone else besides Adrian caught it. "Besides, Jess seemed to really warm up to him and I trust her instincts."

"Instincts, schminstinks," said Celeste. "This isn't the way to solve crimes."

"Okay," Sam put his two cents in. "Let's look at the facts. First, your dad was seen at the college at the time of your mum's death, and Mr. Barstow was definitely at your house at least a half hour before your mum died."

"And he proved it by mentioning the teabags, which was one of the few bits of evidence they found," I added.

"But," put in Paul, now following Annie's lead, "He said he left before the storm, which we know from Pru's memory of that day hit just about the time Mum died."

"So *if* he is telling the truth, it wasn't him," finished Sam.

"We may just have to accept the fact that we are back where we started from, that we may never know the truth," I said, the discouragement obvious in my voice.

"But there were a couple of other things Barstow said that may help us answer some of the other questions we've had," said Annie.

"Like what?" asked Adrian.

"Your mum will have to fill you in later, but there was always this mysterious factor that seemed to be connected to Hank becoming increasingly more disturbed over the years," answered Annie.

"But maybe, according to Barstow, it wasn't so mysterious. It was just losing his life-long companion," added Paul.

"A one-eyed pig, no less!" exclaimed Celeste.

"Hey, Cel, pigs make great pets. It would be just as bad for you if it was one of your favorite dogs or horses. I'd be devastated if I lost Velvet." At the sound of her name, Velvet thrust her nose into my hand. I scratched her soft ears.

"Yeah, yeah, I know. It's just the whole pig thing."

"My guess is that the thresher accident was the final straw," said Sam. "Remember at the VA, Pru? Hank was mumbling about the arms and legs in the water? If he was swimming with body parts on D-Day, then having a worker who was his responsibility lose a body part would have been an enormous trigger."

Sam sure had a way of stopping conversations.

"Hank never had much of a chance at life, did he?" I said.

"Besides Dirk, once his dad died we were really the only family Hank had," said Celeste. "Poor Mum. Me, a teenager, a baby, and a worn-out, freaked-out war vet." Celeste glanced at Sam as soon as the words were out of her mouth, chagrin written all over her face.

"Hey, it's all right, Celeste," Sam turned to her. "You call it like you see it *and* you're probably right. No offense taken."

Adrian spoke up. "I feel so sad that Grandmum and Granddad were doing better and then, Bam! She gets killed." He looked at me. "Especially since you could have had a much different life. I can't imagine what mine would have been like without you." He got up and came over to give me a hug. Tears were stinging my eyes. I hugged him back and pushed him away playfully.

"Cut it out, kid, you'll have me blubbering in front of everyone." I looked around. It didn't help that all I saw was compassion on the faces of my family and Sam.

Annie came to my rescue. "Not to change the subject, but there was also the bit about Barstow giving the stones back." She turned to Adrian. "Your grandfather brought back six precious stones from Burma, given to him by one of the mountain men he fought with. Four rubies and two star sapphires which appear to be the ones he lent to Barstow."

"I've never heard of those," responded Adrian.

"None of us had, until we read Dad's war journal," added Paul.

"There was no mention of any sapphires found on Mum the day she died."

"And Dad never mentioned them in the years after Mum's death," said Celeste. She stopped. "Hey, I just thought of something."

"What?" all of us but Sam asked in unison.

"Maybe the stones disappeared with Mum's coat. If she put them in the pocket of the coat when Barstow returned them and if she was mad at Dad about them, I could see her deciding to take them back East just to annoy him."

"That makes sense," said Annie, "except Barstow said your Dad had them years later when he used them to send for that Burmese man's grandson."

"Shoot! I thought I was onto something. Find the stones, find who took the coat." Celeste looked deflated.

Then it hit me.

"I think you just did, Cel. Dad had the stones years later, so *he* must have been the one who took the coat."

"I can't stand the thought that we are back to Dad as the killer," groaned Paul. "I just can't." He put his head in his hands. Annie went over to him.

"Darlin', he didn't kill your mum. Maybe he took the coat for a different reason entirely."

"Oh Jesus! I feel like we are going round and round! I don't know about you, but I'm hungry and I need to go home. This is much too much to digest in this short a time." Celeste stood up and shook her hair out. "Besides, I have to check on the horses. Glen was going to come over to help Josie and Harris. I have to call the hospital to see how Ollie is and find out when he can leave. Let's call it a day, kiddoes." She walked over to her raincoat and put it on. In a flash, she had hugged each one of us and dashed out the door.

"Whoosh!" I said. I looked at my watch. "Wow, it's late. Annie and Paul, you want to stay the night? You can have Mum and Dad's room. Adrian, you're in Celeste's, Sam you're in Paul's."

Paul and Annie looked at each other. Surprisingly, it was my workaholic brother who put his hand to his forehead and said, "I feel the flu coming on. Annie, my dear, I don't think I'll make it to work tomorrow. What about you?"

Annie leaned her head against Paul's. "Ah, Darlin', guess I have to stay home to take care of you, your fever being so high."

"Great," I said. "The sheets and quilts are in the linen closet upstairs. Unless you don't mind sleeping in Celeste's sheets from last night."

Paul made a face. Annie prodded him. "Then it's helpin' me, you are." With that she dragged him upstairs.

Sam stood up. "I think I'll drop by to see Dad and then pick up some gear at the store."

"You okay to drive?"

"Yep. I haven't taken any of the Lorazapam. Just a couple of those new ones. They don't have the same drowsy effect. I'll be fine." He looked at his watch. "I'll be back at 7:00."

"Good. Can you stop at Dahlin's and bring back some French bread?" He nodded. "Adrian can help me wrassle up some vegetable soup in the meantime."

Adrian nodded in agreement and added, "Then, after a good night's sleep, Sam, I'll cut that tree, so you can check the space under the moonshine car."

"That's a deal, Adrian. Later." Sam put on his coat and squeezed out the door, trying to keep Velvet from following him.

"Stay here, Velvet. I'll take you out in a bit." Velvet slumped down, her face on her paws, looking so sad that I handed Adrian her leash and shooed them out the door. I decided to attack the soup by myself. Besides, I had some serious thinking to do.

THE COAT IN THE WOODS 239

CHAPTER THIRTY THREE

Cooking my favorite recipes is like meditation for me. My hands seem to chop and stir and add all by themselves, leaving my mind free to wander amid my thoughts, watching the ones that pass through, noticing the ones I grasp.

My vegetable soup is one of those recipes. As I pulled out the onions, garlic, carrots, and celery from the fridge, I found I was grateful to be alone. My thoughts wandered to David and our marriage, wondering what I was going to do about it. I caught myself before my teeth began to shred my cheeks again. Ah, progress. The upside to the revelations of the past week. I didn't know how long it was going to take for me to grieve all the losses I had experienced in my life, but I knew I could no longer ignore them.

Professionally, I had a career I enjoyed. Like my mother, I also volunteered for the Democrats from time to time. A few close women friends kept me upright, and I dabbled in watercolors and weaving in what spare time I had. It was my personal life that was a mess. It had been a search for the mother I hardly knew, for a father who was present only sometimes, and for someone to provide me with a security I had never felt. No wonder I fell for David. At first he was so calm and comforting, like no one else had been. It took me a long time to realize he did this to avoid giving much to the relationship. When I started asking more from him, he looked elsewhere for the superficial connection he craved. But hey, good old Pru ignored it because she thought she had found the security she was looking for. A steady life, a good job, a successful husband, and two marvelous children.

So what if the successful husband cheated a little, was only a part-time partner? I didn't really know anything else. Besides, the affairs were always short-lived and each time I'd hope he was done with them. I was afraid if I set a limit on my tolerance for David's activities, I'd be left alone, so most of the time, in order to keep from getting hurt, I just shut down a part of myself. In these past days, I had felt more pain, given more of myself to a relative stranger, and let things go that were out of my control in more situations than I ever had before. I was even alone in a way I had never been and was surprised that I actually felt comfort in that solitude. As unfamiliar as it was, it felt good and I didn't want to lose that feeling.

I thought of Adrian's mild rebuke when I expressed cynicism that Barstow could be telling the truth about Mum and Dad. He had a point, I was cynical. I thought about Sam's comments. He was right, too. I *didn't* trust men. Not a pretty picture when I looked at it that way. It made me wonder why David had stayed with me. But part of me knew Donna was right. He could no more cut the cord that held us together than I could. I wondered what would have happened if I had drawn the line sooner, been more open about how much his affairs hurt me, read him the riot act like Mum had done to Dad.

Shoulda, woulda, coulda. It was time to decide what I should, would, and could do in the present, not keep munching over the past. With that last thought, I stirred the broth and barley into the soup pot, and set it on simmer. I headed upstairs and heard low talking and giggling coming from behind the closed doors of Mum and Dad's room. Sounded like Paul and Annie were taking advantage of their playing hooky from work. I knocked loudly.

"Dinner in half an hour. As soon as Sam returns, okay?"

"Thanks, Darlin!" More giggles. "Paul, stop it."

"I'm out of here, kids. See you later." I thundered down the stairs, hoping I wasn't going to have to endure squeaking bedsprings tonight as I tried to get to sleep.

Adrian came into the kitchen, followed by Velvet. "She found the fur tree again, Mum. You were right, it is the smell thing. She led me off the track right to it and rubbed her ruff against it. The wind rustled the trees a bit, then I thought I caught a strong smell like the scent that's in this house. You haven't changed your perfume, have you?"

I shook my head.

"Then whose…?" Adrian stopped, then ventured, "Grandma's?"

"That's what I think. The others think I'm nuts."

"Maybe she's trying to tell us something," my open-minded son replied.

I wanted to believe that more than anything. I took a risk and told Adrian what had happened to me that morning.

"Don't discount it, Mum." He gave me a hug. "Oh, and I checked out that tree that fell over and pushed the car further down. I think I can get the chainsaw to it without churning up too much dirt. It'd be great if there was some moonshine loot buried under there. By the way, I found that old jug Sam told me about under a tree by the side of the path. Are there others?"

"Back in the still where we found that one."

"Something else we can do tomorrow."

Thank God for youthful energy. I heard the sound of a car outside.

"Sounds like Sam is here."

"Good, I'll tell him I put the jug in the woodshed." Adrian headed out the door

"And I'll call the two love birds," I said to the empty room.

That night I climbed the stairs early. I woke up once during the night and listened. I could hear Velvet snoring from the deck and the television on downstairs. I opened my door and peeked out, noticing that Paul's old bedroom door was still ajar, no one in there. Sam must have fallen asleep in the den again to the sound of the TV, his comfort blanket. I liked the feeling of having the house full. I went back to bed and slept soundly until morning.

CHAPTER THIRTY FOUR

The next day was clear. The rain had refreshed the woods and although it promised to be a warm day, it seemed as if the storm had chased away the high summer heat and left just a hint of the fall to come.

After scrambled eggs with waffles and sausages, made by Paul, we all trooped out to the woods. Sam had his ear mufflers around his neck and carried a shovel to dig up whatever he was hoping to find. Adrian carried the saw and Paul, Annie, and I followed with Velvet, the rope, and the bucket with the gas and chainsaw tools. About a hundred feet into the path, Adrian stopped and started the saw. Sam slipped on his head gear, and he and Paul helped Adrian buck up the first tree across the road.

Three trees later, Adrian called, "Mum, let Velvet lead now. I think we are close to where she veered off to the coat tree."

"Good. I don't think she's real happy about the chainsaw sound. I may have to take her home once we find the place."

"And miss what could be an amazing discovery?" said Sam. "She can have my ear mufflers."

I gave him a look. "Sam, this car has been here for ages. Not even the police found anything but the silver when they looked."

"But that was *in* the car, not *under* it!" Sam was dancing with excitement. His amazing smile replaced the vague look of a couple of days ago and a twinkle shone in his soft brown eyes.

Another thing I was learning about PTSD. Symptoms came and went depending on the triggers and the effectiveness of the medications. Both factors seemed to be in Sam's favor this morning. Velvet was pulling me through the brush, so I needed to concentrate on my footing. The woods were calm and quiet except for our thrashing feet. I could hear the others behind me.

Then, there it was again. The sun reflecting off the bark, the little tufts of fur sticking out at odd angles. Paul and Annie hadn't seen it in years. They stood side by side, hands linked.

"Sure shrunk since I saw it last," commented Paul.

"What did you expect Darlin?" replied Annie. "Actually," she added, with a grin, "if you are talking about the tree, it grew."

Paul tapped her affectionately on her bottom. "It's just one of those things that in my mind never changed. It will always be a full-length coat hanging on its hanger." His tone was wistful. Then his nose went in the air, a bit like Velvet catching the scent of a deer. "Do you smell that? Like lavender?"

"It's just the flowers," Annie said.

Paul moved up to smell them. He pulled Annie closer. "No, they're different." Annie put her nose to the flowers, so did Sam.

"I told you that the other day," I reminded Paul, but you just pooh-poohed me."

"She's right," chipped in Sam. "The flowers have a different smell than the one in the air or on the trunk. That smell was even vaguely on the pieces we plucked from the tree."

It was then that the breeze started to rustle the basswood leaves. Adrian and I looked at each other. Then Annie caught on, tugged at Paul. Sam looked at us all.

"Okaaay," Paul said.

"This is just what happened to me yesterday morning," I said.

"And me," added Adrian.

"Who was the only one I dared tell about my experience," I said pointedly.

"Well, M'dears, if it isn't Leprechauns, then I think someone is trying to talk to you." Annie's eyes were soft and excited.

"Mum?" Paul asked. The breeze intensified. The perfume wafted under my nose.

"I wonder how she'll feel about cutting the other tree up," Adrian commented.

"Only one way to tell," added Sam. He wasn't going to be deterred by a ghost, no matter how friendly. He motioned to Adrian to follow him down the hill. Adrian told him he had to re-sharpen the saw teeth first, so we all watched Sam as he used the shovel to steady his descent towards the car.

"It's pretty solid down here," he called up. "We'll only have to make three or four cuts to clear out the space the car occupied before it was pushed over."

Adrian finished sharpening. He hefted the saw in his hand. Paul followed with the rope. Annie and I looked at each other.

"I think this is one of those times I'm not going to fight for equality of the sexes," I said.

"Me neither." Annie agreed. We'll watch and call the ambulance if anyone else needs to join Ollie at the hospital."

"Mum," Adrian called up. "Keep an eye on the coat tree. See if our activity affects the movement or smell."

"Right, Ade," I replied. "That's a bit too much even for me to believe," I said to Annie.

"Hey, you never know. I'll keep watch. You take Velvet, get her away from the noise of the saw."

"Sounds good to me. I'll count how many more trees we have to take down to get to the farm." With that, Velvet and I pushed our way back to the path. We climbed over tree after tree. I counted ten more in all before I came to the bottom of the pasture. Time to go back. Maybe the guys would have finished the job by now. Maybe they'd find a box with what was left of the rubies and sapphires. Right. And maybe Prince Charming would appear around the corner. As we arrived back in the clearing, I could hear the sound of dirt being shoveled and flung into the woods.

"Any change in the tree?" I asked Annie.

"Nope. Same level of breeze and smell," she replied. I looked around. It was the only tree moving in the gentle wind.

Then a sound out of a hundred films rang out. "Clunk!"

"What's that?" I called, "a rock?"

Silence except for scraping and some lighter clinks. Mumbling from the guys floated up.

"What?" Annie leaned over the edge of the gorge.

I followed. Velvet pulled ahead of me and I had to hold her tightly to keep her from dragging me down the hill. I could see them all leaning over a hole. The tree chunks were thrown to one side. The car looked naked and exposed on the other side of the indentation in which it had rested all these years. "Hey guys, what did you find?"

"It's a box wrapped in oilcloth," Sam called back. He handed it to Paul.

Paul unwrapped the cloth. "It's metal and surprisingly the padlock isn't rusted. We might need a bolt cutter."

I suddenly remembered the key in my pocket. Good thing I hadn't worried about wearing the same pants two days in a row. Still fantasizing that Dad had kept some of the stones, I called, "No we won't! Bring it up here. The key from Dad's desk. I have it in my pocket."

At that, the three of them hauled themselves up the ravine as fast as mountain goats, equipment and all. Sam and Adrian plunked down the saw, shovel, and rope. Paul handed me the box. I looked at them all, as I fitted the key in the lock.

"I feel like I'm in the middle of a B movie," I commented.

"Or a Humphrey Bogart one," Sam added.

I turned the key. It opened the lock. I gave everyone one more dramatic look.

Paul looked like he wanted to strangle me. "Pru, for God's sake, you're worse than Celeste."

"Yah, yah, sorry. Just couldn't resist." With that I lifted the top of the box. Inside wrapped in yet another piece of oilcloth was an old, only slightly mildewed notebook, like the one we found in the attic. I took it out and checked the rest of the box. No stones. Just the book. I opened it carefully. The familiar writing jumped off the front page. "Arthur Dillen, Journal, December 28, 1945."

We were all speechless for once. I handed the notebook gently to Paul. He thumbed cautiously through it until he came to the last page that had any writing on it. "May 28, 1959," he read. He looked up. "Three years after Mum died."

I could hear the blood pulsing through my head.

At that moment, the breeze that had been riffling through the coat tree became a wind that blew directly at us, enveloping us in the lavender scent.

CHAPTER THIRTY FIVE

The next hour flew by. We left the rest of the sawing until later and hustled back to the house. Annie was the first to pick up the journal. As she thumbed through it, I called Celeste to tell her what we had found. Within ten minutes of talking to me, she careened into the parking space next to the other cars. She clumped onto the porch in her barn boots, shucked them off outside, and joined us in the living room. Paul got up and fetched a cup of tea for her. Then he sat down beside her on one of the love seats. Sam and I were on the other one with Velvet at our feet. Annie sat in the armchair and Adrian pulled in a chair from the dining room. There was an electric air in the room, and a faint smell of lavender, as if we had all brought some of it back into the house on our clothes. Celeste noticed it.

"Did someone open up the spare rooms?" she asked.

"Yes, for sleeping. Why?" I responded.

"Because it smells like Mum's toilet water, and one of her old bottles I kept is still in the top drawer of my old dresser."

I guess that gave me an explanation for the scent I had detected in that room. Too bad.

Adrian, who had been the one sleeping in her room said, "The smell was definitely there when I went upstairs. But the fragrance was a bit too much for me to sleep with, so I looked for the source and took the bottle up to the attic before I went to bed. I put it on the old sewing machine up there. I hope that was okay."

"No problem, kid," Celeste replied, "but then why does it smell that way down here?"

Very carefully, to avoid as much of Celeste's cynical response as possible, I told her about all of our experiences out by the coat tree – the breeze, the wind, and the increasingly heavy lavender smell. I gently suggested we might have carried it back with us. Celeste looked from one of us to the other. She didn't say a word. Paul was the first to break the silence.

"I already had to endure Pru's reminder of our disbelief earlier."

"Mine wasn't really disbelief, just self-protection," Celeste replied.

"What do you mean, Cel?"

Celeste directed the next comment to Paul. "You were so adamant, I wasn't about to stick my neck out along with Pru and get thought of as nuts. Happens enough as it is."

"Okay, okay." Paul had the grace to look sheepish.

"What do you mean, it wasn't really disbelief?" I was torn with annoyance at Celeste for not supporting me and curiosity about her experience.

"What I mean, Pip, is that every time I have ventured into the woods and happened upon the coat tree, usually when the dogs were with me – I never seem to be able to find it without them – the same thing has happened to me. A breeze only in the basswood leaves and Mum's lavender smell."

If I thought it was quiet before, it was nothing compared to the next few minutes.

Paul finally spoke up. "I owe you both a huge apology. I obviously need to find a different lens to look at things and people."

"Maybe your Mum is trying to teach you all how to do that," offered Annie.

Paul answered her, "I'm not sure I'm ready to go as far into that dimension as you seem comfortable with, Annie, but she sure seems to be trying to tell us something."

I started thinking about all the coincidences that had led me to sitting in this room at this time. "It sure seems to me that my recent experiences have been leading somewhere, but I haven't been able to figure out where." I nodded to the journal. "Maybe the key is in there."

"And," said Annie, holding her hand up to arrest any protests, "maybe your Mum's spirit can't rest until we find that key and she knows that you all can move on."

"Parenting from beyond the grave – next on Oprah!" Celeste couldn't resist.

I couldn't help it. I suppressed a giggle, but too late. Annie caught it and chuckled, then Celeste. Finally even the guys were hooting and hollering with laughter. When we finally wound down, Celeste said, "So, who's going to read this one? I don't think I can do it this time."

"We were waiting to see if you wanted to," I said. "None of the rest of us did. We decided that if you didn't, we'd ask the poet of our group to read," I nodded towards Annie. Celeste smiled and clapped her hands.

Annie held the journal up, as if she knew she would be the one to read it. "I already glanced through it, I hope you don't mind. This covers fourteen years. Your dad obviously didn't write in it often, which he comments on. He seems to have written only when he was burdened by something. Are you ready?"

She looked around the room. As she came to each one of us, we nodded. I was finding it hard to breathe. This would not be a good time for an anxiety attack. I tried to relax and as I sat back, I found myself in the crook of Sam's arm. His hand rested easily on my shoulder. I took a deep breath. As I exhaled, I suddenly couldn't think of a more comforting place to be to listen to my father's words from years ago.

CHAPTER THIRTY SIX

Arthur Dillen, Journal
December 28 1945

I wasn't very good at keeping my journal while in Burma, but perhaps I can improve on that now that I am home. It might help me to put what I have experienced into perspective.

   I am grateful for my lovely Adrienne. My reunion with her and the children went better than I hoped for. One difficulty, however, was that Celeste and Paul asked where I had been, especially when I had a re-occurrence of dysentery, and I couldn't tell them. Also, I haven't been able to bring myself to tell Adrienne about my freezing in combat. It rides somewhat uneasily between us, because I know she senses something is wrong, but is not willing to push me. Many of the Det 101 guys are looking forward to a reunion in a year, but I'm not sure I will be able to show my face there. For now, the only men I have had contact with since the war are Hank and Ed and I haven't told them anything either.

   I am concerned about Hank. He is working well at the farm, dotes on Dirk the pig, and seems like the old Hank. Almost. He has talked openly about how hard Omaha Beach was on D-Day and the days after, but only in generalities – about feeling badly when he lost his men, about the terrible toll it took just to start advancing towards the Germans above. However, at times he seems lost in another world. No doubt he has things he cannot tell me as well.

December 27, 1948

Good thing I am a teacher and not a journalist. I seem to have repeated my pattern of the war, by starting this journal gung ho and then pushing it to the back of my desk drawer and forgetting it. I found it the other day while I was searching for my favorite fountain pen, which I found in the kitchen under a pile of Paul's drawings. He has gone from cartoons to elaborate house and garden plans.

Life has been busy. I have been enjoying the Burmese students at the university, having spent time in their country, even if I cannot tell them that. Interacting with them here brings to mind my Kachin friends. Believe it or not, Naw Hpraw still contacts me regularly on the ham radio. My work with the Japanese Embassy before the war landed me a consultancy contract with our government. I am proud that I have been able to utilize my language skills on its behalf. I am often away from home and miss Adrienne and the children, but I feel I am making more of a contribution than I did in the war.

I fear that Adrienne's patience with my traveling is wearing thin however, as I have had to miss a few of the trips back East, which she always finds difficult without me to ease the tension between her and her mother. I have also missed some of Paul's baseball games. We did buy Celeste a horse, Sunrise, from the young stable owner who has been training them both. Celeste has started show jumping. She has quite a talent for urging that huge horse over imposing fences. I wish I could get to more of her shows as well.

One area in which I have been helpful, I think, has been with Hank. He began drinking heavily when he returned from the war, and he would have lost his job with mother if I hadn't intervened. With him more or less sober and back in charge at the farm, I feel more at ease when I have to leave, especially since Dad hasn't been doing well since his heart attack last month and Mother isn't getting any younger and has her hands full helping Dad.

August 9, 1950

The most amazing and yes, miraculous thing has happened! We just had another baby yesterday! Prudence Eleanor Dillen. The doctors said she was a change-of-life baby and that this is quite common. When we found out nine months ago, we both couldn't believe it. After all we aren't exactly young any more, the older children are all set with their interests and school, and Adrienne's career is finally in full swing. I've still been traveling too much, but last year, Adrienne was able to accompany me to Japan to submit architectural plans for some projects there. We have been excited about the prospects and it has helped Adrienne view some of my other travels in a more positive light. However, children are gifts, so you accept them. Who's to say another child won't bring us even more happiness? The thought of another grandbaby to spoil has already perked Mother and Dad up. His heart attack inflicted more damage than they thought and it has slowed him down considerably, which has been hard on both of them.

I am getting ready to visit Adrienne at the hospital, and cannot wait to hold our precious child again in my arms. She looks just like her mother – except I think she will have my mother's green eyes. Of course you can't really tell yet.

This will definitely change my schedule. Adrienne can't be expected to take care of the baby, the needs of the older children, check up on Mother and Dad, keep up with her career, and deal with Hank all on her own.

Poor Hank. Dirk died last year. He must be the only pig in Stearns County buried in a grave with a granite headstone, but then he did live longer than any pig should. Without Dirk's company, Hank has spent more time after work with our family. He has had a number of drinking binges as well. Adrienne has told me a few times that his constant presence is stressful for her so I have been trying to spend more time with Hank, just us two, so that I can feel more comfortable telling him that Adrienne and I need to have some family time by ourselves. He likes the movies, so we usually attend one a week when I am home.

June 6, 1954

I suppose I have to accept the fact that this journal reappears when I need it. Do others write only when momentous events occur in their lives, or when they are despondent and uneasy?

The Korean War has taken a good deal of mental energy for all of us. The newsreels on the war, shown before the movies, have been difficult for Hank and me to watch, yet for some reason we are drawn to them. For me, the war increased our government's incentive to keep Japan as an ally. As a result, my schedule did change, but not in the way I had intended the year Pru was born. Instead of traveling less, the number of trips increased. In the last two years, I have had to travel to Japan every two or three months, sometimes more. Adrienne's tolerance of this finally ran out. She sat me down this past spring after my third trip in five months, and told me in no uncertain terms that if I wanted to continue to be part of this family, I needed to be PART OF this family. She challenged me that I was traveling for me, and pretending it was for the family. She said if I really wanted to do something for the family, I could stay home more. Pru needed her daddy, Paul needed me around to figure out how to become a young man, and Celeste in her newly won sobriety needed support from ALL OF US to continue on the path she was shakily walking. Then my dear wife added she hadn't even begun on the topic of Hank.

I was speechless at first. I felt like I had always done everything for her and the children. Didn't she see that? I didn't really say anything back, but took a long walk up to the farm. I ended up in Mother's kitchen and without really telling her what Adrienne had said, felt her out about some of the issues that Adrienne had brought up.

Boy, that old Gal doesn't miss a trick!

In her calm but strong manner, Mother basically told me I was a fool not to have figured all this out by myself, and that she would never have been as patient as Adrienne. She also came out and finally told me since Dad died two years ago, she sure could use more support on the farm. Quite an eye-opener. I headed back home through the woods, trying to digest all of this. I walked by the cliff to hear the brook, looked at the old car, and then crossed the path to the old still. I heard a noise and ducked inside.

To my surprise, Hank was sitting in the corner of the still, his knees up, his head down, arms around his legs, just rocking and talking to himself. I asked him if he was all right.

He looked up. Not at me. A thousand yards beyond me. The smell of alcohol hung over him like fog on a clear day. He started talking louder, yelling about the artillery and bodies in the water. I did the only thing I could think of. I shouted his name, told him who I was and told him he was in the old still, not in a bunker.

It seemed to work, as Hank's vision slowly focused closer until it rested on me. He looked so sad. He talked about missing Dirk, asked me why I kept going away, and that he thought he just irritated Adrienne. He asked me if they would make him return to the war. I sat down beside him and put my arm around his shoulders. I told him the Korean War was over and so was his, but then realized that his war might never be over. I had a feeling I knew what Adrienne would be telling me about Hank. And she would be right. He was my responsibility.

And the children were our JOINT responsibility. I thought of my Dad, who never shirked his duty, and realized that my outside consulting, which had started as a need to make up for what I still see as cowardice, had over the years become something else. If I really looked at it, it had turned into glory seeking. Yes. Basking in the praise I missed out on by my foolish behavior in England all those years ago that cost me my career at Yale, feeling a part of something that eluded me after the incident in Burma, and enjoying a freedom that the Depression took from our generation. Well, it's time to reevaluate my priorities.

I helped Hank up and told him I wasn't going away any more. I would be here when he needed me. He looked at me with a mixture of hope and sadness and thanked me. Then he said something about needing a nap before he got back to work. Without any more words, he left the still and threaded his way through the woods back to the path that led to the farm. I watched him leave, wondering how that man's mind worked and how often he had retreated to the still. I decided to let him know about my secret one day. Perhaps it would make him feel less crazy. First, however, I needed to clear the air with Adrienne. I brushed off my suit pants, which I hadn't even had a chance to change before my lovely wife lit into me, and walked back to the house to tell her about the war and that I would resign my consultancy with the government.

After I haltingly told Adrienne of my shame in combat and that my fear of what she would think of me had prevented me from talking to her until now, she hugged me until my tears dried up. Then she put me at arm's length and told me something I still remember almost word for word.

"Arthur Dillen, sometimes I don't think you have the brains you were born with. It is time to get it through that brilliant head of yours that all I have ever wanted is to be with you. The only time I haven't been happy has been during our separation by the war and your subsequent withdrawal when you returned."

With that, she left me to figure out the rest. I should have felt like a puppy running home with its tail between its legs, but instead I felt renewed, as if a fresh breeze had blown all my self-imposed cobwebs away.

As a result, our renewed closeness and my stronger commitment to the family lent a festive air to the summer. Celeste has been doing well, working for Glen, training new riders as well as finding a talent for dealing with difficult horses. Paul was on the Varsity baseball team this spring and has been drawing editorial cartoons for the school newspaper. He can't decide whether to be a journalist, cartoonist, or an architect like his mother. We are encouraging him to go to college at least before he decides. Pru, our "Pipsqueak", is an energetic toddler. She loves coming into the woods when Adrienne and I go clearing, and has found a fellow explorer in Elias' son, Sammy. Elias brings him over when he comes to cut wood for Mother. I even don't mind going out East with Adrienne. Mother Marshall will never change and it helps Adrienne when I go. Oddly enough, perhaps because I am glad to go with her at times, she doesn't mind going alone on some occasions when I have a heavy class load or exams.

Even Hank has been doing better. At least until yesterday, when one of the men lost an arm in the thresher. I have to close now, as I can hear Adrienne on the phone. It sounds as if Hank has disappeared.

December 8, 1954

Yesterday was the anniversary of Pearl Harbor. I expected that it might be a rough day for Hank. He bought a television, and they broadcast the news right into your living room, even some of the old war newsreels. You don't even have to go to the movie theater any more, which is too bad, as Hank has been making some progress since the thresher accident.

I finally found him that summer day he had vanished, huddled again in the still, drunk, muttering over and over again that it was his fault. I decided that I needed some help and took him to the Veteran's hospital. They did a thorough check-up on him and told me what I already knew, that he was suffering from his combat experiences in the war. They don't really seem to know how to treat it, but working on the hospital farm and on the landscaping for the hospital seems to have helped Hank come back to himself. He also has a psychiatrist with whom he can talk, which seems to provide some relief for him as well. I asked to visit him with Hank once, and told Hank about my freezing in combat. Hank appreciated my candor as he often felt that there was something wrong with just him. The psychiatrist reassured both of us that what we had been through - even me - was pretty common. We learned that both of us may have some difficulty in the future if we encounter certain situations that bring our war experiences back to us, such as the thresher accident or seeing the war footage on television. I came away from there feeling better and Hank has been mostly his old self with that impish sense of humor. Even Adrienne has commented on his improvement, enjoying playing the old card games again with him when he comes over on Fridays. He's teaching Pru magic, which she loves. So we will just go on as well as we can. Adrienne's career is blossoming, so I am considering cutting back on my classes to spend more time on the farm with Mother, Hank, and our Pip. She won't be young for long.

Speaking of youth, Pip's presence continues to help mother stay energetic. She had to let Hank go as farm manager after the thresher accident due to his unpredictable behavior, but he has a pension, and Mother has graciously let him stay in the barn apartment, since as she says, "It is his home." She hasn't felt alarmed by his episodes as he has never been threatening or anything - just frightened and confused.

May 28, 1956

I'm not sure I can even put this into words, but perhaps it will help me if I try. God knows I have no one else to talk to.

Since last month I can't sleep. If I do, I wake up with nightmares. I hardly eat and I don't know how to take care of my Pip. I leave her at Mother's all the time to go to work, then I don't go anywhere, except to the woods to sit by the coat that my darling wore, to be with her scent and her presence.

I don't know if what I did was right or wrong. I only know it was the only thing I could do at the time. If only I had gone home before the storm hit. If only I had planned to go East with Adrienne this time. Then I would have been home when Ed came by to return the stones. I would have been home during the storm. Maybe it would have been me who died, not Adrienne, not my darling. How in the world will I live without her? How will I raise Pru? Oh God, what will I do?

I was so pleased with myself that day, deciding to dash home for lunch, bringing sandwiches and a corsage for Adrienne's trip. I tried to call Mother and tell her I would take Adrienne to the train, but I didn't get an answer. That was all right. I figured I'd catch her at the house. As I turned onto our road, the rain was washing off the windshield in waves and there was such a lightning strike and crack of thunder that for a moment I felt like I was back in Burma watching the railroad track exploding from the charges our team had put there. Then I remembered where I was and quickened my pace in case Adrienne was frightened. I'm not sure why, as we have always enjoyed sitting on the porch to watch the storms over the lake. What made me think that day might be different I can't explain. I pulled up as close to the house as I could and ran to the porch. The door was ajar. I pushed it open.

My heart stopped. A man in a hooded raincoat was leaning over Adrienne, my love, who was lying on her side by the cast iron stove, covered by her fur coat, her face turned away from me. In a flash I was on him. This time my hands were ready to break his neck if I had to. I would not freeze. I would do anything to protect her. As I grabbed the man's shoulder, he stood up and spun around, his right hand going up in the air. I ducked, thinking he was going to hit me and was about to grab his other hand when his body went rigid, and he actually saluted me.

The familiar odor of alcohol blew into my face as I looked up and recognized Hank. He was talking to me as if I was his superior officer, something about not meaning to hurt her, that he had to protect her from the shrapnel, from the flashes of artillery. I gaped at him, then leaned down to look at Adrienne's face to see how she was.

Her beautiful brown eyes were open, but seeing nothing. I felt the pulse at her neck. The skin under my fingers was flat. No beat. I gently picked her head up. My right hand came away all bloody. I felt around. She had a deep cut on the side of her head. The collar of her coat was bloody and as I looked up I could see a smear of blood on the corner of the iron stove. I gently laid her head back down and wiped my hands off on my pants. I looked back at Hank. He was trying to stuff Adrienne's right arm into the coat, urging her to put her hand in, as if this would keep her warm. Blood was dripping from a cut over his right eye onto his hands. He wiped them off on the hem of the coat.

Oh God. This was worse than finding a stranger. Much worse. This was my oldest friend and he had killed my Adrienne, my heart. What was even more tragic was that he killed her because he thought he was trying to protect her.

A renewed rush of adrenaline pushed my grief aside. With Oxford and Burma, I had failed to do the right thing. This time would be different, even if it was the most difficult thing I ever had to do. I couldn't save Adrienne, but I could help Hank. I reached for his shoulder again, but this time with a different intention. I told him I knew he hadn't meant it, but that Adrienne was dead, and we had to get him out of there. He looked beyond me with that stare until I shook him and told him that I needed his help. This finally seemed to register, so I asked him to fold the fur coat up and wrap it in Adrienne's raincoat, hanging by the door. In the meantime an idea sprang into my head.

Racing into the dining room, I pulled the heavy, wooden silverware box out, emptied the silver from the drawer into it, and put it on the table. I had to work fast, since Mother was due to come over between twelve-thirty and one to take Adrienne to the train, and it was already eleven forty-five. Hank was standing by the door, the wrapped coat in his arms, just waiting. His face lit up when he saw me again.

It was still raining, so I slipped on my Anorak. Then, with the silver box clutched to my chest under my coat, I led Hank and his bundle out of the house and down the path towards the farm. Thank God, the lightning had passed on, but the rain made pushing through the brush a chore.

Painstakingly, we made our way back to the still. I knew Hank would feel safe there, would probably have come here on his own had I not appeared. His eyes cleared up a bit as we hunched into the old concrete bunker. I pointed to the spot where he liked to sit and directed him to stay there until I returned. He settled back, clutching the coat, and opened the raincoat cover enough to bend his head down into the fur beneath, seemingly soothed by its smell and texture.

I backed out through the opening, still holding onto the silver box and crossed the woods to the path. I ran a few dozen yards towards the farm, then turned left into the woods again, towards the old moonshine car, making sure I broke some branches on my way, so it looked as if someone had come this way in a hurry. I found the car and made my way down to it. I pried up the half-open trunk, slipped the silver box in, and closed it again.

My heart was beating nearly out of my chest, but I knew I had to keep going if I was to save Hank from going to jail. He would never survive. I climbed back up the hill and ran across the path to the still again. Hank was almost in the same position as I had left him. I called to him from the doorway. He looked up again and smiled. I told him we had to get him home, that we could leave Adrienne's coat here. He didn't question this, just handed it over. I hope like hell he won't remember any of what happened that day. Sometimes shell shock can have a good side.

I took the fur coat from him and, just for a moment before covering it again with the raincoat, inhaled my darling's scent, kissing the soft fur. I mentally shook myself, realizing I couldn't collapse yet. I put the coat gently on the floor of the still, pulled Hank up and together we stumbled into the drenching rain back to his barn apartment.

By the time I had settled Hank in his bed, it was twelve fifteen. I raced home, dialed the sheriff's office, and in a voice finally breaking down with grief and guilt, told them I had come home to find my wife dead on the kitchen floor.

I went back into the kitchen and sat with Adrienne's head in my lap, my tears running down her face, mingling with the blood from the wound at the back of her head.

I don't remember a whole lot about the rest of the day. I vaguely remember the sheriff and ambulance coming. I told the sheriff what time I had found Adrienne, that our silver was gone, and that I had run outside to see if I could see anyone getting away, to no avail. The sheriff told me to get some rest, and that we could talk tomorrow. Then the doctor who arrived took me upstairs, gave me a pill and got me into bed. As I was fading out, I momentarily wondered who would get the children, who would tell them they had lost their mother.

When I awoke the next morning, I remembered everything. I felt emptiness unlike any I have ever known. It was like someone had sneaked in during the night and cut out my soul. I will never be the same. God help me.

* * *

Annie thumbed through the rest of the pages. She looked around the room at our numb faces. "There's just one more entry. Shall I read it?"

What the hell, I thought. Might as well hear it all. The others nodded with me.

* * *

April 26, 1959

It has been three years to the day since Adrienne died. I shoved this journal far back into my desk so no one would find it and just yesterday retrieved it again.

I just re-read the last entry. That emptiness still haunts me. At times, when I am with Pru, I can forget about it for a while, but then she tosses me a look so much like her mother's that my stomach twists up all over again.

I still think I couldn't have done anything different that day. I made up a story for Mother, Hank, and the older children about a robber. Luckily the sheriff took my hint and went looking in the woods. He discovered the silver box and even though the technicians at the laboratory couldn't detect any fingerprints on it other than the family's, the sheriff made the assumption that the man who had recently escaped from the Reformatory was responsible. Fortunately he has never been found. As for Pru, I convinced Hank, Celeste, Paul, and Mother that we should tell her that Adrienne died of a heart attack. She is too young to have to deal with anything else.

Hank has good and bad days. He doesn't like to go into the woods any more, mostly because he seems to have accepted the robber story and says he is frightened, but he often asks about Adrienne's coat. After he recovered enough from the day of the accident to go about his usual routine, I realized there was simply no telling when another triggering event might send him to the still, so I took the coat into the woods and hung it up on a pretty basswood tree that Adrienne liked. It is right up the hill from the moonshine car. Hopefully if anyone happens upon it, he or she will think it is left over from the thief's rampage. Of course I took the sapphires out of the pocket long ago. They wait in a safe-deposit box along with the rubies until Naw Hpraw's grandson is old enough to come to this country for college. Adrienne had agreed to that long ago. A promise is a promise.

I still have trouble sleeping. I dream about that day over and over and wake up in a sweat – far worse than my war dreams. I know Pru has heard me in the night and noticed the whisky glass by my bed. After all, I am right next door to her. She is very bright and inquisitive, not to mention caring and nurturing, and she is becoming more aware of her surroundings every day. The other day, she and Chloe were in the woods with me while I was clearing some of the undergrowth. Chloe ran off and when I told Pru to go find her, I realized too late where Chloe probably was. And I was right. Pru dragged me to see the coat, thinking she had found something out of one of her stories. She even noticed the car. I hope I was stern enough with her to discourage any further exploration or sharing of her discovery with anyone else, as I can't bear to take the coat down. I still go and sit by it and talk to Adrienne whenever I can. It's the only peace I have. I swear I can smell her scent, and there is usually a small breeze in the tree when I am there. Is she at peace? I pray that she has forgiven me.

When I talk to Adrienne, I ask her what to do about Pru. She needs a woman in her life. She is getting to those years where just having her old Dad isn't enough. Celeste has her own life. I tried having her take care of Pru when she was younger, but that worked about as well as trying to mix oil with water. Mother took over with Pru, but she is getting frailer and I don't know how much longer we will have her. Pru has a right to a more lively life than living with a sad old man. Adrienne always said that if something happened to us, Hugh and Alice would take care of the children. Maybe I need to call Hugh. Ask him about Pru spending the school year out there once Mother passes on. During the summers, we could camp or work on the farm together. Summers are easier. I can't stand the thought of being without my Pip, but I have to provide for her, give her the best chance to grow up as normally as she can, given the circumstances.

In the meantime, this will be my last entry in the journal. I can't bring myself to destroy it, but I can't chance that Pru might one day discover it, so I will find a way to bury it under the moonshine car. Literally burying the past. How ironic. I feel certain that this journal will be undetected there, ensuring that Hank will be safe, and that both of us can live the rest of our lives as freely as our ghosts will let us.

CHAPTER THIRTY SEVEN

Within minutes of Annie reading Dad's last words, Celeste exploded, "That dirty son of a bitch! I inherited the job of taking care of the man who killed our mother? How could he do that?" She sprang up and paced back and forth in front of the French doors.

"Who? Dad or Hank?" asked Paul, his face drawn and white.

"Both!" Her pacing continued.

"Although," inserted Annie more quietly, "if what your father said was true, Hank doesn't remember what happened."

"That doesn't make it all right, though," Paul argued.

Sam got up and went out the French doors to the deck. He stood looking out at the lake with his back to us. Adrian fidgeted in his seat and followed him out. He didn't do well with conflict. I focused back into the room. I was having trouble finding my voice. I felt both so sad at the tragedy of it all, and at the same time relieved to hear in his own words that my father had loved me. I finally spoke. "Dad was doing what he thought best in an untenable situation."

"But you weren't used and lied to like we were," shot back Celeste, still visibly fuming.

"Wasn't I? You all agreed to tell me Mum had a heart attack. I didn't even get to hear the official lie."

"You're right, Pru. There were lies upon lies, all supposedly to protect us from the ugliness of the truth." Paul's color started returning to his face.

"But we deserved the truth. We might all have had different lives if Dad had told the truth." Celeste was still pacing.

"Different, Celeste, but you don't know if life would have been better or worse." Annie's calm voice was like the sun coming out from behind the clouds.

"At this point, I don't know anything. I've got to get out of here. I need time to think. I can't just decide in a split second how I feel about this." Celeste strode out the door without a backward glance. The rest of us were left looking at each other. Paul was on one settee, I was alone on the other. Velvet was wandering about, reacting to the commotion. Annie sat on the chair, her hands resting on the journal. My mind went to the picture of my mother, sprawled on the floor, her head oozing blood, my father cradling her in his arms, and tears started to run down my face. Annie must have noticed, because soon she surrounded me on one side, Paul on the other. As I cried, I could feel them both shaking on either side of me. Finally, taking a breath, I looked first at Paul and then at Annie. Tears streaked their cheeks and their noses were dripping just like mine. Annie grimaced and popped up. She returned with a tissue box that she generously shared.

"How come letting your feelings out becomes such a messy endeavor?" I asked.

"Who knows?" answered Paul, wiping his nose. "Maybe to help us get back to the present. Hard to ignore it when you can't breathe."

I joined the nose-blowing serenade. When we quieted down I thought about the present. Sam. I checked outside. His car was still there but I couldn't see him or Adrian, for that matter, on the deck any more.

"Hey, guys, did you see where Sam and Adrian went?" They both shook their heads. I got up, put on my jacket and grabbed Velvet's leash. "Hold the fort, I've got to find them."

Velvet and I took a turn around the house. No Sam. No Adrian. I did notice that the chainsaw was missing and then heard the distant sound of one. That must be Adrian. Action was his antidote to emotional turmoil. He was probably cutting the trees across the path. But where was Sam? As we walked along, I suddenly knew. And so apparently did Velvet. She pulled me in the direction I had already decided to go. To the still.

We wound our way through the brush. The windfall from the storm had obliterated the path Sam and I had made earlier, but we finally came to the broken-down structure. Velvet pulled me down the steps and headed straight towards the large figure sitting against the wall, knees up, head hunched down on his arms. She pushed her nose between Sam's head and arms and licked his face. He reached up and scratched her ruff. She then sat down next to him on one side. I sat on the other. Sam looked up. Surprisingly, his eyes were clear, blazingly clear. He nodded towards Velvet, keeping his hand on her back.

"No wonder Hank loved his pig. Nothing like an animal's unconditional love."

"You aren't Hank, Sam," I said.

"How do you know, Pru? Jesus, I almost did the same thing to you the other night. Except it was a wooden desk instead of an iron stove and you just missed hitting your head by inches."

Even though I had a hunch this was why he had left to come here, when he said it out loud, I was speechless.

Sam went on. "Your Dad kept writing about Hank's eyes. The political cartoonist, Bill Maudlin once said, 'Look at an infantryman's eyes, and you can tell how much war he has seen.' I know I get that look too. I can tell by the way others look at me when I'm like I was the other night. I know because on one level I am aware that I am way off somewhere else, somewhere scary. You say I'm not like Hank. But look at me. I left my job to come back here because the explosion up North made it difficult for me to function the way I used to. So I am starting a second hand store. What is it but a place full of junk? I tried to fool myself that I came back for my Dad. Hell, he's fine. I'm the one who's not. He even got a two bedroom apartment in case I wanted to stay with him."

I remembered something. "But I thought you said his place was too small for you."

Sam looked at me. The dimple on his right cheek appeared without the smile. "I lied about that. I'm embarrassed to stay with him because of the nightmares. When I stay at the store, there's no one around at night to hear me." He looked at me. "And I can't hurt anyone when I get confused."

"You know, there is another option."

"I'm listening."

"Let your dad in. He already knows more about you than you think. Tell him what happens. Bring him with you to talk to Dr. Slovak so he can learn how to help you."

"It's been a long time since I've needed him to be my dad."

"You never know, you may be giving him a gift he never dreamed of."

"Yeah, maybe."

We were quiet for a few minutes. I could still hear the chainsaw in the distance. With his energy, Adrian would have the path cleared by dinner.

I put my arm around the back of Sam's shoulders and gave him a friendly squeeze. He added his smile to the dimple.

"You're a good old friend, Pru. And a good new one."

I squeezed his shoulders again. Then I felt a bit self-conscious, so I moved my arm back. We sat side by side in the silence for a while, motionless except for Sam's fingers pushing through Velvet's fur. Finally, he looked at me. "What about you? How are you doing?"

"I have a lot to absorb. I think it will take a while to even know the answer to that question. In the meantime, I'll be glad to lend a hand at the store, that is, if you'll still help me get that fence up."

Sam smiled at me again. A wide one this time. "It's a deal."

I stood up. "Sam, if you're okay, I need to find Adrian."

He stood up too, as far as he could. "Sure. In fact, I think I'll head over to Dad's to see how he weathered the storm. Do you mind if I give you a call about hanging out here for another night?"

"Not at all. I'll see you later." With that we patted each other's arms. Sam bent down to give Velvet one last scratch, and she and I ducked back out to find Adrian. I heard Sam exit after me and scrabble through the brush in the other direction. I thought about what he had said and realized it was probably a good thing he was going to see his dad. My guess was that he would find some way not to stay with us tonight, given his present state of mind. I hoped that he would follow up with the doc.

As Velvet and I walked, bucked logs scattered the path, some pushed to the side, others creating an interesting maze. I found Adrian at the last two trees just before the bottom of the pasture at the farm. His shirt was drenched with sweat, his hair slicked back from his face. For a minute he looked like a young version of David. A pang went through me. And I wasn't even sure I loved David any more. I couldn't imagine what it was like for Dad to look at me and see Mum looking back at him when he least expected it. Sadness still sat like a boulder in my gut. I called out to Adrian. He stopped the saw.

"Need some help with these last two?" I asked.

He tossed me a grin. "Sure, I'd like the company. How are things at the house?"

"We had a good cry, then I left to look for you and Sam."

"Is Sam all right? He looked kind of funny when we both left."

"I think he will be," I said over my shoulder as I tied Velvet to a tree away from the noise, but close enough for her to see us. Together Adrian and I bucked and moved the last two trees blocking the road. The physical effort was calming.

As we finished I commented, "Now we can get Cel's truck in here and carry the wood to both places to split."

"Got plans to stay the winter, Mum?" Adrian's words were loaded.

I sat down on a log. Velvet whined to come closer. Adrian went over and untied her from the tree. "I'm beginning to think so, Ade. As I told Sam, I need some time to digest all this, and I would like to do that with the basswood tree to visit, and with the rest of Dad's papers to go through." I looked at him. "With each event that has touched me here, it feels less likely that I will return to Washington."

"You mean to Dad?"

"You'd think that would be clear, wouldn't you?" He nodded. "But, oddly it isn't yet. At this point I just need to trust the process."

"Whatever works for you, Mum. You know we love you no matter what. Just like we still love Dad, which some days is hard, given how much he's hurt you."

"I know. It's never simple, is it?" Adrian sat on the log beside me and put his arm around me. I leaned my head on his shoulder. We sat there until Velvet started pawing at my knee. "Somebody's hungry. Let's go back and see what we can find to eat for ourselves as well."

"Good, I'm starving. I think I'll take off tomorrow. I have some friends up in Duluth I'd like to touch base with before I fly back to Vancouver Island. They're working construction up there."

"Any hope you might relocate?" I asked.

He smiled. "You never know. You obviously get into too much trouble without one of us around!"

"Oh right. Hey, none of this was my doing!"

"No? Mrs. Inquisitive – digging into papers, taking blood samples, rediscovering fuzzy fur-bearing trees."

"Well, when you put it that way."

Adrian laughed and squeezed my shoulder. "I'm mostly kidding, Ma. You've been doing just fine on your own."

"Speaking of blood samples, I never told Celeste that I put her name and number on the ones we mailed."

"Then, let's go." Adrian stood up and grabbed the chainsaw with one hand and the gas can in the other. I had Velvet and picked up the bucket of tools. Together we walked a crooked path through all the cut-up trees back to the house.

CHAPTER THIRTY EIGHT

When Adrian and I walked into the house, we found Annie heating up the rest of the soup. I inhaled the smell of something marvelous baking in the oven, Annie's herb bread. Adrian went upstairs to shower. Velvet walked over to her dish, picked it up and took it over to the pantry door. I got the hint. I patted her, took the dish from her mouth and filled it. Annie smiled indulgently at this scenario then said, "Sam went to his dad's."

"I know. I found him in the still."

She raised her eyebrows.

"Maybe later, Annie. Where's Paul?"

"Up in the attic."

"I hope he remembered to shut the door." I wasn't in the mood to deal with bats tonight.

Annie laughed. "My Paul? He's way too anal to forget something like that." She turned back to the soup.

"I'll go upstairs and see what he's up to." I climbed the steps, opened the attic door, and called to Paul that I was on my way up.

"Don't forget to close the door!" he called back. I smiled to myself. I clumped upstairs and there was Paul, sitting on the floor, Mum's old drawings spread out in front of him.

"I didn't realize she had designed so many of the buildings in St Cloud," he commented. He lifted up a paper to expose cartoons, and other pictures of houses, gardens and patios. "Look, she even kept my old drawings."

"Maybe you found them for a reason."

"I'm not really into your whole thing of there are no coincidences and all that." He drifted off.

"I hear a 'but' in there."

Paul grinned. "But," he said, "I think I might look into taking one of those CAD classes at the vocational school when I get back. Cut back on the consulting engineering a bit."

"CAD?"

"Computer Assisted Drawing." That's how plans are drawn up these days. If I decide to go into architecture, I have to learn that first."

"Go for it, Big Bro. Are you staying here tonight?"

"No, I think we both want to get home. We'll leave after supper. Annie has a couple of poetry readings coming up she needs to prepare for. I told her I'd be going with her whenever I can."

I hugged him. All sorts of changes happening around here. "Could you give me a hand with something before you go?" I walked over to the sideboard and Mum's portrait. "I want to bring these down again."

"Sure." Paul gathered up the papers, put them back into the folder, and stuck the folder under his arm.

We started with the sideboard, carefully hauling it downstairs. As we opened the door, Adrian was standing in the hall. "I was wondering what all that noise was. I thought we had really big bats up there."

"Funny," I responded. "Here, you take this end. I'm going to get Mum's portrait.

As we carried the sideboard and hung the portrait, our joking counteracted the heaviness in my heart, and in the end served to ease it a bit.

Finally, there we were, sitting at the table for dinner, the sideboard back in its place, Mum's brown eyes looking down at us. Paul raised his glass of wine. We followed.

"Here's to you, Mum. Glad to have you back."

I looked at the portrait. Yes, in a way, we all finally had her back.

Just as we were finishing dinner, the sound of Celeste's truck blasted into the quiet, and there she was, larger than life, bearing a pan of carrot cake.

"I had to cook. Helped me sort through some stuff. Couldn't stay away. Want some? Where's Sam?" She plunked the cake down on the table and sloughed off her boots and jacket. I informed her of Sam's whereabouts.

"Good, I was worried about him." She looked at me. She was the only other person who knew about the similarities between the past and present veterans. "Do you think he'll see that doc tomorrow?"

"Hopefully." Paul, Adrian and Annie were looking back and forth between us. Cel and I looked at each other. I sighed, and filled them in with as few details as possible about Sam's service and the night of the storm. It was hard to let them know what had happened while trying to help Sam keep his dignity. I shouldn't have worried.

"He's a really neat guy. Too bad he had to go through all that, said Adrian."

"The funny thing is," I added, "he said he wouldn't be who he is today if he hadn't."

"The paradox of war," added Annie.

"Sounds like the title for a poem, Annie," Paul said.

"Might be."

We all quieted, thinking our separate thoughts.

Then Celeste noticed Mum's portrait. She stared at it for a bit, a soft look on her face. "Hello, Mum," she said. She looked around. "Is it just me, or is Mum's scent back?"

Paul answered, "I wasn't going to say anything. I figured we had just brought it down from the attic with us, even though I noticed the toilet water bottle was still up there."

"We did," I said. We looked at each other and smiled. I felt more at ease than I had in a long time.

After consuming most of Celeste's cake, Annie and Paul prepared to leave. Just before they opened the door, Celeste spoke up, "Oh, I almost forgot. The lab called me this afternoon."

"That was quick," I commented.

"The only reason they called so soon was they said they don't often get fur bits in baggies. They were intrigued."

"Did they get any results?"

"Just blood type, no DNA. That takes longer. They wanted to know if we still wanted to try for it."

"I expected that," said Paul.

"They found two different blood types. They asked if I needed to know what they were."

"What did you tell them?" Annie asked.

"By that time I had calmed down from this morning." She paused. "I told them that it wasn't necessary."

We stood there, nobody saying anything. Finally Paul said, "Well that's it, then. I'm okay with that." The rest of us nodded. We hugged Paul and Annie, and they went on their way, promising to keep in touch weekly. There were still a few threads dangling. Adrian went upstairs with my cell phone to update Jess.

"So you aren't angry any more?" I asked Celeste.

"I don't think it's a matter of anger. You know me, I just blow off the top of my head sometimes."

"No, you?"

"Anh anh, anh! Watch the attitude."

"You're right. I can start my day over at any minute."

"You've got it. As I was cooking, I had time to think. I obviously need more time to digest how Dad's secrets impacted my life, good or bad, but I did some checking on the Internet once the cake was in the oven, and I think you can call Donna and tell her she can close the case on Mum."

"You mean tell her the truth?"

"We have to start somewhere, don't we? Otherwise we are just carrying on the same old, same old. I wouldn't suggest it if there was a chance Hank would go to jail. It is a 45-year-old case, Pru. If they need it, we have proof it was an accident. Hank is in the VA, stored away with the rest of the old guys. I don't think anyone is going to waste the taxpayers' money on this one."

"Okay. Donna will also be glad to know I'm thinking about staying around for the winter."

Celeste raised her eyebrows and tucked her hair behind her ear. I expected the third degree, but all she said was, "Damn, I really will have to share that firewood. Lucky I'll have extra strong hands to help split it."

It was my turn to do the raised eyebrow thing, but I didn't say a word.

"Glen and I have been talking. He wants to sell his stable and bring his horses over here. Live in the other wing."

"Right," I said. We laughed, then took our spoons and fought over the last few pieces of carrot cake.

EPILOGUE

Labor Day, a year later

I'm still in the family house on the lake. I bought myself a new queen-sized pillow top bed. Ah, so cozy. I moved my stuff into our parents' bedroom. It felt right. I fixed up my old room for when Jess or Adrian comes to visit, complete with a new bed. My plan is to slowly renovate as I find the funds. Jess is moving up the food chain in the production business, and Adrian's contact in Duluth finally offered him a job in a construction company. Adrian started last spring. He may still go back to Vancouver Island to log in the winters.

 Sam and I finished the fence before winter last year. *That* was a learning experience. Velvet can run around to her heart's content, and I know that any deer who decides to jump in can just as easily jump out, without Velvet following it. I kept my end of the bargain and worked at Sam's store in return. Turns out he was selling himself short when he said it was full of junk. Much of the "junk" is in demand for the antique-hunting Stearns County collectors. Speaking of collections, we split up the Red Wing jugs among the family and Sam sold the rest for us at a good price. This summer he has been going to lots of garage sales. When I have time, I've been volunteering at the Stearns County Historical Society. I'm enjoying learning more about this area I grew up in. I'm also working on a new watercolor of our lake loons.

 Sam moved in with Elias and kept his appointment with Len, who referred him for a complete going-over. It turns out that some of the newer medications are very effective with the flashbacks Sam was having, and the others do help the anxiety and depression better than the old standbys. He's also been going to group for about a year. He doesn't talk much about it, but I can see in his face that it's helping him.

 He didn't tell any of us for a few months, but Sam started

visiting with Hank. He talked with Dr. Slovak, who encouraged the psychiatrist on the elderly unit to try some of the medications on Hank that were helping Sam. In June, Sam told me what he had been doing, and asked me if I would visit Hank with him. He promised me he had prepared Hank with pictures and descriptions of me, so there would be less chance that he would get upset. I went, although I was a bit nervous.

The man I met sure did not resemble the person I visited a year ago. Yes, he's old, but he is no longer feeble or disoriented. There is a light in his eyes, and my family was right – a very quirky sense of humor. Let's hear it for modern drugs. Although to give him credit, Sam has been responsible for much of Hank's progress. Sam slowly reintroduced Hank to Paul and Annie – Celeste he never forgot – and brought Adrian in when he visited once. Finally, we had Hank back to the house for a picnic. Hank tired out after about an hour, but everyone looked as if they were having a good time. I certainly enjoy him. He has great stories about when he and Dad were young, so I feel closer to Dad when he talks. Having him over Sundays has become a habit. Sam and Elias bring him. If Celeste and Glen can come they do, and if Paul and Annie aren't busy they drive up.

Two weeks ago, at Sam's urging, Paul, Cel and I sat down with Hank and told him we knew what had happened the day Mum died. He looked a bit confused for a minute. Then a big tear started down his cheek, followed by another. As he cried, we all held on to a part of him, weeping as well. When he was done, I told him we knew he had gotten confused between the storm and the war and that he thought he was trying to save her. We said we forgave him, and thought maybe Mum had, too. It was a pretty emotional day.

Since then, Hank has seemed almost relieved. He has remembered more family stories – about Mum as well as Dad. It was fun this past weekend seeing Ed and Hank together. For two guys in their nineties, they sure were chatting away. Ed's grandson accompanied him, as did Jess. They seem pretty interested in each other. Ed tracked down Naw Hpraw's grandson, Joseph Hpraw. Of all things, he is in graduate school at St John's, here in Avon. He came over after the memorial ceremony yesterday. He may turn into a regular on our odd family Sunday get-togethers.

Donna was ecstatic that I stayed over the winter. I gave her Dad's journal to read. She did the necessary paperwork and Mum's case is closed. We have had some good girl talk, and she has become another Sunday regular. She introduced me to the eccentric principal of the school to which she is a liaison. As a result, after Christmas, I will be subbing for their school psychologist who is going on maternity leave. Who knows? It might lead somewhere else. At the very least I can keep renovating a little at a time.

David wanted me to come home to work things out. I wanted him to visit out here, as I wasn't sure I would be strong enough even now, to separate myself from him again if I went home. But he wouldn't bother, which was fine. That told me something right there. So we have telephone conversations instead, which has actually worked better. I usually sit at the dining room table, facing Mum's portrait, and feel a sense of security that helps me continue to be assertive with him about what I want to do with my life. I can also make notes, so he can't get me off track as easily. Sounds absurd, doesn't it, what it takes for some of us to take care of ourselves? Donna recommended a good lawyer whom she used in her divorce. I scribbled his number in my telephone book and look at it every so often. I'll get there one of these days. David sold the house and already gave me my half. Besides keeping some money out for income until winter and splurging on the beds, I invested the rest should no full-time job appear in the near future. David is living on the boat, and Jess and Adrian travel every so often to sail with him. They say they insist on spending time with him when no girlfriends are around.

Everyone left this morning, but yesterday, we had a houseful.

Ed, Brian, Jess, and Adrian all stayed here. Velvet was in seventh heaven. Then in the afternoon, Paul, Annie, and their son, Bill drove up. Hank, Sam, Elias, Celeste, Glen, Josie, Ollie, and Donna came over. We had been given permission to dig up the urns that contained Mum and Dad's ashes. Sam and Ollie did a great job clearing the area by the basswood tree. It is a regular little grove now. If you look down the ravine, you can still see the old car, but no one wants to drag it up. We all trooped out there. We took scoops, and those of us who wanted to, took turns scattering the ashes around the basswood tree. Annie read a poem. Mum's lavender scent was very strong during this process, and the breeze busily shook the basswood leaves.

I looked around at the faces of the people who had become so important to me over the past year. My parents' tragedy had touched us all. None of us would ever be the same. I, for one, had finally come home to myself. My mother had completed the job she had stayed to do. As the last few ashes sifted to the ground, the breeze died and her fragrance faded into memory. Adrienne could finally leave.

AVALANCHE

By Annie Dillen

The conditions for an avalanche
Exist far beneath the surface,
Long before the blanket of snow
Starts its downward slide.

Once in motion, the avalanche
Scourges everything in its path,
Rock, earth, plants, trees, wildlife,
Human beings.

Even after the roar of the slide
Gives way to the silence of the mountain,
At the edge of the destruction,
Small rocks and tiny pebbles
Keep rolling.

Some pebbles fall off the edge into the abyss.
Some are halted by larger rocks and sit
Among a barren landscape,
Exposed to the elements.
Still others come to rest
Among a formerly grassy meadow
Or shaded grove
That with luck springs up again
Around them.
Flowers grow near them.
Birds peck at insects beside them.
Animals dig beneath them.

We are like those pebbles.
What sent us rolling
Was not of our choice.
But unlike them, we can choose our direction.
We can avoid the abyss,
And can move beyond the barren landscape
To find our own meadow or grove.

"War is at best barbarism ... Its glory is all moonshine. It is only those who have neither fired a shot nor heard the shrieks and groans of the wounded, who cry aloud for blood, more vengeance, more desolation. War is hell."

WILLIAM TECUMSEH SHERMAN
Graduation Address, Michigan Military Academy, June 1, 1879

ACKNOWLEDGEMENTS

Although Arthur's experiences are fictional, the details and personal touches about Detachment 101 in Burma during World War Two would not have been possible without the direction of Sam Spector of Rome, Georgia, who was one of the members of the real Detachment 101 and generously shared his experiences and those of his fellow Det 101 compatriots. Any changes are mine, for narrative purposes. If you are interested in more information about the Det 101, their website is <http://oss-101.com>.

Thanks too, to the Vietnam veterans who shared their experiences with PTSD and the VA hospitals in St. Cloud and Seattle (both excellent). This whole project would never have started rolling without Patsy Ludwick and her writing class <http://mypage.uniserve.com/~writershaven>. My first readers were invaluable, including my children, and above all my husband, Ed, whose patient listening and concise comments kept the revisions going. I couldn't have done it without Clayton, Keven and Will of Eternal Flow Computers <www.eternalflowcreations.com>. Thanks to Ellie Speare for her cover photo and book trailer <www.elliespeare.com> and to Ben Speare for his ideas on how to use the photo on the cover. The book was designed by Toby Macklin <www.tobymacklin.com> and first printed by Regan Lall at Gallery Press <www.galleryprinting.com>, both of whom I highly recommend. Thanks also to Jenny Gisler for her website design.

Two books that proved helpful and might interest those who want to know more about the American OSS during WWII are: *This Grim and Savage Game*, by Tom Moon, DaCapo Press, 1991, 2000, and *Behind Japanese Lines: With the Oss in Burma*, by Richard Dunlop, Rand McNally & Co., 1979. This last one is out of print but you can get it at the library or through Amazon.com.

For the details of the history of Avon, Minnesota, I found the book by Jeannette Blonigen Clancy, *Nestled between Lakes and Wooded Hills: the Centennial History of the Avon Area*, very interesting. It and *3 Towns into 1 City, A Narrative Record of Significant Factors in The Story of St Cloud, Minnesota,* compiled and narrated by John J. Dominik, Jr, Edited by Ed L. Stockinger, can be obtained through the North Star Press or the Stearns County Historical Museum in St Cloud, Minnesota.

For links to related information and to order copies of this book, visit <www.thecoatinthewoods.com>.

Made in the USA
Charleston, SC
23 May 2010